THE QUIET MOTHER

ALSO BY ARNALDUR INDRIDASON

The Girl by the Bridge

The Darkness Knows

The Shadow Killer

The Shadow District

Into Oblivion

Reykjavik Nights

Strange Shores

Black Skies

Outrage

Operation Napoleon

Hypothermia

Arctic Chill

The Draining Lake

Voices

Silence of the Grave

Jar City

Arnaldur Indridason

THE QUIET MOTHER

Translated from the Icelandic by Philip Roughton

MINOTAUR BOOKS
NEW YORK

This is a work of fiction. All of the characters, organizations, and events portrayed in this novel are either products of the author's imagination or are used fictitiously.

First published in the United States by Minotaur Books, an imprint of St. Martin's Publishing Group

EU Representative: Macmillan Publishers Ireland Ltd, 1st Floor, The Liffey Trust Centre, 117–126 Sheriff Street Upper, Dublin 1, DO1 YC43

THE QUIET MOTHER. Copyright © 2019 by Arnaldur Indridason. English translation copyright © 2025 by Philip Roughton. All rights reserved. Printed in the United States of America. For information, address St. Martin's Publishing Group, 120 Broadway, New York, NY 10271.

www.minotaurbooks.com

The Library of Congress Cataloging-in-Publication Data is available upon request.

ISBN 978-1-250-40376-6 (hardcover)
ISBN 978-1-250-40377-3 (ebook)

The publisher of this book does not authorize the use or reproduction of any part of this book in any manner for the purpose of training artificial intelligence technologies or systems. The publisher of this book expressly reserves this book from the Text and Data Mining exception in accordance with Article 4(3) of the European Union Digital Single Market Directive 2019/790.

Our books may be purchased in bulk for specialty retail/wholesale, literacy, corporate/premium, educational, and subscription box use. Please contact MacmillanSpecialMarkets@macmillan.com.

Originally published in Iceland under the title *Trégesteinn* by Vaka-Helgafell

First published in the English language in Great Britain by Harvill Secker, an imprint of Vintage, a Penguin Random House company, 2025

First U.S. Edition: 2025

10 9 8 7 6 5 4 3 2 1

1

And there by the living-room window stood the young woman, looking out into the evening darkness. She was smoking a cigarette and exhaled the smoke leisurely, her outline clear in the dim gleam coming from within the flat. Her hair fell about her shoulders and her thin body filled out her tight dress as she took a sip from a glass she'd placed on the windowsill. Maybe she'd just come home from a party. She looked stately, standing there at the window with her cigarette. Behind her appeared a man of her age, who went to her and took a drink from the glass. Then he put his arms around her, and they kissed.

  Most of the people were watching the quiz show that was on telly. In the lower-floor apartment of the house next door, a middle-aged couple was sitting on a couch, watching telly. The man was bald, and wore glasses, a shirt and loosened tie. The woman, whose hair was in a ponytail, sat close beside him and yawned. She got up and went to the kitchen, pottered a bit at the sink and put dishes into cupboards. Suddenly, at the same moment, they both looked up.

In the flat above them, kids were playing in the living room, two boys and a girl. They'd spread a large collection of Lego blocks over the floor and were building something out of them, but suddenly stopped and looked at the kitchen door, which was closed.

Their parents were in the kitchen and seemed to be arguing. The woman said something and the man shouted back and slammed his fist on the table before stepping menacingly towards her as if he was going to hit her.

In the living room, the older boy stood up from the Lego and led his siblings into the bedroom hallway.

In the kitchen, the two people continued to argue, and suddenly, the man hit the woman.

Downstairs, the man stopped watching television, stood up, and looked at the ceiling. Apparently, the noise of the argument in the kitchen upstairs had carried down to him. At the same time, the woman stopped what she was doing, went to the man in the living room and exchanged a few words with him. The woman seemed to be encouraging the man to go up and calm down their neighbour. Judging by their body language, this wasn't the first time such a thing had happened.

The man in the kitchen kept yelling and hit his wife a second time, knocking her to the floor.

The well-dressed young couple in the house next door kissed more passionately and the woman started unbuttoning the man's jacket. He hesitated a moment and looked at his watch as if they had limited time, were late, had to get going. Not about to stop, the woman started unbuttoning his shirt. A moment later, her dress fell from her and she pushed the man down onto the sofa. The man lay stretched out on the sofa with his trousers around his ankles and watched the woman undo her bra before she had second thoughts, stopped what she was doing, went to the living-room window and drew the curtains shut. Shortly afterwards, the light went out.

The man in the kitchen stood threateningly over the woman, yelling at her. The children were nowhere to be seen. The man abruptly stiffened and listened. Something had disturbed him. The woman lay there on the floor and now he pulled her up and fixed her tousled hair, then ordered her with hand movements to stay in the kitchen. The woman was wearing a grey skirt and white blouse. She smoothed out her skirt and the man opened the door and went into the living room. Glancing around, he saw that the children were no longer there, only the Lego blocks, abandoned and scattered over the floor. Then he looked at the front door and went and opened it. His wife stood dejected and motionless in the kitchen.

The woman downstairs stood in her doorway and listened. She seemed very worried. The man had gone upstairs to the neighbours'. There, the woman hid in the kitchen, seemingly unsure of what to do. Help was so near. Maybe this had all happened before.

At the front door, the men were speaking to each other. Finally, the woman inched her way to the kitchen door, opened it, and came out. The men turned and looked at her. In the hallway, the older boy was looking to see what was going on. His siblings stood behind him. The man from downstairs said something to the woman, but she shook her head as if to say he needn't worry. The husband, apparently having had enough of his neighbour's nosiness, started to shut the door. His neighbour wasn't about to leave it like that. The two men appeared to argue while the woman and children watched.

The thick curtains concealing the couple in love remained in place.

Having lost his patience, the man shooed his neighbour and tried to push him out the door. The woman stood there silently, doing nothing. The children went to her and put their arms around their mother. The woman downstairs remained standing in her doorway, listening to what was going on. Finally, the man succeeded in pushing his neighbour out into the hallway and slammed the door in his face. He turned to his wife, standing there surrounded by their children, and stared in turn at her and them before disappearing into the corridor.

In a block of flats across the street, a scantily clad woman sat at her dining table, her face buried in her hands. She seemed to be feeling poorly. She looked regularly around the flat and appeared to be speaking to someone, and soon a man walked into the room and kissed her on the mouth. He was wearing dark trousers and a sweater, and now slipped on a jacket. The woman followed him to the door and the man stepped hurriedly into the hallway. It was as if they wanted to keep things secret and no one to see him. Left alone in the flat, the woman sat back down at the table, but was restless and stood up and looked at her watch. She grabbed a mobile phone, checked it, and put it back down.

Above her, an older woman sat in front of the telly. She was illuminated only by the light from the device. She looked in the direction of her front door, stood up and walked hesitantly into the hall.

She opened the door, and before she could react, a man attacked her and knocked her to the floor. Indistinct in the darkness, the man crouched over her.

Soon afterwards, the shadowy figure rushed around the flat with a plastic bag in his hands. The man dashed at lightning speed from one room to another, pulling open drawers and tearing out the contents of cupboards before running back out into the hallway, making sure to shut the door behind him.

The living-room curtains of the couple in love were drawn open and the young woman stood naked in the darkness, looking out the window and smoking, with a soft glow falling across her peaceful face.

2

Marta parked her car in front of the stairwell and stepped out, taking her e-cigarette with her. She was in one of the city's neighbourhoods that alternated between blocks of flats and terraced houses, with a detached house or two thrown in for those whose pockets were better lined. The neighbourhood was built in the early seventies and had seen better days. Police were dispatched there sometimes to deal with rowdiness and drunkenness, and graffiti artists had a free hand there with their particular form of vandalism. Break-ins and theft also found their way into the police department's case files on the neighbourhood, but no real serious crime had ever been committed there. The residents were both surprised and shocked when news of what had happened got out, after police vehicles, their sirens blaring, an ambulance and a car from the police department's Forensics Unit began lining up in front of the block and people in uniforms started streaming up the stairwell to the second floor of the building, where cameras began flashing.

The woman was lying in the hallway in front of her door, making it nearly impossible to enter the flat without taking a big step over her. She was probably about seventy years old, wearing a cardigan over a blouse, brown trousers and glasses on a slender chain around her neck. Her hair was almost completely grey. Her face reflected the violence that precipitated her death. Her eyes were bulging and her mouth was wide open as if she'd used the last bit of her strength to draw in oxygen.

Her flat had been trashed. The woman's belongings lay on the floor, some broken. Drawers were open, books had been shoved off the shelves, furniture overturned. The woman owned a number of paintings, some of which hung askew on the walls. Apparently, none had been stolen.

Marta stood at the door of the flat and raised her e-cigarette to her lips. She'd stopped smoking slender menthol cigarettes, having fallen for the hype that e-cigarettes were healthier for people than regular ones. She liked vanilla best, but otherwise, the flavour didn't matter. She used fairly strong nicotine and got a bit of a buzz from it if she inhaled fast enough, sucking the vapour in deeply. Sometimes she trailed plumes of vapour as if from a geothermal power plant.

'Do you have to do that here, while we're working?' asked a Forensics tech, obviously irritated.

'Relax,' she said, before turning to the district medical officer, who'd come to verify the woman's death. 'Can you determine the cause of death?'

'Isn't it obvious? She couldn't breathe,' said the doctor. 'Suffocated. And it happened a short time ago, maybe half an hour or so. How did you all get here so quickly?'

'So she was strangled, you mean?'

'No. It's more like something was put over her head. A plastic bag, maybe. Tightened around her neck,' he added, pointing to a line faintly visible there. 'She tried to defend herself. Her fingernails are broken. But the autopsy should determine exactly what happened.'

'Who called this in?' Marta asked.

'It was anonymous,' said a police officer standing in the hallway, and who had been first on the scene. 'The caller said that there'd been an assault here, and that a woman might be lying injured in her flat.'

'Can we trace the call?'

'They say it could be difficult.'

'Maybe it was the person who did this?' Marta said. 'And then regretted the outcome? Hadn't intended to go that far?'

Her questions weren't directed at anyone in particular, and no one had an answer to them. It had been a short time since the woman was attacked, and there were no witnesses apart from the assailant himself. Or assailants. Maybe there'd been more than one, and they'd decided to let the police know. The woman had opened the door without checking who it was first, and someone immediately attacked her and knocked her to the floor. Or she'd been fleeing the assailant and made it only to the door. If that was the case, then she'd probably let him in. Had possibly known him.

E-cigarette in hand, Marta stepped out into the hallway and looked up the stairs and then down towards the floor below. She walked down the stairs, then continued down to the basement. She switched on a light in the dark basement hallway, which had storeroom doors on both sides. At the end of the hallway was a spacious laundry room with a casement window at chest height, which looked out onto a large back garden. The window had a holder set halfway open, and there were signs on the windowsill – dirt and shoeprints – that someone had recently entered through it.

'Did you crawl in here, you sleazebag?' Marta whispered to herself as she ran her eyes over the signs. The offender hadn't been in such a hurry that he didn't take the time to reset the window holder, as if that would suffice to cover his trail. Marta tried looking through the window to see if the grass in front of it was trampled, but it was dark outside and she saw nothing.

After going back upstairs, she let the Forensics techs know about the basement window. They were dressed in thin white coveralls, with hoods over their heads, and one of them immediately took his equipment and went downstairs. Before long, they gave Marta permission to enter the flat, as long as she promised not to touch anything. People in that stairwell's flats had been kindly asked to remain in them, but a number of spectators were clustered in front of the block. The woman's body was carried down the stairs and taken to the National Hospital for an autopsy. The name Valborg was printed on the doorbell.

Marta regarded the destruction that met her eyes. More often than she cared to remember, she'd gone to investigate a house that had been broken into and, at a glance, it was impossible to see that this was any different from them. Nooks and crannies had been searched for things of value, and no effort had been spared to find them.

Marta wondered if the criminal had been looking for something special. On the bedroom floor lay a small jewellery box that had been emptied. A handbag had been dumped out and its contents strewn over the floor. Nearby was a wallet, empty of banknotes and credit cards.

In the bathroom, the medicine cabinet was bare; everything

torn from it in the same frenzied way. An empty medicine box was lying in the bathtub, and there were several items in the toilet as well: nail clippers, a soap dispenser. A blister pack of Atacor cholesterol tablets was floating at the top of the bowl. The woman had had high cholesterol. Marta reached for the box lying in the bathtub, and as far as she could tell, the woman had also been suffering a serious illness.

She found no computer, neither a desktop nor laptop. No mobile phone or tablet, either. She presumed that the woman hadn't had profiles on Facebook or Twitter. An old-fashioned telephone that had been standing on a table in the hall had toppled to the floor. Marta knew elderly people who didn't want any of that computer rubbish in their houses and believed the internet was evil. Still, she thought the woman in the flat was a bit youngish to have denied the computer revolution altogether.

There was a desk in one corner of the living room, and papers and newspapers lay scattered around it. Prescriptions and bills from medical specialists, all sorts of memos, shopping lists and other notes lay either on top of the desk or under it. Marta picked up a few of them and looked them over, until, in one of the memos, she noticed a phone number that she knew well. No name was written along with it, and Marta stared at the number for several moments, wondering what connections there could possibly be between it and the woman. Deciding not to wait to find out, she took out her mobile phone and called the number. After a moment or two, a familiar voice answered the phone.

'Konrád.'

'Am I disturbing you?'

'What's up?'

'Do you know a woman named Valborg?'

'No.'

'She seems to know you,' said Marta.

'Hmm? Valborg? I don't remember . . .'

There was a short silence on the line.

'Yes, hold on, is she an elderly woman?' Konrád asked.

'I found your number on her desk. She's dead.'

'Dead?'

'Yes.'

'Are you at her place? Did something happen to her? What are you doing over there?'

'Her house was broken into and she was suffocated,' said Marta. 'With a plastic bag, probably.'

'Are you serious?!'

'How do you know her?'

'I don't know her at all,' Konrád said, and Marta sensed over the phone how startled he was at this news. 'If it's the same woman. She knew I'd been on the force and wanted to meet me. It was around two months ago, I guess . . . Did you say a plastic bag?'

'What did she want from you?'

'Is she dead?' Konrád stammered. 'It took me a moment to place her name, but I remember her well because what she wanted was rather unique. She asked if I could find her child.'

3

They met at the Ásmundur Sveinsson Museum.

Konrád remembered how reluctant he was to help her when she called. He said he was retired and not taking on any new projects, but she didn't give up and called again about a week later and asked if he might have changed his mind. Konrád was surprised at her stubbornness, but didn't want to be impolite. He sensed the pain in her voice and suspected that it hadn't been easy for the woman to contact him.

'Weren't you in charge of the case up there on Langjökull Glacier?' she asked, disheartened, after he'd twice tried to end the conversation. He couldn't deny that he was. It was one of the more difficult of his cases and had been given a lot of media coverage, as almost three decades went into solving it. Konrád had sometimes been pestered by people who had all sorts of ideas for him, garish conspiracy theories about disappearances, deaths, fraud and deceit traceable to the Icelandic criminal flora.

Shortly afterwards, they said goodbye and Konrád thought the matter was over and done with, but two months later the woman called again.

'I don't know if you remember me,' she began, 'but I've called you before to ask for your help.'

He vaguely recalled their conversation, remembered the pain in her voice, and dreaded having to refuse the woman his help for the third time. He hadn't given her request any thought, mainly because she'd never had the chance to go into detail, just asked if he might be willing to help her with a little matter that had been bothering her for a long time and was personal. He hadn't wanted to ask anything more about it because he feared it would be the start of further business between them. Now he had to admit that his curiosity was piqued.

'What is it that you're so concerned about? What would you like me to do for you?' he finally asked, when their conversation became awkward.

'I prefer not to talk about it on the phone,' she said, finding his attitude to have changed slightly in her favour. 'I would appreciate it if you could be so kind as to meet me. Maybe at a cafe in town. Or wherever you like. And please excuse these interruptions; I know I'm bothering you, but I just don't know where else to turn.'

She mentioned that before she stopped working, her job was a short distance from the Ásmundur Sveinsson Museum and she occasionally went to that quiet place to unwind at the end of the day. They agreed to meet there one afternoon. When Konrád arrived, no one was at the museum but a few tourists. A busload of the same was driving away and, of course, more were expected. Reykjavík was drowning in tourists, and tourism companies desperately sought destinations to drive them to and from. The Ásmundur Sveinsson Museum was one of the more interesting ones, located where the city used to end and surrounded by a sculpture garden.

The building itself was strangely timeless and alien; there was none other like it in town. There, severe surfaces and soft lines collided, and over them rose a domed roof that resembled an astronomical observatory. It was as if a ship from a distant galaxy had been stranded there.

Valborg sat on a bench next to one of the sculptures in the gently curving exhibition hall. The statue was of a mother holding a child on her knee and gazing at it affectionately; its name was *Motherly Love*. When Konrád came in, he gestured hesitantly to Valborg; they greeted each other and she invited him to sit down beside her.

'To think that it's possible to change an ordinary rock into such beautiful art,' she said, admiring the sculpture.

Konrád had once seen part of an interview with the artist on his old black-and-white TV and noticed the sculptor's strong fingers, his broken nails with dirt beneath them, and scars of cuts made by his chisel and hammer. Rugged hands that ground down rock and changed it into stories and poems.

'He crafted such beautiful images of women,' said Valborg. 'Mothers especially. Strong women who hold their children and admire them and shelter and feed them. The love between a mother and her child, carved in stone.'

'Is it something you think about a lot?' Konrád asked, looking at Valborg after a few moments of silence. Her countenance was kind, her forehead high and intelligent, and her eyebrows dark and arched.

'More so as the years go by,' she said. 'I didn't even want to hold it. I never saw it.'

'What did you never see?'

The woman didn't take her eyes off the artwork.

'I've gone from one specialist to another and they tell me that the time I have left is growing shorter. They have medicine to slow down the disease and reduce the pain, but it can't be turned back and I have to accept that. I've tried. It isn't easy. I've been putting my affairs in order lately and . . . I don't really know how to say it. I had a child and it was taken away from me immediately after birth, or rather . . . it wasn't taken from me, I gave it up. I'd actually agreed to do so before the baby was born, and I thought it wisest not to see it or hold it, in order to avoid any chance of making a connection. I've never stopped thinking about it even though I've never made any serious attempt until now to find out what became of the blessed child. It's been forty-seven years and . . . I don't know. I don't even know if it was a boy or a girl. I accepted it all because it was my decision and I couldn't keep the baby, I knew that, but now I want to know if it's been all right and maybe tell it . . . tell it what happened and why things happened as they did and find out how it has coped with life, to stop me from worrying. That it was the right decision. That I did the right thing, despite everything.'

'Forty-seven years is a long time.'

'I always say "the child",' Valborg said softly. Konrád sensed how tired and worn out she was and thought of the painkillers she'd mentioned. 'It's nearly fifty years old, but I still say "the child",' she said. 'Naturally, I never knew it otherwise. The things I say! I didn't get to know it at all.'

'What have you done to find out about it?' Konrád asked.

'I lived in Hveragerði, actually moved there because of this, and gave birth at home. It went really well and the midwife was there and she was good to me and understood my situation. She actually encouraged me to go that route rather than have an abortion. I last saw the child in her hands. I've found out that she passed away and I can't find any information about the child, which isn't strange really, considering how we dealt with it. Of course, I know the date and year of birth, but they haven't been of any use and I wonder whether the date of birth was changed. I tried asking the police, but no crime was committed. It was all done with my consent. The police are drowning in work and advised me to make it public; go to the newspapers, the television stations. I can't. I would never do that.'

'Why did you give up the child?'

Konrád put the question so bluntly that he immediately regretted it.

'Do you think you can help me?' Valborg asked, without answering him.

'I don't see how,' Konrád replied, reluctant to become involved. 'From what you've told me, it seems you've explored all your main options. And I don't know, maybe it would be best for you to let it go. If no documents are found and people who could help you are deceased, it might be best to let this rest in peace. Besides, you never know what you might discover after all this time. Maybe you would be happy and satisfied and everything would have worked out for the best. But you might possibly end up feeling much worse than you do now.'

'I know that, and I'm willing to take the risk,' Valborg said, looking at him as if she'd already thought these things through. 'I'm willing to do anything it takes to find out what happened to my child. I can pay you. I've put money aside for this.'

'This isn't about money,' Konrád said.

'You solved the case in the end, that one on Langjökull. Even if it took thirty years. You didn't give up.'

'I actually gave up on it many times,' Konrád said. 'Made mistakes. I'm far from proud of that case.'

'But the papers said that –'

'Well, not everything the papers say is true. Why did you give up the child? Was it your own decision?'

Valborg gave the sculpture of the mother and child a long look.

'You won't help me?' she said without any pushiness, although her disappointment was obvious.

'I'm just struggling to see what I can do for you. Unfortunately. I don't deal with these sorts of things.'

'And you think I should let it be?'

'Of course it's not for me to say.'

'No, probably not.'

They sat there silently, admiring the artwork, as the day's fading light fell on them through the slanted windows.

'Have you heard the story of the crag Tregasteinn – the Rock of Sorrow?' Valborg asked.

'No,' Konrád said.

'It's on a mountain out west,' said Valborg. 'I sometimes think of it when I look at this beautiful sculpture.'

She stopped when she noticed Konrád glance at his watch.

'I'm not going to take up any more of your time,' she said, standing up.

'I don't want you to leave here upset,' said Konrád.

'I'm not at all upset,' said Valborg. 'Thank you for meeting me.'

'Won't you tell me why you gave up your child?'

'I see no point in it if you're not going to help me.'

'I don't even know where I would start.'

'No, I understand, don't worry. I wanted to test this path fully, but see that it's closed. Thank you again for meeting me. And I'm sorry for the trouble. You won't hear from me again.'

Looking back in his mind's eye, Konrád saw the woman as she left the museum, short-statured and helpless and tormented by a painful past. She kept her word and Konrád heard no more from her. After Marta called with the unbelievable news that she'd been murdered in her home, he wondered whether he'd failed her somehow. He sat there dumbfounded, incredulous that anyone could have attacked that gentle woman as violently as Marta described. Nothing in his conversations with Valborg suggested that she could have been in any danger. Konrád was reluctant to accept tasks like the one she'd proposed to him. Reluctant to involve himself in other people's private affairs, as if he were still on the police force, with everything that entailed. It could be a real strain, delving into people's tragedies. He preferred to be free of such things.

Eventually, he turned back to the papers he'd been reading when Marta interrupted him, and now he saw more clearly than before a part of himself in Valborg's ordeal. He himself was looking for answers. In his hands, he held a printout of the testimony of a young woman in a decades-old criminal case that few remembered and was still unsolved. The woman was walking along Skúlagata Street one evening in 1963 when she came across the body of a man lying in his own blood in front of the facilities of the Butchers' Association of the South. The man was Konrád's father. He'd been stabbed twice and died there on the pavement. The wounds were deep and in the right places for causing as much damage as possible, and the woman who found him spoke repeatedly about all the blood that ran into the gutter.

The woman was still alive. Konrád had never met or spoken to her. Lately, he'd thought a lot about whether he should meet her or let it be, and was contemplating this again when Marta called. He hadn't paid the matter any attention in all his years working for the Criminal Investigation Department, but it had never strayed far from his mind, and recently he'd been trying to muster up the courage to contact the woman and ask if he could bother her.

He still hadn't gone for it. Konrád knew that if he did, it would be the biggest step he'd ever taken in the search for his father's murderer.

And he feared there would be no turning back.

4

While listening to Konrád's story, Marta scrolled through photographs of the crime scene. This was the day after the discovery of the body, and Konrád had hardly slept a wink since hearing about the murder. His mind turned constantly to Valborg and the sculptures at that quaint art museum, which turned out to have been her refuge at the end of her working day. He tormented himself for not having done anything for her. Over and over, he'd thought of her in the weeks since their meeting, and when he heard of her death and how it occurred, it was like a heavy blow to his chest. The violence and ruthlessness in no way fitted with the quiet, polite woman who had sought him out and borne her grief for so long in silence. Now he wished he'd been more understanding, and more sympathetic to her suffering.

'So did she have – what did they call it in the old days – a love child?' asked Marta, completely unmoved by the story, as she placed two photographs on the table in front of him. They were sitting in her office at the Hverfisgata Street station, where Konrád had come to tell her more about his interactions with Valborg, as meagre as they were.

'She didn't tell me anything about it. I didn't get to hear the whole story. I guess she would have told me if I'd been more receptive to her request. Unfortunately, I pushed her away. I regret it now. I should have listened better to her.'

'Are people contacting you about such matters?'

'It happens.'

'But you aren't particularly obliging?'

'No.'

'I see,' said Marta. 'Do you find anything strange about these photos?' she then asked, handing him three photos of the scene.

He looked at them and saw how the thief or thieves had trashed the woman's flat. He noticed the wallpaper and the paintings still hanging in their places. It gave him a very peculiar feeling, seeing into the woman's flat like that.

'I assume she lived alone,' he said.

'Yes, sixty-nine years old. Unmarried. Childless. On her own. Her parents died long ago. She doesn't seem to have had many relatives, and she had few friends. We know of one sister, who's in a nursing home. And that's all we know. I'm going to visit her later. Over the last two decades or so, Valborg worked as a secretary at a medical centre on Ármúli Street, but had recently retired. We talked to the staff there, who were stunned by the news, of course. We need to question them more closely. Gather information. Find out who she was, this woman.'

'Now you know that she gave birth to a child,' said Konrád. 'You could try determining that person's whereabouts.'

'Yeah, we'll see what comes of that.'

'And her neighbours?'

'They have nice things to say about her. Good with children. Helpful. As far as we can tell, none of them did this. The block is four floors, two flats on each floor at each stairwell. The occupants of two of the flats are travelling, either here in Iceland or abroad. Others weren't at home or aren't under suspicion, have never run foul of the law and had no apparent reason to attack the woman, but we may have to go over all of it more closely.'

'And no one noticed anything?'

'There was a popular quiz show on TV,' said Marta.

'Have you found out who reported it?' Konrád asked.

'No. It was someone with an unregistered phone number, a man; otherwise, we know nothing but are working on it. I spoke to Valborg's GP this morning and he said she'd been diagnosed with advanced pancreatic cancer. It had spread and was untreatable. If the person who attacked the woman knew her well enough to know that . . .'

'Then he would only have had to wait for what, a few months, and she would have been dead? Death had already got a grip on her.'

'Exactly,' said Marta, before taking her e-cigarette, lighting it, and starting to blow out jets of vapour.

'They didn't know each other, you mean?'

'I think we can say, at least, that they hadn't been close.'

'I found her to be quite reticent about herself – at least from the little that we spoke to each other,' Konrád said. 'She may not have told anyone about her illness.'

'The staff at the Ármúli Street medical centre had no idea about it. They didn't know she was ill and didn't notice any changes in her the last few days she was there. She just acted normal. Pleasant. Friendly. They said goodbye to her with a cake and flowers.'

'It's like he went berserk in the flat,' Konrád said, flipping through the photos.

'It's typical. I've seen numerous break-ins and this is no different from the others, apart from the woman's body,' said Marta. 'We don't know exactly what was stolen; something from her wallet, probably something from the drawers.'

'And the drugs?'

'We got a list of the painkillers she took. They're very strong and much sought-after by addicts, and are sold for a high price. Morphine-related drugs. All prescription stuff. The thief took all of it. The burglars on our repeat-offenders list seek out such stuff. We're questioning them. They'd drink from the toilet for it. So, yeah, what can I say? Typical squalidness.'

'And the call?'

'We don't get it,' said Marta, exhaling nicotine vapour. 'There are no witnesses to the crime except for the perpetrator. It happened at the door to the flat. He must have called it in himself. Why did he want us to find the body right away? Why didn't he want to leave it there for a few days, until people started wondering about her? What was the rush?'

'Maybe he didn't intend to go that far,' said Konrád, 'and when he saw that he'd killed her, he was so shocked that he called.'

'Yeah, he's a fool, whoever he is.' Marta sighed. 'A goddamn fucking fool.' She slammed the photos on the table and looked at Konrád. 'Do you know about the plastic bag? I shouldn't be telling you all this.'

'What about it?'

'They found traces of soft drinks and beer on the woman's face and in her hair, which they believe was from the plastic bag that was used to suffocate her.'

'Oh?'

'It's like it was full of empty cans or something.'

'Good luck figuring that out,' said Konrád. 'You need look no further than the entire population.'

'I heard you were asking for all sorts of printouts from the archive,' said Marta, a little annoyed by Konrád's comment. 'Is having nothing to do getting to you?'

'I try to keep busy.'

'Or your dad's ghost?'

'I don't believe in ghosts,' said Konrád.

5

Eygló had expected more people at the coffin-closing ceremony. She went into Fossvogur Chapel, where less than ten people had gathered; no one she remembered from the Society for Psychical Research.

The coffin was open and there lay Málfríður under a snow-white sheet, with a bit of a stern expression, as if she still had something she wanted to say. She'd been the oldest member of the Society for Psychical Research and a good friend of Eygló's despite their considerable age difference, but they hadn't been much in contact recently. Málfríður said that she herself wasn't clairvoyant, but had been married to a well-known psychic healer and was in charge of organising his séances and house calls. Eygló knew few people who had a richer interest in the next life or spoke more passionately about the etheric world. When she had looked to the society for guidance back in the day, it was Málfríður who welcomed her and taught her not to fear the visions that troubled her, but rather to enjoy being cast in a different mould from all others.

The old woman died in the nursing home where she'd been living in recent years, and Eygló visited her there for the last time shortly before her death. Málfríður had sent for her. It was she who'd decided that Eygló should start holding séances, which she did hesitantly at first, unsure and insecure. Her father had worked as a medium but didn't have a good reputation and was said to be in cahoots with a swindler who had no qualms about taking advantage of the misery of those who mourned. That was Konrád's father.

Eygló wished to make as little as possible of the psychic abilities she possessed and that both her father and Málfríður said she needed to cultivate. She would have preferred to be free of them, and didn't want that clairvoyance of hers to interfere with her life, but Málfríður encouraged her and said she shouldn't resist it, but try to harness her abilities and use them for good.

Upon her arrival at the old woman's nursing home, Eygló asked about her health and was told that she probably didn't have much longer to live. She slept a lot and was sometimes out of touch and confused, talked to herself or even to imaginary visitors in her room, as if delirious. She had very few visitors apart from her son, who looked in regularly. Eygló was the only one who had come to see her that day.

When Eygló came to Málfríður's door, she saw that the old woman had a visitor. Apparently, visits to her weren't as rare as the staff had indicated. The visitor was an elderly woman, wearing a veil on her head and a rather tatty green coat, sitting on a chair by the bed with her hands in her lap. Eygló noticed how gentle her expression was.

Just then, Eygló's phone rang in her pocket and she ambled over to a waiting room while answering the call. When she returned, the woman at Málfríður's bedside was gone, and she sat down in the chair she'd occupied.

There were a few personal items on Málfríður's bedside table. A photograph of her son and some audio books – Icelandic sagas and thrillers, it looked to Eygló. She didn't want to wake her. The room was dusky. Málfríður was nearly blind and no longer perceived anything but shadows and movements in front of her.

Finally, Málfríður stirred, opened her eyes, and asked if someone was there with her.

'Is that you, Hulda dear?' she said. 'Are you still there?'

'No, it's Eygló. How are you?'

'Dearest Eygló,' said the old woman. 'How lovely of you to look in on me.'

'I didn't want to wake you.'

'I thought I'd crossed over. I feel like that every time I fall asleep. I was back with my mother and it felt so wonderful.'

Málfríður groped for Eygló and gripped her hand.

'I look forward to my dreams,' she said. 'In them, I can see perfectly again and everything is so alive and colourful around me.'

Málfríður smiled and began to tell Eygló about her dreams, that they were all bright and warm. She was so old that she didn't fear dying, but was curious to find out what came next. She'd spoken along those lines before, when she said she'd had a good life and now another plane of existence awaited her, whether it was the cold grave devoid of heavenly bliss or the world of the souls who had gone before and in which she believed so steadfastly.

'I'm not afraid at all,' she said. 'Do you remember the sick girl in the Þingholt neighbourhood?'

'The sick girl? Why . . . ?'

'I don't know why I'm thinking of her,' said Málfríður.

'That was many years ago,' said Eygló. As far as she could tell, the woman wasn't delirious or confused.

'Probably because I've been thinking so much about my dear Kristleifur, whom you went with then. How he took it all so close to heart. I've been dreaming about him,' said Málfríður. 'He's standing here in my room, clear as day. Do you remember Kristleifur?'

'Yes, of course, I remember him well,' said Eygló.

'I think my time here is almost up,' said Málfríður. 'I think he has come to fetch me. I've dreamed him twice recently, standing here next to my bed, smiling at me.'

'He was a good man.'

Málfríður fell silent and closed her eyes. Several moments passed.

'Do you still see that policeman?' she asked.

'No, not much,' said Eygló.

'Well,' said Málfríður, with a clear touch of disappointment in her voice. 'You don't like him?'

'I simply don't give it any thought.'

Eygló had told the old woman about her association with Konrád, the retired policeman. That their fathers had known each other at one time and worked together to swindle money out of people – a very sad story.

'Who is this Hulda you mentioned?'

'She's a dear old friend who always believed more than anyone else in life after death and just took it as self-evident,' said Málfríður. 'We talked about it for years – how it would be to cross over to another plane of existence following this one here. That's why I'm thinking so much about the world of the departed. And you and I have done no little talking about it either, and I'd like to ask you to do something for me if possible.'

Eygló nodded. As the years went by, Málfríður had become more and more interested in what happens after death.

'What is it that you want me to do for you?'

Eygló had begun to suspect what Málfríður wanted from her.

'We've talked about it before. I want to get messages through.'

Fixing her nearly blind eyes upon Eygló, Málfríður squeezed her hand.

'I have nothing left but curiosity,' she said, lowering her voice. 'I'd like to ask you to keep your eyes open should it come to it.'

The priest entered the chapel, greeted the few people sitting there, and made the sign of the cross over the coffin. Then he opened the Bible and began reciting the verses on the resurrection and everlasting life. He briefly eulogised the deceased, mentioning that she'd always had a wholehearted belief in spiritualism. Then he prayed and asked those present to turn to the hymn about the flower. Someone behind Eygló cleared his throat, and soft-voiced, awkward singing began. When it was finished and those gathered had made the sign of the cross over the deceased, the funeral-home staff closed the coffin and fastened it with decorative gold screws. Friends and relatives were invited to tighten them into the coffin lid and Eygló took hold of one of them, turned it as she said a short prayer and bade farewell to her old friend, and thought about the promise she'd given her.

When the ceremony was over, she expressed her condolences to Málfríður's son, but was stopped in the foyer on the way out when someone grabbed her arm.

'Are you Eygló, by any chance?' asked a man of her age whom she'd never met before.

Eygló said yes.

'I'm sorry to disturb you. My name is Jósteinn and I knew Málfríður and her husband through the Society for Psychical Research. She talked sometimes about you and Engilbert. I didn't know your dad, but knew who he was.'

'Yes, right,' said Eygló with a smile, intending to go on her way.

'Have you sensed anything since she died?' the man whispered. He was almost impolite in his eagerness.

'Sensed anything?'

'Have you made contact with Málfríður?' The man was dressed in a long black coat that had seen better days, and his hair was messy. 'Is she here? Is she here with us, maybe?' he asked, pulling a wool cap over his head.

Eygló was surprised at the man's forwardness. She didn't care for his aggression. She found it particularly inappropriate to speak of the dead in this context, in this place.

'I don't think so . . .' she began, but was unable to finish her sentence.

'I know about your dad,' the man said softly. 'Málfríður told me what happened. That you and that friend of yours were looking for information. Isn't he a policeman? Málfríður said he was a cop.'

'I don't know what –'

'Málfríður said that you might hold a séance. That you would try to make contact with her. That you'd promised to receive messages from her.'

'You said you know about my father?'

'Are you going to do that? Are you going to hold a séance?'

'I haven't given it any thought,' said Eygló, trying to calm herself. 'What do you know about my father?'

'Yes, Engilbert,' said the man. 'I was at a séance a while back, maybe three years ago, and heard then that he'd tried to finagle money from a widow in Hafnarfjörður, some Hansína, by means of séances, not long before he died. Wasn't that in the sixties?'

Eygló stared at the man.

'What do you mean? Finagle money?'

'Well, that's what someone said. And that you were a considerably more effective medium than he ever was.'

'Listen –' Eygló had had enough of this man.

'I don't know if that's true or not,' he hastened to add apologetically. 'Someone knew her son, this Hansína's,' Jósteinn said, before mentioning a name that Eygló memorised. 'I don't know any more. Would you advertise the séance at the Society for Psychical Research, do you think? That is, if you're going to hold one, now that Málfríður is dead?'

'There will be no séance,' said Eygló, before telling the man goodbye.

Shortly afterwards, she walked across the church's car park and was opening the door of her car when she saw a ragged-looking woman come out of the cemetery and head towards her. Eygló was taken aback when the woman asked if she'd been at the coffin closing.

'Did you know Málfríður?' asked Eygló.

'We knew each other. She came here often.'

'To the cemetery?'

'Do you think she's crossed over?' asked the woman.

'Over? I suppose so,' said Eygló, hurriedly getting into her car, having had enough of strangers who presumed they had business with her.

She saw the woman standing there watching as she backed out of her parking space, but when she looked in the rear-view mirror as she drove away, the woman was gone.

6

Konrád had had no intention of involving himself in the case when he sat down with Marta and told her about his association with Valborg. He gave his report and had a cup of coffee with his friend and watched her inhale the vapour from her e-cigarette. Then he went home and tried to forget it all, unsuccessfully. His meeting with Valborg came back to him over and over, the conversations he'd had with her, her sad situation and his refusal. He could just as well have spoken to her encouragingly and promised to explore for her the options that were available but that she may have missed. Instead, he chose the easiest path and acted as if she was of no concern to him. Now, every time Valborg came to mind, he felt a deep pang of regret.

Which is probably why, two days later, he stood in front of the block of flats where she'd lived. The crime-scene investigation was finished and the police had packed up their equipment and gone. The area had been photographed back and front, samples taken, fingerprints searched for, an incident description drawn up and everything else done to help shed light on what happened when Valborg was murdered. The residents of the flats at that stairwell and indeed the entire building had been spoken to, as well as others who lived in the immediate vicinity and most of those who were known to have been acquaintances of Valborg or with whom she'd had some contact.

He'd spoken briefly to Marta over the phone to enquire about the progress of the investigation and learned that the police were nowhere closer to solving the crime. Many habitual offenders or others well known to the police were interrogated, especially those who'd committed break-ins. It was rare for such crimes to be accompanied by gross violence. Not far from Valborg's block was a shelter for alcoholics and the homeless, where two men who'd had repeat dealings with the police over the years were interviewed. Both were able to account for their whereabouts at the time of the attack on Valborg. It appeared that a rumour she'd been hoarding money at her place had been going around the neighbourhood, and could possibly have precipitated the burglary.

'She'd visited the shelter several times with food and clothing and the like,' Marta had said, 'and some stories were spun about her. We're looking into that.'

A woman pushed a pram up to the block of flats and started fussing with taking it down the basement steps. She was carrying stuffed shopping bags, making things much harder for her, and Konrád offered her his help, then took the bags and held the basement door open. A baby girl lay awake in the pram and looked up at Konrád with mistrustful eyes, and he hoped she wouldn't start crying.

The mother, who, naturally, also had her guard up due to the incident there, thanked him for his help, and Konrád asked if she'd been at home when the woman on the second floor was attacked.

'No, I was abroad,' said the woman. 'Did you know Valborg?'

'Yes, I knew her a little and was shocked when I heard the news,' said Konrád, before offering to carry the woman's shopping bags to her flat. 'I would never have thought a woman like her could be subject to such an attack.'

'Yeah, it was really unbelievable,' said the woman, who had thick red hair and freckles. She took the child from the pram, said that she lived on the third floor and thanked Konrád for his kindness. 'She was always so nice and quiet. I hardly ever noticed her. And then this happens.'

'No one noticed anything?'

'The woman in the flat below hers said she heard some commotion and thought she was moving furniture. That was all, I think.'

They went into the basement hallway. The woman held the baby and ascended the stairs ahead of Konrád, and he sensed that she wasn't entirely at ease about having let a stranger into the building with her. He explained to her that he was a retired policeman and had been assisting the police due to his acquaintance with the deceased woman. That appeared to calm the woman down a bit and she thanked him for carrying her bags up to the third floor. The child, on the other hand, continued to give him the same mistrustful look and held tightly to her mother.

'My husband and I have of course talked to the police,' she said. 'We had very little information for them.'

'You didn't notice anything unusual in connection with Valborg the last few days or weeks? No visitors, or anything?'

The woman shook her head.

'I don't recall her having any visitors at all,' she said. 'I think she was pretty lonely, but as I said, she was always really nice. Showed Lilla a huge amount of interest,' she added, referring to her child. 'Offered to babysit her and so on.'

'And did she do that?'

'Yeah, a couple of times, just briefly, if I had to pop out.'

'Yes, of course. Was she good with children?'

'Yeah, she was.'

'Did she ever tell you if she had children, now or in the past?'

'No,' said the woman thoughtfully. 'Never.'

Konrád thanked her, went down to the first floor and knocked on the door of the woman who'd heard a commotion in Valborg's flat. No one answered, and he left the block and got into his car. It wasn't his intention to question everyone in the neighbourhood. The police had already done their job and he didn't actually know what he was doing there. He looked up at the building, which hadn't been painted in a long time, at the concrete damage and weathered yellow surfaces that appeared to match the worn linoleum in the stairwell. Graffiti artists had defaced the building's gable ends and an attempt had been made at one time to paint over their scrawls, but it had only created a new canvas for the vandals.

Konrád's mobile phone rang and he saw that it was Eygló. The last time he heard from her, she'd told him she was going to attend the coffin-closing ceremony of a friend of hers who'd died in old age.

'Did your dad ever talk about a woman named Hansína?' she asked as soon as he answered.

'Hansína? No, I don't think so,' Konrád said, without remembering for certain.

'A widow. Lived in Hafnarfjörður,' said Eygló.

'I don't remember. What about her?'

'I don't really know. I was coming from the coffin closing and there was a slightly unusual, intrusive man who said that Dad had tried to dupe her. It was at the time when he started hanging around with your dad again.'

Konrád listened attentively. He'd got in touch with Eygló a few years ago because both of their fathers were a brief footnote in a criminal case from the war years. They held séances that turned out to be scams and made a lot of money from them, but when the truth came out, they went their separate ways and probably had no contact until the early sixties, when it appeared that their paths came together again. Konrád had wondered if they'd taken up their old scheme of fleecing people at séances. It was just a hunch that prompted this question, as he and Eygló had very little information about this latter period of the two men's acquaintance. That's why all the news about their interactions and collaboration woke his curiosity. Especially in light of the fact that over a period of just a few months, one of them had been found murdered in front of the slaughterhouse run by the Butchers' Association of the South on Skúlagata Street, while the other had been pulled out of the sea at Sundahöfn Harbour and appeared to have died accidentally. No injuries were found on Engilbert, Eygló's father. He had sometimes wandered down to the boats in Reykjavík Harbour to scrounge for booze, and the police thought it quite possible that he'd been doing the same when he died, perhaps having fallen between a ship and the pier and drifted into the bay. A significant amount of alcohol was measured in his blood.

'Tried to dupe her how?' Konrád asked.

'Through séances,' said Eygló.

'Do you think they were working together to deceive her?'

'He only mentioned Dad, but . . .'

'But what?'

'I can't imagine that Dad was working alone,' said Eygló. She'd always maintained that Engilbert had been a useful innocent in the hands of Konrád's father, who could be a brute and was one of the police force's most familiar acquaintances for many years. 'We know that they were colluding a bit at the time,' she said. 'Maybe Hansína was easy prey; I don't know.'

'What are you going to do with this information?'

'The man I met thought that her son was still alive. I was thinking of talking to him. Find out if there's anything to this. Then we might be able to determine if our fathers had started scheming together again and targeting victims who were easy to deceive and swindle.'

7

During the call, Konrád had watched a young woman walk towards the block of flats and disappear into the lobby. Soon afterwards, a light came on in the flat on the first floor whose door he had knocked on without result. He got out of his car and rang that flat's bell. After a moment, the door phone crackled and a woman's voice said hello. Konrád introduced himself and asked if the woman had time to speak to him about the incident there in the building; he'd known the dead woman. There was silence on the door phone, and Konrád was about to ask again when another crackle was heard and the front door opened.

When he reached the landing, he saw that the woman had opened her door slightly and was watching him nervously.

'I don't know what I can do for you,' she said, and Konrád sensed the same mistrust from her as from the mother with the baby. It was understandable. A terrible thing had happened there in that building, filling the general population with both disgust and fear.

Not only was the act horrific and merciless, but the perpetrator was still at large and it wasn't known who he was or what he might be up to.

Konrád tried to calm the woman and say all the right words. He had considerable experience in doing so, having worked as a police officer for decades, and it wasn't long before she invited him in and they sat down in the kitchen. The woman said she'd lived in the building for only a year or so, and she liked it very much. She lived alone, worked at a shop nearby and had been rather distracted the night Valborg was attacked. Her sister had been in a car accident and she'd been with her at the hospital for twenty-four hours, but then come home and paced her flat while waiting for news of her. She'd tried to take a nap to make up for her lack of sleep, but had done nothing apart from stare at the ceiling, and just when the hospital called, she heard some noise from the flat above but paid little notice until afterwards.

'I told the police officers who came here and questioned the neighbours that I hadn't noticed anything because I was on the phone.'

'I hope you didn't get bad news,' said Konrád.

'It's not . . . not really possible to answer that yet,' the woman said. 'She was buying me a birthday present. My sister. It's my birthday tomorrow and a car hit hers from the side . . .'

She stopped.

'Was it a coincidence that Valborg was attacked?' she then asked, and it was clear from her appearance that she'd been under great strain over the last few days. She spoke wearily and had rings under her eyes. Konrád thought it best not to trouble her any more than he thought necessary, and half regretted being a nuisance.

'Most likely,' he said, 'but it's impossible to confirm anything under the present circumstances. The police are a bit perplexed by it. Did Valborg ever say anything to you about her friends or relatives? Did you ever notice anyone visiting her?'

'No, I don't think she ever had any visitors.'

'And you haven't noticed any unusual people here around this building? Anyone in the back garden? Anyone on the street who stood out?'

'No, nothing like that,' said the woman. 'How did you say you knew Valborg again?'

'She came to me with a particular problem,' answered Konrád, unsure if he should tell the whole truth. 'I could have done more for her.'

'What was it?'

'It was personal,' said Konrád. 'I don't know if she would have wanted me to talk about a private matter.'

'No, I understand,' said the woman. 'She was always so friendly, ever since I moved into the building, and I never heard of her having any difficulties or struggling with any problems. We're always so silent about what's wrong in our lives, instead of talking about it. We hope no one finds out about it and that it just goes away one day.'

'So she didn't tell you about her illness, then?' Konrád asked.

'No – was she ill?'

'She didn't have long to live, apparently. You weren't told about it?'

'No, not at all. I didn't know that. Poor woman. And then this.'

'Yes. She had cancer. Endured it quite well but knew that her time was limited and wanted to settle certain issues.'

'Is that why she contacted you?'

'Yes.'

'If only I'd known. I might have been able to help lighten her burden.'

'I'm sure she would have come to you if she'd needed any help.'

Shortly afterwards, Konrád thanked her and got up to leave. He said he hoped he hadn't bothered her too much and walked towards the door, looking at the same time into her living room, at the sofa and flat-screen TV and the few pictures on the walls. He noticed a handsome pair of binoculars on a table by the living-room window and she saw that his curiosity was piqued.

'I'm not spying on anything,' she said, going and picking up the binoculars. 'I'm trying to see if anyone is watching me.'

'What do you mean?'

'Maybe I'm being overly sensitive, but two or three times, I've seen a gleam from one of the buildings over there, as if from a mirror or binoculars or something like that, but I haven't been able to see exactly where it's coming from.'

'From a building over there?' Konrád pointed to where three five-storey blocks of flats were lined up side by side.

'I feel like it could be the one in the middle,' said the woman, 'but it's like they're kind of on top of each other, so I'm not entirely sure.'

Marta answered breathlessly after several rings.

'Did you notice the curtains in Valborg's living room?' Konrád asked as he sat back down in his car.

'What about them?' Marta panted into the phone.

'Am I disturbing you? What are you doing? Is there someone with you?'

'Ehh . . . jogging.'

'When did you start jogging?'

'What's with the questions? What do you want?'

'Were the curtains open?' Konrád asked.

'Open? Yes, the curtains of all the windows were open.'

'I think someone witnessed the murder from the outside,' said Konrád, 'and called immediately. And I think I know why he doesn't want to talk to the police.'

'Who?'

'A man with binoculars.'

'A man with binoculars? And why doesn't he want to talk to us?'

'It's very simple. He's a peeping Tom.'

8

The man led the psychic healer up the narrow staircase and into the dark attic flat. Eygló followed behind with a weight on her chest that she'd been carrying all morning, a feeling of anxiety whose source she didn't know, but that became more noticeable with every step she took. The woman rented the flat from the man who'd met them at the door. She had two children and the older one was terribly ill, and the woman had called for the healer in an attempt to help the child. It was the flu, which was going around town. The girl had caught it and stayed in bed for a few days, but then had got up and about too soon and been struck back down by it. Now she was twice as bad as before, with headaches and muscle aches and a high fever. Earlier that day, she'd thrown up twice. She was seven years old.

 It was a cold February day in the Þingholt neighbourhood in 1978, and a little light snow cover swirled up now and then on the streets. The healer's name was Kristleifur; he was a short-statured, chubby man, and wore a thick coat and a hat on his head. Kindness and care radiated from his round face. Eygló liked him because he was friendly and unpretentious. He was the husband of Málfríður from the Society for Psychical Research and it was her idea that Eygló accompany Kristleifur on house calls in order to learn from him. Eygló hadn't taken the idea badly and accompanied him on a few visits, but kept a low profile, for the most part. The healer was in contact with physicians from the other world, seven of them, who wanted to use him for good works. Wherever he went, he pointed out that he was no physician himself, but only the tool of the physicians from the beyond for helping the sick and weak.

The girl was lying in a small room in the attic, in a bed that she shared with her mother and younger brother. The woman lived under straitened circumstances, with her two children to support. The girl went to school in the mornings and the boy went to a babysitter, allowing the woman to work in a fish-processing plant out on Grandi, in the western part of town. She was tidy and took good care of her children.

Taking off his hat and coat and placing both on a chair, the healer spoke softly to the woman, asking about her daughter's medical history. The mother's worried expression could not be concealed as she told the doctor how the illness started, and she said she should have taken better care of the girl and not let her get up so soon. She hadn't realised that the poor child hadn't completely recovered. She'd seemed healthy enough and had felt well enough to go to school, but when the woman came home in the evening, she found her daughter lying gravely ill in bed. The girl had a key and had got herself home to the attic after school and lain there alone and helpless half the day. Her mother had rung a doctor on call, who gave the girl something to bring her fever down and told the mother to keep a close watch on her.

'She started having bad stomach pains this morning, my poor darling,' the mother said. 'I've called the doctor, but he can't come right away. I gave her aspirin.'

Eygló sensed the mother's intense fear, and without immediately realising it, started to smell something peculiar, but had no idea where it was coming from.

The healer asked if he could wash his hands, and, that being done, he went in to the girl's room and sat down on the edge of her bed. She was in a drowsy haze and barely noticed it when he put his hand on her forehead, bowed his head and began praying. His lips moved and his fingers held the girl's small forehead, making her face practically disappear under his palm. He closed his eyes and his expression was stern and focused, like a priest exorcising the devil.

'Was she cooking here recently, do you know?' Eygló whispered to the landlord as they stood in the living room. The mother watched the healer from the bedroom doorway. Her son was sleeping on an old sofa in the living room, apparently unbothered by it all.

'Cooking? No,' the man whispered back. 'I don't think she's prepared any food since the girl fell ill.'

'What about you?'

'What about me?'

'Have you been cooking?'

'I've boiled haddock for the last three days now,' the man whispered.

'And brought some up to them?'

'Yes,' he whispered. 'I've made enough for all of us, but she hasn't had much of an appetite. Understandably. They're very close. She and the girl.'

'Do you live alone downstairs?'

'Yes.'

Eygló fell silent. The smell grew stronger in her nostrils and she eased her way into the kitchen. A pot of curdled milk stood on an electric hob. The odour she smelled wasn't coming from the house. It evoked memories of the cheap food her mother would buy in the autumn and fry. The offal. Liver, heart and kidneys. It was food that Eygló found particularly unappetising, besides the fact that she didn't like the thought of eating animals' organs.

In the bedroom, the healer held the girl's forehead and his lips moved in supplication. The girl opened her eyes halfway and the healer smiled at her and asked her not to fear, her mother was with her. Wearing a serious expression, the girl clutched her stomach and groaned in pain.

'Does it hurt, dear?' asked the healer.

The girl nodded.

'In your stomach?'

Again the girl nodded, and it was clear that she was suffering.

The healer moved his hand to her stomach and continued praying, and the girl groaned again in pain and looked tearfully at her mother, who was standing in the doorway, trying to smile encouragingly at her.

Meanwhile, Eygló stood motionless in the kitchen and thought of her mother and the entrails, and of the girl in the room, the healer and the prayers.

'We need to get her to the hospital,' Eygló said to the mother as she came out of the kitchen. 'You should call an ambulance.'

'What . . . ?'

'Call an ambulance now!'

The healer looked up.

'What commotion is this?' he asked.

'She needs to see a doctor,' said Eygló. 'This isn't just the flu. This is much more serious than the flu.'

'Why do you say that?' the healer asked in surprise.

Eygló turned to the mother and ordered her again to call an ambulance. The mother looked from her to the healer and back again before rushing to the phone and calling.

'Are you sure?' the healer asked Eygló.

'The girl needs to get to the hospital,' she said. 'That's all I know.'

The girl moaned in agony, and the healer tried to calm her down and looked at Eygló. She wanted most of all to take the child in her arms, but instead gave way to the mother, who reappeared in the doorway with a blanket and laid it over her daughter. The healer stood up from the bed and the mother was about to lift the girl and carry her out of the room, but Eygló stopped her.

'Leave it to the paramedics,' she said.

'What?'

'It's better that they take care of this,' said Eygló in a soothing tone.

She bent over the girl and stroked her forehead. The girl, who was both fearful and on the verge of passing out, gave Eygló a questioning look. Sweat sprang from her forehead and she grimaced in pain.

'Try not to worry,' said Eygló, smiling reassuringly.

The girl looked up at her and tried to smile back, but groaned again and clutched her stomach.

A few moments later, an ambulance parked in the street in front of the house, sliding a bit on the thin covering of snow. Two paramedics started to carry a stretcher up the stairs, but realising it was too awkward, they left the stretcher behind, went into the flat and lifted the girl gently from her bed and then carried her down the stairs and out to the ambulance. The girl's mother went with them, sitting with her daughter in the back of the ambulance, which soon headed down the street, lights flashing.

The healer took his hat and coat.

'I understand you'll look after the boy?' he said to the landlord, glancing at the girl's brother, who was still sleeping on the sofa and hadn't stirred the whole time.

'Yes,' said the landlord. 'I'll be here at home. I'll take care of him.'

'Good,' said the healer. 'Hopefully the girl will be fine. Would you mind letting us know?'

The man promised, and the little group went back down the stairs. The healer and Eygló said goodbye to the landlord with handshakes, and at that, their house call was over.

It wasn't until they were driving home that Eygló discovered that the healer resented her for her intervention, even though he tried to handle it well. He said he'd let her come along on Málfríður's recommendation, but it had been his understanding that she wouldn't interfere with his work or disrupt it in any way, but just observe and learn. Eygló apologised. She hadn't been aware of those conditions regarding their collaboration, and had only been concerned about the girl's welfare. Their goodbyes were rather curt when he dropped her off at her home.

She didn't expect to hear from him again. Late that evening, the phone rang. It was Málfríður.

'Kristleifur called the hospital and spoke to the sick girl's mother,' said Málfríður. 'She was still there.'

'How is the child?'

'They think she'll recover,' said Málfríður. Eygló breathed a sigh of relief.

'Was it her kidneys?' she asked cautiously.

'Yes, it was . . . how did you know? Is that why you had the mother call an ambulance?'

'I don't know . . . I smelled something. I experienced a very strong sensation. I don't know why. I have no idea why.'

'The doctors diagnosed her with a serious infection in both kidneys,' said Málfríður. 'She's been given IV antibiotics, and they've probably managed to save her life. It was very close.'

They said goodbye shortly afterwards, and as night drew over, Eygló went to bed but had a hard time falling asleep. The weight she'd felt on her chest all day was still there.

9

Now and then on her way through the Þingholt neighbourhood, Eygló passed the house with the attic flat and recalled the story of the sick girl. The house had long since fallen into complete disrepair, and no one had lived in it for years. The windows and doors were boarded up and the graffiti artists had been ruthless with it, and in addition, someone had apparently even tried once to set it on fire. When Eygló stopped in front of the house, memories slowly crept into her head of the narrow stairs to the attic, the mother's worries and the girl's illness. Málfríður had mentioned Eygló's visit to that house the last time Eygló saw her in the hospital. She'd dreamed of her husband shortly before her death and believed that Kristleifur would escort her into the afterlife.

Eygló wasn't going to make any more such house calls. She knew the history of those who were at the forefront in psychic healing but realised, following her visit to that attic flat, that when life hung in the balance, she didn't want to be the one holding on to that thread.

That was in line with her feelings about the abilities that both her father and later Málfríður wanted her to develop better. She had long repressed what she sensed, the visions that she saw as a child and discussed with her father while he was still alive. She resisted them and wanted nothing to do with them, as they could arouse fear and uneasiness in her. Over the years, her attitude changed and she began to acquaint herself better with the theories of psychological causes for such visions or hallucinations that weren't at all related to life after death, but also stories about the afterlife and seers and incidents that occurred for which no explanations could be found unless people believed firmly in an afterlife.

Her house call with Kristleifur was a part of her learning process. Eygló couldn't explain her strange perception of the disease that was harrying the girl. It came to her unbidden and in the oddest way. She'd gone on house calls with Kristleifur before, but hadn't experienced anything like it.

Nor did she know anything more about the people who'd called the healer and once lived in the house that was now so dilapidated. She'd never run into them afterwards.

She'd come to Þingholt to meet Hansína's son, who lived one street down. His name was Böðvar and she hadn't been able to reach him by phone, so she set out in the hope of meeting him. Jósteinn, who told her about Hansína, had given her the son's name, and when she couldn't find him online, she looked him up in an old phone book she still had. There, she found him listed along with an address, and hoped he would still be living there.

The house at the address listed for him didn't look much better than the one that Eygló had just passed by. It was a two-storey house and hadn't had any maintenance done on it for what appeared to be ages; the gutters were rusty and the window frames were rotting. The gable was in particularly bad shape, with cracks and peeling paint. There was a small front garden that was untended and overgrown.

The house had one entrance, and Eygló knocked on the door without anyone answering, so she stepped into a small hall, where she found a door to the flat on the ground floor and a wooden staircase to the upper floor. She didn't know which floor Böðvar occupied, and when no one answered on the ground floor, she climbed the stairs and knocked on the first-floor door. When nothing happened, she knocked again, harder this time, and heard a rustling sound inside. She was about to knock a third time when the door opened and an angry eye stared at her through a small gap.

'Böðvar?' she said.

The eye stared silently at her.

'Sorry to bother you,' said Eygló, 'but I wanted to talk to you about your mother, Hansína. Wasn't that her name?'

The eye took her measure.

'Are you Böðvar?'

The eye continued to stare at her through the chink.

'Was your mother Hansína?'

The eye disappeared, but the door didn't close. After several moments, Eygló ventured to push it open. She was immediately met by the stench of years of neglect, mingled with the odours of sewage, dampness and mildew that had seeped out onto the landing but erupted once the door was opened all the way. She just managed to cover her nose, so awful was the stench. The man was seated on a filthy sofa in the living room, where there was an old tube television. The room wasn't particularly well lit, but when Eygló got used to the darkness, she noticed all sorts of stuff that the man had collected and that filled every nook and cranny: metal junk of various kinds, cardboard boxes of newspapers and piles of books reaching from the floor to the ceiling.

'What the fuck do you care about my mother?' the man asked.

'I wanted to know if she'd been in any contact with my father,' said Eygló.

'Who was he?'

'His name was Engilbert,' Eygló said, instinctively not going too far into the flat, but staying close to the door.

'Doesn't ring a bell,' said the man. Eygló assumed that he was the Böðvar she'd come to visit. He was almost completely bald, but made up for it with a big beard that reached high up his cheeks, grey and unkempt. He was particularly repulsive as he leaned back in blue sweatpants and a red T-shirt that bore the logo of a foreign football club and swung his knees casually open and shut as if revealing his crotch to her. 'I don't know any Engilbert,' he said.

'He was a medium. I heard that he visited your mother.'

Böðvar stared at her from the sofa.

'A medium?'

'A seer. He held meetings and séances. I understand he paid visits to Hansína.'

'Who did you say you were?'

'His daughter. Was your mother interested in such things? Séances?'

His knees swinging open and shut, Böðvar continued to stare at her.

'Mum died thirty years ago,' he said.

'This happened much further back,' said Eygló, glancing around at all the junk in the flat and the man's miserable living conditions. It all made her feel very ill at ease. 'Did she have . . . did she have a lot of money?' she asked.

'A lot of money?' the man snorted. 'What gives you that idea?'

'There was a story that they . . . that he'd intended to fleece her,' said Eygló. 'She was a believer in the afterlife and my father took advantage of that to finagle money from her. Does that ring any bells?'

Böðvar had stopped swinging his knees open and shut.

'Hold on, was that your dad? Weren't there two of them?'

'Could have been,' said Eygló, thinking of Konrád's father.

'Damned con men. I remember them. They tried to take what little she had from her. Fucking bastards. They pretended to be in contact with our grandma in the beyond and knew all about her, somehow, and all kinds of orders came from her about giving money to this and that charity and they said they'd take it and get it into the right hands. Mum paid them some money until me and my brothers got wind of it and were there waiting for them at home the next time. They didn't pay any more visits to Mum after that.'

The man stood up. He seemed drunk to her. There was an open bottle of vodka on the table. Empty wine bottles and beer cans lay strewn about the flat.

'What did you do when they showed up?' asked Eygló.

'One of them was just some wimpy loser. Was that your dad?! He immediately started wailing excuses to us. The other was rock hard and clearly controlled him. Bastard. Fucking maggot. He came at us. Wasn't he killed afterwards? Wasn't that him? Aren't you talking about him?'

'He was stabbed to death, if it's the same man,' said Eygló.

'At the slaughterhouse, wasn't it? Why are you asking about all this now?'

'Were those two working together?'

'Sure were. We threw them out. The bastard wasn't going to have any of it and we had to rough him up a bit. Why are you asking about this now?'

'Do you know if they swindled others . . . maybe other women at that time? Are you aware of any such thing? Other visits?'

'Mum wasn't the only one. Her friend Stella was another. They played her badly. There were probably more. Those kinds of guys are everywhere, with their nets out. Fraudsters and losers.'

'Is she alive? This Stella?'

'Are you like him, your dad, maybe? Are you swindling people, too? Pretending to be some kind of medium, maybe?'

'Can you tell me where I can find her, and –'

'Do you see all kinds of ghosts in here?!' said the man, raising his voice and pretending to look all around. 'Are there ghouls hovering around here? What are they saying? Where are they? What do you see?'

Eygló looked at the man calmly, but had to settle herself before saying anything. The only ghoul in there was the sad picture before her.

'Can you tell –'

'I can tell you to get the hell out of here!' the man shouted, stepping threateningly closer to her. 'Get out! Leave! I don't want to see your face here again! Piss off! Out!'

Eygló was relieved to get back out into the fresh air and walked back past the derelict house where the sick girl had lived. Again she stopped in front of it, and was standing there regarding the graffiti and the dereliction when a middle-aged man stepped out of the house next door and noticed her standing there looking at it.

'It's in damned awful shape,' he said.

'How long has it been since anyone lived in it?' she asked.

'Two decades at least. Apparently it's going to be torn down and a new one built. Do you know anything about the house?'

'No, not much. I went there once,' said Eygló. 'A woman with two young children was living there. It was in the seventies. It's been a long time.'

'Did she have a girl and a boy?' said the man.

'Yes, that's right.'

'I got to know them a little when I lived here. I just bought my childhood home here next door and I'm going to fix it up,' he added as if in explanation, smiling.

'Do you know what happened to her?'

'No, she was divorced, I recall,' said the man, taking out a key fob, 'but I don't know what became of her. We actually moved to another neighbourhood.'

'I don't remember much about the boy,' said Eygló. 'His sister got sick and it was so sad . . .'

'They weren't actually siblings,' said the man, and a car behind Eygló beeped as he unlocked it. 'He was a foster child. He told me that when I ran into him a number of years ago. He was pretty confused, the poor fellow, and didn't look good. Had been hitting the bottle, I'm afraid,' the man remarked, before getting into the car and driving off down the street.

10

The woman immediately realised who Konrád was and agreed to meet him, but was somewhat surprised by the call. She admitted that she'd never expected him to contact her after all this time.

She knew he was a policeman. Many years after the incident at the slaughterhouse, someone had mentioned to her that he worked as a detective, which made her think he might call her one day. She found that quite natural in the small society that Iceland was in those days – and indeed still was – in which everyone knew everyone else and was acquainted in some way or bound by family ties. When the years passed and she came across his name in connection with criminal investigations that had made it into the media, she sometimes wondered why he'd never called.

When he finally got in touch after so many years, she wasn't just surprised, but also curious. She couldn't refrain from asking about it when they met at a cafe in the city centre, saying that she hoped he didn't take it as presumption on her part. Pointed out that it was none of her business, of course, what he did or didn't do. She just wanted to quench her curiosity and he mustn't take it amiss, but he'd worked for a long time as a detective and his father was murdered. Why hadn't he ever looked into that case? And why was he doing so now?

'Or maybe you did without my being aware of it,' she quickly added, realising that that was a possibility, as well. That he'd delved into it without talking to her. 'Of course, there was no reason why I should have known about it.'

Konrád smiled, getting the feeling that she wasn't prying, but wanted to help him if possible. She was the woman who had found his father dead outside the slaughterhouse. She was very straightforward and had been receptive to his call, listened to him with an open mind and agreed without hesitation to meet him once she'd got over her surprise. 'Just let me know when,' she'd said.

Konrád, however, hadn't expected that she would press him in this way and found himself tongue-tied, as had sometimes happened when this case came up in conversation. His father was the sort of person who was difficult to be around and Konrád sometimes thought that he'd brought on himself the cruel fate he'd suffered, despite nothing justifying such violence. He left behind him a long trail of petty crimes and misdemeanours, prison terms and dealings with the dregs of society. Family life wasn't much better: drunkenness, domestic violence and, finally, abuse, which Konrád didn't find out about until much later. The last interactions between the father and son were full of anger and hatred, due to the fact that Konrád's mother had finally told him the truth. Many years before, she'd saved her daughter from her husband's clutches, moving out east to

Seyðisfjörður after she discovered that he'd started molesting the girl. Neighbours described a loud argument between the father and son only a few hours before the murder. It so happened that Konrád's mother was in town that night. Early the next morning, she was on a bus heading back east. The police stopped the bus in the village of Blönduós. During repeated questionings, she denied all involvement in and knowledge of the matter. Her sister and brother-in-law confirmed that she'd stayed with them and not gone out that night. Konrád had also been summoned for questioning. His friends said they'd been with him all night.

There at the cafe, the woman sipped her coffee. They sat off to one side and the question hung in the air.

'I don't know,' said Konrád. 'Maybe it's something that's grown over the years. The need to know. I have more time on my hands and sometimes think about what happened. My father wasn't a pleasant man, and made enemies easily.'

'Have there been any developments in the case?' asked the woman who had once come across his father lying in his own blood. Her name was Helga, and she'd been running a dance school for the longest time. She smiled easily and moved gracefully.

'No, none,' Konrád answered. 'This case is a real mystery, and I haven't really given it any serious thought. It was dealt with quite well at the time. I can't fault the investigation. It's more like fiddling around, on my part.'

She seemed satisfied with his explanation, as imperfect as it was, and recalled what had happened that fateful night. It was vivid in her mind's eye, despite decades having passed. She would never experience anything like it again, and had nightmares about it for a long time afterwards.

Back then, she was taking dancing lessons in the evenings at Jón Þorsteinsson's gym on Skuggasund Street with two of her friends, and went home with one of them after practice and sat with her until late that night. The woman lived on Lindargata Street, whereas Helga lived in one of the blocks of flats at the eastern end of Skúlagata Street, not far from where the new police station was later built. The two friends lost track of time choreographing new moves for a dance competition to be held the following week, and when Helga saw how late it was, she decided to take the shortest way home along Skúlagata.

'I went that way almost every day and knew the route like the back of my hand,' said Helga. The Völundur woodshop with its tower, the Klöpp petrol station down by the sea, the old Kveldúlfs-skáli building and the slaughterhouse. 'On the other hand, I was hardly ever there that late at night, and at the time, it was a pretty shady part of town. The street lighting was poor and there was almost no traffic on Skúlagata, as there were far fewer cars in the city back then. I remember that long before I got to the slaughter-house, I could smell the odour of the smoking kilns, which hung over the entire area,' she added – contradicting her testimony in the case files, which made no mention of the kilns having been running.

'I remember the smell well,' said Konrád. It was inescapable when they lit the kilns.

'There was supposed to be a light over the entrance to the slaughterhouse, but the bulb was out, the police told me later, so I'd come quite near before I noticed the heap on the pavement in front of the gate. I had no idea what it was and slowed down. I was afraid it might be a dog and I was scared of them, but then I saw that that wasn't what it was at all.'

Helga took a sip of coffee.

'There was a man lying there in the street and I thought it was a tramp dozing by the gate.'

'So you hurried across the street?' asked Konrád. He'd read her testimony numerous times.

'I was afraid of tramps,' she said. 'Dogs and tramps. There were tramps in town back then. Now you hardly ever see them.'

'And when you crossed the street, you saw that there was something wrong with the man.'

'I saw the black puddle. The blood under him. It was awful, all that blood. Instead of running away as fast as I could, I went closer and saw that he was badly wounded. I thought he was dead, but he wasn't.'

'You saw that he was alive.'

Helga nodded.

'He looked at me and tried to say something but I didn't hear what it was, and when I moved closer, I stepped in the puddle of blood and got it on my shoes. It's one of my strongest memories of that horror. Of course I was just a child. I never wanted to wear these shoes again and my mum had to give them away. She never threw anything away, my mum.'

'And you never knew what he was trying to say?'

'No. He saw me, stretched out his hand and opened his mouth and died right before my eyes. I was the last thing he saw in this life. A sixteen-year-old girl who happened to be walking down Skúlagata.'

'I can imagine how awful it was for you, so young,' said Konrád.

'It was just horrendous.'

'I hope you'll forgive me for making you recall it.'

'Well, it's just good to be able to talk about it with you, finally.

I've known about you for a long time and I think it's good that you got in touch. I think it's great.'

'I'm sure you've often wondered what he was trying to say.'

'I still believe that it was the name of the person who stabbed him,' said Helga.

'You mentioned that he made a peculiar sound.'

'Yes, it's hard to describe.'

'Wasn't he just groaning in pain?'

'I felt like he was trying to say something.'

Helga continued to describe what had happened. She told Konrád that the petrol station and every other business on the street had been closed, so she'd run up to the residential area on Vitastígur Street and knocked on the door of the first house she came to. She woke the residents and they called the police, once she'd been able to speak calmly and clearly.

'I was so surprised that the police knew immediately who the man was,' she said, again contradicting her testimony in the police reports. 'One of the first officers to arrive said: "Oh, it's him." Somehow, it didn't surprise them to see him lying there in the street.'

'He was one of their close acquaintances, as they're called,' said Konrád.

'Yes, and they acted like it. As if it was all his fault. That was the feeling I got, and I always remember my astonishment at the way they talked about him.'

'Did a crowd gather at the slaughterhouse?'

'No, I couldn't say that. Just people who lived on Vitastígur and a few passers-by. There weren't many. I remember newspaper photographers. Somehow, it all went by so quickly. Then the police brought me home and talked to Dad and Mum, who had of course started getting worried and had called my friends. I became a bit famous in the family and at school. I'd found a body. Stumbled on a murder. It was all thought so exciting. I thought it was terrible. And I still do.'

'Did you notice anything or anyone peculiar there at the scene or in the vicinity? Someone who stood out? Was hanging around? Acted strange?'

'No.'

'You say that the smoking kilns were running?'

'Yes, I think they must have been.'

'You didn't see any Butchers' Association employees inside the gate?' Konrád asked. He remembered that the kilns were on Skúlagata, east of the gate.

'No.'

The reports noted that there was an iron gate at the entrance to the slaughterhouse on Skúlagata, and that it had been tightly locked. Employees of the company were interviewed, but no link to Konrád's father was found and most of them had alibis. Only a few couldn't account for their whereabouts at the time of the murder, but they were loners who didn't know the victim, had clean police records and no reason to commit such a crime. On the other hand, the murder weapon was never found and the only hypothesis was that it had been a butcher's knife. But that couldn't be determined by the two wounds found on the body. Such analyses were primitive in those days. The depth of the wounds, the width from the back of the blade to its edge, possible contamination from previous uses that the weapon left behind, all of these things were taken into consideration without it greatly reducing the types of knives possible. The attack seemed to have taken Konrád's father by surprise, been purposeful and done without any hesitation. He hadn't been able to defend himself against it at all. No wounds were found on his hands, there was nothing under his fingernails to indicate that he may have grappled with his assailant, scratched his face or grabbed his hair. There were no marks on the hard pavement that could be assumed to belong to the assailant, and he hadn't stepped in the pool of blood as Helga did a short time later. He was unidentifiable and had been so ever since the murder was committed.

'This experience has always been with you,' Konrád said.

'But not in as bad a way as it has for you,' said Helga, smiling as if any such comparison was absurd.

Marta called late that evening to ask Konrád more about his interactions with the deceased, as she worded it so professionally. Konrád said that he thought he'd told her everything he knew about Valborg, which was really very little. He sensed an awkwardness in Marta, as if she were in two minds about this phone call of hers.

'You really shouldn't be involving yourself in this investigation,' she finally said.

'I'm not,' he said.

'No, right, that's why you're hanging around outside her block and pestering her neighbours.'

'Are you calling about that?'

'Did she seem all right to you, I mean Valborg? When you met her. Balanced?'

'I think sedate is the word I would have used for her,' said Konrád.

'Did she seem to be in pain?'

'What's going on, Marta? It's late and I was about to hit the hay.'

'Aw, damn it, I know I can't say anything because you're retired and these things are all confidential and I'm bound to secrecy, but then I just blurt everything out to you as usual.'

'What are you going to blurt out to me?'

'Your friend had old scars on her inner thighs. Very old and faded, but they were found during the autopsy. It looks as if she hurt herself at some point. Cut her own legs.'

'How old are those wounds?'

'Old as hell. But that's not all. She'd been at it again, because they found a more recent scar in the same place. That was actually the reason why they started looking into it.'

'What the hell.'

'She can't have been well,' said Marta.

'Self-harm?'

'You didn't hear it from me,' said Marta.

'Was she punishing herself?'

'That's one explanation. Anxiety. Depression. Suicidal thoughts. It seems she was struggling, the poor woman, for whatever reason.'

11

Konrád took a bite of the sandwich. It wasn't good and he looked at the sell-by date. It was well past it, and he envisioned the satisfied face of the kid at the petrol station who sold it to him. He actually considered eating it, all the same, because he was starving and it didn't smell rotten, but he didn't want to take a chance on old mayonnaise and put the sandwich down. He opened his Thermos and took a gulp of the coffee, lit a cigarillo and blew the smoke through the crack in his window. The entire time, he'd kept his eye on the three blocks of flats standing practically on top of each other. It was evening, and he was watching for a gleam from one of the windows. Ideally, he wanted to catch the peeping Tom with his binoculars in hand.

Two days ago, Marta had sent officers to those buildings to check whether any of the residents had witnessed Valborg's murder and alerted the police. The building where Valborg lived was about three hundred metres away, and a person with good binoculars could easily see into her flat, as Konrád said when he spoke to Marta. It took a good deal of persuasion to get her to promise to look into the matter, as she considered some gleam in the neighbourhood to be irrelevant to her investigation.

The officers still didn't know who it was that Valborg's neighbour thought was spying on the neighbourhood's residents. They went from one flat to another and spoke to those who were registered at those blocks, and the residents allowed them to enter. Most of the flats were occupied by married or unmarried couples of various ages, with or without children, most of whom were very surprised by the policemen's visit. Some dug out binoculars or spotting scopes that they'd acquired during their lives for various reasons; a few had travelled a lot around the country or were birdwatchers, others had been given them as a confirmation or graduation gift and never used them. From the flats that were on the third floor or higher, one could easily see over to Valborg's building and in through her window.

Konrád sighed heavily.

His son, Húgó, had called from the United States. He and his family were in Florida, visiting friends, a doctor and his wife whom Konrád didn't know much about, but who had a house out there. Apparently, they were great golf enthusiasts, and Húgó and his wife were slowly heading in that direction, too. The twins, Konrád's grandsons, were with them and he'd spoken to them on the phone and asked if Florida wasn't a terribly boring place. He enjoyed teasing them. They practically shouted 'no way' over each other and talked about the sea and the beach and said they'd gone to the movies. Konrád missed them.

He looked at the sandwich and didn't know how long he could keep up this stakeout of his. It was an awful lot of windows that he had to keep his eye on. He was cold and hungry and his concentration wasn't at its best. His mind went back time and again to his conversation with Helga. She hadn't been able to tell him anything new, except about the smoking kilns. They must have been filled that day with brined pork bellies and legs of lamb before being lit, and then the smoke transformed the meat into delicious bacon and juicy smoked lamb.

Konrád took a sip of coffee and, as often happened when he let his mind wander, his consciousness filled with memories of Erna.

It took him a long time to tell her about his father and he didn't actually do it until a week before their wedding. He'd managed to deflect her questions about his family by speaking in general terms about his mother and sister who had moved east. He hardly mentioned his father by name, saying that he was dead and had been a labourer, which wasn't entirely untrue. Konrád didn't want to ruin his relationship with Erna with stories of his father. He feared losing her. As time passed, his silence became deafening and she could tell how difficult it was for him when family matters came up. In the end, he gave in and tried to choose his words carefully when he told her what happened at the slaughterhouse. She remembered the murder and admitted that she'd never been so surprised in her life. Little by little, she got Konrád to tell her the whole story of his father's criminal activities, the domestic violence and divorce, and little Beta, who'd fallen into their father's clutches.

'But . . . how could you stay with him?' was the first thing she said, as sensible as she always was.

'He wouldn't let me leave,' Konrád said. 'And that's how he got his revenge on Mum. He kept me there, and Mum didn't have the energy to deal with him any more. She tried her best and always met me if she was in town, and kept track of how I was feeling. She contacted the child welfare authorities but Dad played them and got things postponed indefinitely, and when I was asked, I said I wanted to stay with him. But I didn't know everything. He was clever in that way, how he got people on his side.'

'Why didn't you tell me this earlier?'

'Isn't it obvious?' said Konrád. 'I didn't want to ruin anything for us. It's all one big sad story.'

'You wouldn't have ruined anything.'

'I didn't want to take the risk.'

'So you grew up with that horrible man?'

'He treated me OK,' said Konrád, 'but yes, he wasn't an easy person to be around. On the other hand, I had a certain freedom that my friends didn't. And I didn't know about Beta. My mother told me much later. The day Dad died,' he added hesitantly.

What that might insinuate didn't escape Erna.

'What did the police say about it?'

'They don't know,' Konrád said. 'They know that Dad and I argued that day because the neighbours heard the commotion, but they don't know the reason why. By that time, we argued quite often. I was on the verge of moving out.'

'And was it because of Beta that you two argued that day?'

'Yes.'

'Who knows that, then?'

'No one. Mum. Beta. You.'

Erna looked into his eyes. A week later, they would be married. The question hung over them, but she refrained from asking it. Nevertheless, Konrád answered it, and then they never talked about it again.

'I have an alibi,' he said. 'It wasn't me.'

Konrád noticed at the wedding how caring Erna was of his mother. They'd only met very briefly once before, but became good friends that day, and from then on, Erna made sure to keep in almost daily contact with his mother and see to it that she lacked none of the affection she could give, despite the two of them living in different parts of the country. The same went for Beta, who could be difficult to get to know. Over time, she and Erna became good friends.

Konrád sipped his coffee and the memories came to him like microwave background radiation from the distant past.

'Why don't you try to find out who murdered your father?' Erna asked one winter's night a few years later, after they'd gone to bed. Konrád's mother had just died, and a storm was hammering the house. The topic had come up earlier that evening and, as always, he'd been reluctant to discuss it. Erna hadn't given up. 'No one is in a better position to do so,' she said. 'What are you afraid of?'

He didn't answer her, and all that was heard for a long time was the whining of the wind. The city's residents had been urged to stay indoors while the storm did its worst.

'The truth,' he finally said.

'Did you ever ask your mother about it?' whispered Erna after a moment's thought.

'It would have been like an accusation.'

'Is that why you've never wanted to look into it?'

'Yes. Among other things.'

'But . . . can it be . . . ?'

'Sometimes, I can't think who else it might have been,' Konrád whispered, his words almost drowned out by the storm.

He finished the coffee in the Thermos and was fishing a cigarillo out of his pocket when he looked up at the blocks of flats and saw a gleam in one of the windows on the fifth floor.

12

Keeping an eye on the window, Konrád got out of his car and calculated where the gleam came from, fifth floor, end flat, the middle building, from Valborg's point of view. He'd checked the building's floor plans, how the flat numbers were arranged according to stairwells, and thought he could find this flat on his first try. The doorbells were marked with the flat numbers, with the names of the residents on a board next to them. Konrád pressed the bell to a flat on the top floor, and when no one answered he tried the one next door. The owner was quick to answer the door phone and Konrád said that he'd locked himself out. It was enough. The door was opened for him and he entered the stairwell.

He waited a moment before walking past the lift and then slowly up the stairs, until he was standing in front of the flat that the gleam came from. He knocked politely on the door. A man of around twenty, dressed in sweatpants, with a baseball cap turned backwards on his head, opened the door and gawped dumbfounded at him.

'Emanúel?' Konrád said hesitantly.

'Dad!' the young man shouted into the flat, before scratching his crotch and disappearing into a bedroom.

After a moment a man came out of the living room and, with a bit of a questioning look, over to Konrád. He was about fifty, and was wearing a grey fleece jacket. His temples were greying and he seemed respectable enough, like an office worker relaxing after the hustle and bustle of the day. He remarked that no solicitation was allowed in the building, and that promotions or proselytising were banned, too.

'Yes, I'm not selling anything. Quite the contrary. I'm looking for some good binoculars,' said Konrád, forgetting that he meant to be careful. 'They would preferably need to be able to see into the building opposite.'

The man stared silently at Konrád.

'Does your son have such binoculars?' Konrád asked. 'Could I have a word with him, by any chance?'

The man looked towards the room that his son had disappeared into. His shoulders slumped and he looked sheepishly at Konrád.

'Are you with the police?' he asked. 'I heard they were asking around in these buildings.'

'They're looking for witnesses,' said Konrád, without answering the question.

'I'm no pervert,' the man whispered, to make sure that the words couldn't be heard in the hallway.

'Be that as it may,' Konrád said, 'may I come in?'

'Can I talk to you outside?' the man said, glancing again at the door to the bedroom. 'If you wouldn't mind.'

Konrád agreed and took the lift down and waited in the vestibule for Emanúel, who appeared shortly afterwards. Konrád suggested that they go sit in his car, and the man agreed. Konrád grabbed the expired sandwich and threw it in the back seat, started the car and turned up the heater.

'All I saw was that he attacked her,' said Emanúel. 'I didn't know she'd died until I went online later that evening. You can't imagine how shocked I was. I've actually been on my way to the police ever since. It's just hard to . . .'

'Admit that you spy on people?'

'I'm not spying on people,' Emanúel said firmly. 'It was a complete coincidence that I was trying out a new spotting scope when I saw it happen. Complete coincidence.'

'A new spotting scope?'

'Yes.'

'It must be powerful, with a big lens that gleams. Like a telescope.'

'Yes, it is, actually. Not so big. Very manageable.'

'And you were just trying it out?'

'Yes.'

Konrád had questioned numerous witnesses and knew when they came prepared with excuses for behaviour they weren't particularly proud of. Knew when they'd practised their spiel, had gone over it a thousand times in their heads until they themselves believed what they said.

'Do you live alone with your son?'

'My wife left me. Moved out. She'd cheated on me for two years without . . . and left the boy with me. I can't connect with him at all. He never comes out of that cave of his except to ask for money. I used his phone to report the attack.'

Suddenly Emanúel remembered that he hadn't received an answer to his question.

'Are you with the police?'

'I was with the police,' said Konrád. 'The woman you saw being attacked was a friend of mine. You didn't want to contact the police because you were trying out your new scope? If you had, it would have sped up the investigation, and then we wouldn't be sitting out here like idiots.'

'No – I was on my way to doing so,' said Emanúel. He'd clearly prepared himself for that question, too. 'I even tried to get in touch, but was put on hold.'

Konrád had a very limited interest in the man's excuses, and instead asked him what he'd seen through his lens when he pointed it at Valborg's flat. Emanúel described as best he could what he'd witnessed. He didn't hold back on any details, but turned out to give an effective, descriptive account.

'Did it seem to you as if the attacker was looking for something in particular?' Konrád asked.

'He was in her flat for only a short time,' said Emanúel. 'I was just about to report it when he ran out again. He was in a big hurry and I didn't see him too well; it was so shadowy in there. I wouldn't be able to recognise him. I never saw his face.'

'Young? Old?'

'I don't know. Not necessarily young. He moved pretty stiffly. Skinny.'

'Maybe you were looking at something else at the same time?'

'No.'

'And did he attack the woman immediately?'

'As soon as she opened the door. I was terribly worried about her, and more than a little shocked when I heard that she'd died. I had only a vague view of the attack, actually just through the window of the stairwell. I couldn't see into her hall.'

'Did you see any other residents of that building?' Konrád asked.

'No,' said Emanúel. 'Except for the woman on the floor below.'

'The one who was on the phone?'

'The phone?'

'Yes.'

'I didn't see that,' said Emanúel. 'She wasn't on the phone when I saw her. She wasn't feeling well, or that's the impression I got.'

'Her sister was in the hospital, injured.'

'Oh, I see. But she wasn't on the phone.'

'Are you sure?'

'Absolutely. There was a man with her.'

'A man? What man?!'

'I don't know, of course,' said Emanúel sheepishly. 'He was dressed in black, and then he left the flat. I didn't get a proper look at him.'

'Do you think they knew what was going on on the floor above?'

'I have no idea,' said Emanúel. 'The man left shortly before it all happened.'

'Did you see him leave the building?'

For a moment, Emanúel was tongue-tied.

'No . . . I didn't. I guess I was looking . . . looking at something else.'

'Do you think it was the same man who attacked the woman, Valborg?'

'No, that . . . I just don't know.'

'You need to talk to someone I know on the police force,' said Konrád, taking out his mobile phone and calling Marta. He looked at his dashboard clock. 'She'll be happy to hear from you,' he added, knowing that it was a waste of a good joke.

13

Konrád had a slight edge and he decided to take advantage of it. He headed to the building where Valborg had lived and died. Her neighbour on the first floor was coming up from the laundry room in the basement when Konrád showed up, giving her quite a shock, seeing him again when she walked by the front door. She opened the door for him and Konrád asked if he could bother her for a moment. She was holding the laundry that she'd taken off the clothes line and he asked if he could help her; she declined but he followed her up to her flat on the first floor.

She was wary and didn't invite him in, so he stood in her doorway and said that she'd been right about the gleam from the blocks. She wasn't quite sure what he meant at first, but then glanced at the binoculars still standing on the table by the living-room window.

'You revealed a bit about yourself,' Konrád said.

'What do you mean?'

'Do you really have a sister?'

Upon entering her flat, she'd put the laundry down on the living-room table. The TV was on; a cooking show with a smiley host putting a rack of lamb in the oven.

'I found a single father, divorced, who has no real contact with his annoying son. He finds some comfort or fulfilment in spying on the lives of others. He saw the murder being committed and it was he who called the police. He saw you here, too. Right now, he's talking to the policewoman who's investigating the case, and as a result, I'm sure she'll want to talk to you, too. Probably straight away, tonight.'

The woman looked at him and didn't say a word.

'Those gleams you saw from the buildings over there came from him.'

She looked back at the binoculars on the table.

'What did he see?' she then asked.

'You should close your curtains in the future,' Konrád said. 'I'm not sure he'll lose his urge to peep despite being given a talking-to by the police.'

The woman looked out the window.

'He saw the man who was here with you,' said Konrád.

The woman smiled faintly, but there was no pleasure in her expression.

'There's probably no way to talk about this without it sounding bad.'

'Try it.'

'I have a sister,' she said. 'That's no lie.'

'In the hospital?'

'She was involved in an accident, yes, but it may not have been as serious as I said it was.'

'And the man?'

'He's her husband.'

'Your sister's husband? He's your brother-in-law? And what, were you consoling him?'

'We've been meeting for the past few months,' said the woman. It took Konrád a moment to realise that she meant she was having an affair with her brother-in-law.

'And he was here with you right before the break-in on the floor above you?' he asked.

'Yes.'

'Why in heaven didn't you tell the police about this right away?'

'Because I didn't want my sister to know. I'm sure you understand that.'

'It's never good to lie in such matters,' Konrád said.

'But you don't think he did it? He had no reason.'

'He was seen leaving your flat,' Konrád said, 'but wasn't seen coming out of the building. Soon afterwards, Valborg was attacked.'

'Did you get this from that pervert?' said the woman, glancing at her living-room window. 'It's nonsense. He could never do such a thing. It's out of the question.'

'So your sister mustn't find out about these meetings of yours?' said Konrád. 'In other words, they're still together, your brother-in-law and her?'

'Does she need to find out?' asked the woman. 'Because if she does, I want to tell her myself. I've been meaning to do it for a long time – in fact, both of us have – but it's difficult, of course, and we've pushed it aside. And then there was the accident. She was on her way to see me when it happened, and I was going to tell her about the relationship. It's all a big mess.'

'You should hurry up and tell her,' Konrád said. 'The police will probably want to talk to you and your brother-in-law, and then it will all come out. The two of you should omit nothing. You're already on thin ice for not coming clean and saying that a man was with you.'

'But this has nothing to do with him. Or with us. We didn't do anything.'

'It's your word against his,' Konrád said. 'And you're saying a lot less than when we last met. Did Valborg ever say anything to you about her money?'

'Money? No.'

'She told me that she'd put money aside, and it crossed my mind that she may have kept some of it in her flat.'

'I had no idea about that. We never talked about money. Never.'

Konrád was out on the pavement when Marta drove up and stepped out of her car. With her was another detective who'd recently started in CID and whom Konrád hadn't met. Marta, clearly unamused, sucked on her e-cigarette.

'Why are you always bothering me?' she said. 'Why aren't you at home playing Solitaire or something?'

'Didn't you enjoy meeting Emanúel? You guys managed to miss him completely.'

'That bloody pervert,' Marta muttered.

'What, I get no thanks at all?'

'Oh, please. First of all, you shouldn't be poking your nose into this.'

She stuck her e-cigarette between her lips.

'What did the girl say?' she asked, as if immediately forgetting that Konrád shouldn't be sticking his nose in police matters.

'She told me one of those beautiful love stories that you never get tired of hearing,' Konrád said. 'I'm sure you'd enjoy it. Boy meets girl, boy falls for girl, boy starts sleeping with her sister, too.'

'How sweet,' Marta snapped, blowing out two plumes of vapour in a row before dashing like a locomotive towards the stairwell.

'How is it, working with Marta these days?' Konrád asked the young man.

'Fine,' the detective whispered, slowly setting off after her. 'It could be worse.'

'Oh, yes,' Konrád said. 'It could be.'

14

Konrád had switched off his mobile, and when he switched it back on, he saw that Eygló had called twice. He decided to call her back even though it was late in the evening. She was quick to answer, and asked if he could stop by her place in Fossvogur. She'd found out what they'd suspected, that their fathers had started collaborating again, and now she knew what they'd been up to.

She welcomed Konrád, poured a glass of red wine for him, and told him about the widow in Hafnarfjörður whom they'd tried to fleece. Their fathers. That they'd held a séance in order to cheat a gullible widow. And not just her. Her son, that Böðvar, had mentioned a friend of the widow's named Stella, who probably would have been no less easy prey for the fraudsters. Eygló said that she'd gone to the Society for Psychical Research in search of information about this Stella and discovered that a woman by that name had several connections to the society. Late that afternoon, Eygló had found out that she'd died many years ago.

Konrád listened silently to his friend. He and Eygló had often talked about their fathers, and once he'd angered her by daring to insinuate that her father may have played a role in his father's death. At the very least, it couldn't be ignored that their collaboration may have led to Engilbert or someone on his behalf having stabbed Konrád's father to death. Konrád had nothing to go on other than that the two men had possibly started in again on swindling money from people. She always maintained that Engilbert had been compelled into the collaboration during the war years, and felt awful about it. Konrád's father had been the kingpin in their scheme, a thug whom even Engilbert feared and dared not provoke. Engilbert was an incorrigible drinker who was practically destitute, so Konrád's father must have coerced Engilbert into depending on him again and using him at will.

Such were the things they discussed about the two men: Eygló's father, who'd left nothing behind for her but questions and sorrow, and Konrád's father, who'd sown in his son's mind only anger and bitterness. In a strange way, their fathers' shared story had brought them together, as different as they were otherwise. She, open to the unexplained because of the things she'd experienced and her psychic abilities. He, a law-enforcement officer who believed only in what he could see and touch. Konrád tried not to let her sense how little faith he had in everything that had shaped her world. Eygló tried to hide from him what a limited view of life and existence she thought he had. Yet their different views didn't sunder the two, and they knew each other well enough to be able to see the humorous side of the contrasts between them.

It was past midnight when Konrád put down his glass and said he needed to get going.

'It might be possible to talk to some of that Stella's relatives,' he said. 'Let me know what you decide to do, will you?'

'I will,' said Eygló, showing him to the hall, where he'd hung his jacket in the cupboard. 'It wasn't so long ago that I went online and looked up articles about the murder,' she added.

'Yes, I did a bit of that myself.'

'Have you thought about tracking down the photographers who were there? I'm sure only a fraction of the photos appeared in the newspapers. There must have been a lot more taken at the scene. It might be possible to get a look at them. If they still exist. Naturally, not everyone is as interested in keeping such things.'

'Yes, of course. The idea occurred to me, too,' Konrád said. 'For a long time, it was the same photographers year after year who eavesdropped on the police channels and even beat us to the crime scene.'

'Why do I feel the need to ask you about the smell of smoke?' Eygló said as he slipped on his jacket.

'Smoke? Maybe you're smelling Marta's e-cigarette?'

'Is that what it is?'

'Or my cigarillos? I smoked too many of them, sitting in my car tonight.'

'You brought it in with you. Quite a strong odour. But it's not . . .'

'Unless it's the smoking kilns?' Konrád smiled as if the suggestion was far-fetched. 'At the slaughterhouse. I talked to the woman who found Dad,' he added. 'I forgot to tell you that.'

'So you went to see her? Did you learn anything?'

'Not much. She's a very nice woman and it was good to talk to her, but it added nothing significant. Although she did say that the smoking kilns down on Skúlagata had been running. I didn't know that.'

'I don't remember any smoking kilns. But then I knew nothing about the Butchers' Association slaughterhouse.'

'No. I remember them quite well, there on Skúlagata.'

'Does it matter that they were running?'

'Hardly. They were a part of the normal operations there. They were fired up earlier in the day, long before my father was attacked. I can't imagine it was of any importance to the investigation, and it was never mentioned in the reports. But it kind of gave me a stronger sense of how little time had passed from when he was attacked until Helga, that is, the witness, came across him. He was still alive, tried to say something, and then died right before her eyes. I knew that, of course, but talking to her about it made it all clearer.'

'Which means?'

'That the murderer couldn't have got far. He was either on the next street over or hiding down at the shore. The sea came up to Skúlagata in those days.'

'And snuck away from there?'

'I've sometimes wondered about that. He had to be in the immediate vicinity.'

'But she didn't see him?'

'No, she didn't see anyone.'

Konrád hesitated, standing there at the door.

'It's best that I get going,' he said. 'Unless you . . .'

He looked at Eygló.

'What?' she said.

'Unless you have more . . . wine,' Konrád said.

'What do you mean?'

'Well, then I could . . . stay a bit longer . . . if you want,' he said, stepping closer to her.

'No, I don't think so, Konrád,' said Eygló, smiling at his attempt. 'I don't think I have anything more for you tonight.'

'Are you sure?'

Eygló nodded.

'Fine, then . . . I'll just say goodnight,' said Konrád, backing out the door and shutting it behind him.

15

The old woman stared fearfully at Konrád. She hadn't understood a single word he'd said and it soon dawned on him that she wouldn't, no matter how he tried. No one had bothered to tell him what state she was in when he asked about her in the hallway and where he could find her. When he walked into her room, she was sitting up in her bed, looking out the window. He introduced himself and told her what he was doing there and then noticed that she was frightened of him. It looked as if she was going to start sobbing. He immediately slowed down and told her that he hadn't meant to startle her, but she just stared at him like the intruder he was there in her room and in her lost world.

'Who are you?' Konrád heard someone ask behind him, and when he turned round, he saw a woman of about fifty in the doorway, looking at him. 'Can I help you?'

'I was going to talk to . . . umm . . .'

He momentarily forgot the old woman's name.

'No, there's no point in talking to her,' said the woman, short and plump in an unbuttoned coat. She was holding a mug of coffee, as if having just popped out for refreshment. 'It's been hopeless for a long time. I haven't seen you here before,' she added. 'How do you know my mum, might I ask?'

Konrád introduced himself and said that he didn't know her, but her sister.

'You knew Valborg?' The woman was clearly surprised. 'Poor Valborg. It was horrible, what happened to her. And she was so ill, too. Just awful to think that such a thing can happen.'

'Yes, that's true.'

'Her neighbour has apparently been called in for questioning,' said the woman. 'The one living below Valborg.'

Konrád had already heard that. Marta had decided to bring the woman from the first floor down to the station. The police also wanted to talk to her lover, and he was being looked for. It came to light that the man wasn't completely unknown to the police. He'd been an offender from a young age, and finally received a sentence of several years after his involvement in drug trafficking was discovered. Following his release from prison, the police had had no further dealings with him. On the other hand, he'd been on the first floor around the same time as Valborg was attacked, and hadn't been seen leaving the building. This was based on the testimony of Emanúel, who'd been spying from his flat some distance away and may very well have missed seeing the man leave. Konrád couldn't imagine him being a very reliable witness in that regard.

Konrád had spoken to the staff of the medical centre where Valborg worked, but found out nothing other than that she'd been a well-liked and reliable employee, helpful and tireless. Composed in everything she did but reticent about herself, and thought to be something of a loner.

Konrád told the woman in the hospital room that Valborg had approached him about a very personal matter, but that he'd declined to help her and now regretted it. The woman immediately seemed to understand what he was talking about.

'Was it the child?' she asked. 'She spoke of wanting to do something about it.'

'Your family knew?'

The woman walked over to her mother, who looked at her in as much surprise as she'd looked at Konrád before. The woman spoke soothingly and affectionately to her and got her to lie down, then spread the duvet over her. It was as if she were dealing with an infant.

'I don't know ... did you say that Valborg had got in touch with you?'

Konrád sensed that the woman was reluctant to go into family matters with him, a complete stranger, and was sympathetic. He told her more about his acquaintance with Valborg, that they'd met among the works of art at the Ásmundur Sveinsson Museum and he'd got to know her story, though by no means all of it. Unfortunately, he hadn't agreed to help her and admitted that he didn't feel good about it, especially considering Valborg's fate not long afterwards. He was a former law-enforcement officer, still had good connections among the police, and wanted to do more if he could.

'I've thought a lot about what she told me and, if you don't mind, I'd like to do what I can to find the child,' Konrád said.

'But why should you do that?' said the woman. 'Valborg is no longer with us.'

'Yes, but there are two sides to the story. On the one hand, there's her. On the other hand, there's the child. Valborg wanted the child to know of her existence,' said Konrád. 'That she'd never stopped thinking about it and wanted to get to know that person, even though so much time had passed.'

The woman didn't seem entirely opposed to what Konrád was saying.

'We hardly have what you'd call a family,' she said. 'I went over this with the police when they got in touch. Valborg didn't talk to me about it until after she learned of her illness six or so months ago. By then, my mother had been admitted here because of her dementia. Valborg said that Mum had known, but she never told me about it. This matter of Valborg's came up shortly after I was born, and I was raised in large part by my grandma. Grandpa was dead. But Grandma never said a word about it either. Valborg told me that Grandma hadn't known, and that she certainly would never have accepted it.'

For several moments, the woman looked silently at Konrád, as if she didn't know how to react to this strange visit to her mother's hospital room. She asked Konrád to tell her more about his acquaintance with Valborg and he tried to answer as best he could, telling her again of the few times that he'd spoken to her and that he'd more or less waved her off.

'And what?' she said. 'Do you think you can find the child? She herself wasn't able to.'

'I want to try,' Konrád said. 'Even if only to assuage my conscience a bit. If the police are able to find out what happened to the child, that would be great, too.'

The woman considered his words for a moment, then held out her hand and introduced herself. She and Konrád shook hands and she told him everything she knew about Valborg and her child. Valborg had the baby in Selfoss, where she'd been staying temporarily. She'd met a midwife who pretty much took her in after Valborg told her that she wanted an abortion. She gave birth to the baby at the home of that midwife and gave it up, and knew nothing of its fate when she told her sister all of this a few years later. Her sister told her that it was probably best to leave well enough alone. As the years went by, what had happened became an increasingly heavy burden on Valborg and she began to wonder more often what had happened to the child. How it had turned out. What had become of it. Where her child was. She even expected it to try to track her down. She'd read stories about children who found out they'd been adopted and put in a lot of effort in adulthood to find and become acquainted with their biological parents. That was impossible now, in her case.

'Did she mention who it was that took in the child?' asked Konrád. 'How it happened? Who found the foster parents? Was this recorded somewhere?'

'As I said, I think that at first, she wanted to have an abortion, but then she met that midwife, who talked her out of it. The woman convinced Valborg to have the baby, and said she would make sure it was adopted and no one would need to know anything. Valborg accepted that. When she started searching for the child decades later, she found out that the woman was dead. Valborg never told us her name. Valborg's own name was nowhere to be found in the hospital records when she looked. It was as if the birth had never taken place. That midwife seems to have been very motivating during it all. Valborg spoke highly of her and said that she hadn't been forced to do anything against her will. It was more as if the woman had wanted to help her with what Valborg herself had decided that she needed and had to do.'

'When did she have the baby?'

'In September 1972.'

'She started her search late.'

'I think she feared finding something that . . . you know, would only add to her sadness.'

'Did she give any reasons as to why she didn't want to have the baby?' Konrád asked.

'No, not really,' the woman said as she adjusted her mother's pillow and stroked her greyish-white hair.

'Not really?'

'No, I don't know what to say. I know she found it very difficult when I asked her about it. I got the feeling that everything about it had been a real tribulation for her. Even that it had been a kind of last resort.'

'Do you mean that she was coerced?'

'She said nothing about it.'

'That the child's father had been involved?'

'All I know is that she could barely even talk about it.'

For a moment, Konrád stood thoughtfully at the window, then continued to try to fish more out of the woman. But she knew little about her aunt from the time in question and had no idea who Valborg associated with in her younger years. She did, however, have a vague memory of her mother saying that at one point Valborg had been a waitress in restaurants and was working at the nightclub Glaumbær when it burned down.

'And the child's father?' Konrád asked.

'She never mentioned him by name.'

'He was never involved in the decision-making?'

'Involved?' The woman snorted. 'It was more like he never existed.'

16

When Marta spoke to the cuckolded sister, an old saying went through her head, distorted, of course, because she could never clearly remember such things: Hell has no fury like a woman who's been betrayed. The woman's fury was actually directed not so much at her unfaithful husband but at her sister, whom she couldn't stop bashing and calling a slut and a whore in between sniffling through her doll-like, reddish nose.

Her name was Glóey, and according to her, she'd had no idea about the unfaithfulness until detectives from CID showed up and informed her that the police needed to speak to her husband. She said she hadn't heard from him for a few days and they asked if she knew where he was. She wasn't very cooperative, in fact telling them to get the hell out, but they told her the man had probably been at her sister's place at the same stairwell and at the same time that a serious crime had been committed. They asked if she knew what he was doing there and about his movements that evening.

These last questions caught Glóey's attention. She was flabbergasted, and they had to repeat all of it until she realised exactly what they were saying and what they were after.

'The fucking bastard,' she hissed before lighting a cigarette. Her face was carefully made up, with eyeshadow and blush. 'I knew it. Damn it, I knew it! She could never leave him alone! And there I was, in the hospital. Damn it, it figures. Bloody hell! It figures.'

The police had obtained a search warrant because her husband had a history as a drug trafficker and dealer, which raised suspicions. Knives and blunt objects such as a baseball bat were found in the flat, along with some packs of pills and white powder that the woman claimed to have no idea about.

'Did he kill that old woman?!' she shouted angrily at Marta when she came to see her later that day. The search for the husband hadn't yet been successful. 'I'm sure my sister got him to do it. Damn it, I'll . . . damn it, I'll kill her the next time I see her! How long has this been going on between them? Fucking cheating bitch!'

Marta did her best to try to calm the woman down and let her know in a soothing tone that the police were only looking at one aspect of the case involving her sister and husband, and that it was important that they speak to him as soon as possible in order to put to rest a few doubts. She asked if Glóey agreed. Whether it wouldn't be in everyone's best interest. That the sooner this was resolved, the better it would be for all parties. This was a cliché, and Marta didn't try to sound convincing.

Whether it was thanks to Marta's vapidity or something else, the woman calmed down. She sat down on a chair's armrest, sighed heavily, and hung her head. She'd been discharged from the hospital the day before and still bore the marks of the car accident, with a bandage on her head and one arm in a cast. It turned out it wasn't the first time her husband had been unfaithful; but it was the first time her sister was involved. He was an incorrigible ladies' man and she should rightly have left him long ago.

'And that's what I'm going to do,' said Glóey. 'I give up. I can't take it any more. I can't do this. I just can't.'

'No, it's –'

'Fucking bitch.' She sighed again, scratching her cast.

'Did you ever hear your sister talk about her upstairs neighbour?' Marta asked.

'Not that I remember. She's been there for a year or so and I don't think she's got to know anyone properly. Was it there that they met? At her place?'

'So it appears,' Marta said.

'He was with me in the car,' said Glóey. 'When I was hit. I ended up in the hospital. Look at me! Look what happened to me! He escaped completely unharmed. Not a scratch on him. You know . . . some, you know . . .'

'Yes, tell me, is he in any trouble? Financially, I mean?' Marta asked. 'Or the two of you?'

Glóey stopped scratching her cast.

'What? Did she have money, that old lady?'

'Would that be a reason for him to attack her?'

'The fucking idiot. He owes everyone. Everyone!'

A little later, Marta sat down with the woman from the first floor in an interrogation room at the police station on Hverfisgata. The sisters were quite different: Glóey fair-haired, excitable and rather burned out, while this one, whose name was Begga, was darkhaired and quieter and lacking the expressiveness of her sister's face. She'd been picked up by the police at her workplace and went with them down to the station without saying a single word. When she was asked about her brother-in-law, she said she had no idea where he was.

Now, sitting there facing Marta, she asked how long they intended to keep her and if it had really been necessary to come and get her at work, in front of everyone, especially given that she'd done nothing wrong.

'Your sister thinks otherwise,' said Marta. 'She doesn't have much good to say about you.'

'She's one to talk. She's no angel, either.'

'For your brother-in-law to attack a defenceless woman wouldn't surprise her at all, and she told us that he has chronic financial difficulties. Did your brother-in-law attack Valborg?'

'Absolutely not.'

'Did you go along with it?'

'He didn't do anything to her. I didn't do anything to her.'

'Did you know Valborg well?'

'No, not really. But I knew she was a lovely woman. I would never in my life have been able to attack her.'

'Did you ever discuss money matters with her?'

'No. Never. What money matters?'

Konrád had told Marta that when he met Valborg, she'd stated specifically that she'd put money aside. When her bank accounts were examined, it came to light that she had no significant balances to speak of, maybe one million krónur in total, but she'd regularly withdrawn from her savings account, even tens of thousands each time. She had no stocks or government bonds or anything of that nature. When her niece was asked about the matter, she said that Valborg hadn't trusted banks or financial corporations following the economic crash. On the other hand, her niece knew of no special assets of hers or how Valborg would have disposed of any such thing. Yet she mentioned that through the years, she had generously supported various causes touching on child labour and children's diseases, and did so anonymously. It was possible that she'd simply given them the money that she thought she didn't need, which explained the withdrawals from her savings account.

'Is he in financial trouble?' asked Marta in the interrogation room. 'Your brother-in-law? Your lover?'

'Lov— He's going to leave Glóey,' said the woman. 'He's been meaning to do so for a long time. Their marriage is completely dead. That's why he comes to me.'

'Why don't you tell us where your brother-in-law is, and then we can ask him all about this in person?' Marta said wearily.

'I don't know where he is.'

'Did he go from your place up to Valborg's and break into it?'

'No.'

'Did he send someone on his behalf, or you, to Valborg's to rob her?'

'Do you think he'd be crazy enough to be in the building at the same time? We didn't do anything to her. He didn't send anyone to do anything to her.'

'Have you heard from him since then?'

'No. And I don't know where he is. He hasn't been in contact with me.'

17

As Konrád looked around the old nightclub, memories quickly began lining up, one after another. He remembered cold, damp nights outside the place behind the Free Church, endless lines in crazy weather, and puddles on the lot by the entrance. Teased hair like candyfloss and terribly short skirts that came straight from the streets of London. White high-heeled boots that reached up to the knees. He remembered unruly hair that reached down to shoulders and beards of all shapes and sizes; as if free love started with the beard. He remembered the drunkenness. A flask was passed down the line and songs were sung, sometimes on beautiful summer evenings, sometimes in the harsh frosts of winter when the lot transformed into a skating rink and snow collected on people's clothes. That suited the place, which was an old ice house on a street running up from the Pond, from which the blocks of ice were taken. Finally, it was turned into the most popular nightclub in the country, called Glaumbær.

The goal was to drink as much as possible before going into the club, where alcoholic drinks were sold at exorbitant prices. The best buy at the bar before closing, though, was a Chartreuse Green, which guaranteed the highest alcohol content for the least money. Konrád recalled the almost unbearable heat inside the place, and how it never took long to run into a familiar face. People were in constant motion, with music thumping in their ears, from floor to floor, room to room, and bar to bar. The place was on three floors and divided into bars and rooms, with endless little corridors in between. There was a disco on the top floor, and it was there that the fire started that burned Glaumbær to the ground shortly before Christmas 1971. The place never reopened, and just like that, in the blink of an eye, the entertainment headquarters for the hippie generation in the country disappeared. The party was over.

Konrád tried to imagine the old layout of Glaumbær as he stood there in the middle of one of the galleries – the old ice house had recently been given a new role when it came into the possession of the Icelandic Museum of Art. A retrospective was currently being held of the works of the old masters, Þórarinn B. Þorláksson and Jón Stefánsson. A smattering of people drifted around the gallery like a herd of ghosts, stopping in front of the works and regarding them. Now there was a solemn silence where once you could barely hear the person next to you through the noise.

'So you think you know something about art?' Konrád heard a voice say behind him.

Konrád turned, saw the man he'd come to meet, smiled and shook his hand.

'You don't come here often enough,' he said.

'That's true,' said the man. 'This probably isn't the first place that comes to mind when I'm on holiday.'

They strolled over to the cafe and sat down and chatted, recalling their years on the police force. The man's name was Eyþór, and before he worked with the force, he'd been a waiter in the city's restaurants, and Konrád recalled how he sometimes talked about his years at Glaumbær and how fun it had been working there. He'd quit a year before the fire and taken a job at the Naustið restaurant, then applied to the police, where he worked for about a decade before becoming an estate agent. He'd earned a lot and looked good, in an expensive suit and with a tan from Florida. Konrád hadn't heard from Eyþór in a long time, but it occurred to him to call and see if he could do him a favour.

'What's bugging you?' asked Eyþór. 'I hear you've been sticking your nose into all sorts of cases since leaving the police.'

'I'm bored,' said Konrád.

'And what is it now? Anything interesting?'

'I don't know,' Konrád said.

'But not . . . have you got involved in that incident at the block of flats? What was her name? Valborg, wasn't it?'

'Do you remember her at all?'

'Me?'

'She was working at Glaumbær when the place burned down.'

Eyþór looked around.

'Is that why you wanted us to meet here? Because of Glaumbær?'

'Do you remember a woman by that name? Valborg?'

'Does it have something to do with Glaumbær? What happened to her?'

'No, I'm just poking around. She came to me a while ago and asked for help with something and . . . I'm trying to gather information. Just thought a bit of art might do you good. Looks like I was right.'

Eyþór smiled.

'I must have missed her,' he said. 'I can't remember anyone by that name. I'd quit by then. Was working at Naustið.'

'Are you in contact with anyone who worked at Glaumbær?'

'Yeah, a few of them,' said Eyþór. 'Would you like me to talk to them? Ask about this Valborg?'

'Would you mind?'

'I'll try to dig something up.'

'It was unbelievable, hearing about the fire,' Konrád said, taking in the thick walls of the old ice house.

'Yeah, wasn't there some talk about it being cigarette embers here on the top floor? In a sofa? Wasn't that the determination? It was all so sad, somehow. It was shortly after they refurbished the place and it had never been livelier. I saw the musical *Hair* onstage here that December, just before it caught on fire and . . . you know, it was just awful.'

'And they were good people who worked here?'

'Cream of the crop,' said Eyþór. 'I still have good friends from that time. I'll talk to them. Find out if they remember that woman.'

'There was one other thing,' said Konrád, as if thinking out loud. 'I don't know if it has anything to do with it or not, but Valborg had a child that she gave up at birth.'

'Oh?'

'You shouldn't mention it to anyone because I don't know if it matters, and it's probably just a coincidence, but . . .'

'Yeah?'

'The child was born in September 1972, meaning it was conceived in December of the previous year.'

'In 1971?'

'Around the same time she worked in this building.'

'Do you mean . . . when Glaumbær burned down?'

'Yes.'

Two days after the search for Glóey's husband began, he was found. One of his chums informed the Narcotics Unit, in return for some goodwill after being arrested while on probation for drug use, that the man had a half-Danish cousin whom he held in considerable regard. The half-Dane also turned out to have run up against the law, for his involvement in drugs. In that cousin's home, a shabby rental flat in the Efri-Breiðholt suburb, the suspect was found stoned out of his mind along with two handguns, a wheel wrench that he was holding, three baseball bats, and a considerable quantity of drugs that turned out to belong to his cousin. On one wall was a large but rather well-worn poster of the Danish football team that made an unexpected splash at the World Cup in Mexico in 1986.

'We are red, we are white . . .'

18

Engilbert leaned against the piano. He was rather ragged of appearance, and a bit unsteady. Konrád's father had done his best to patch him up and given him a few drinks before they'd left for the séance, and promised more if he did a good job. Engilbert had been uncooperative and said he couldn't do it unless he had something to drink first. Konrád's father had given him a sweet to mask the smell of alcohol while he went over the information he'd gathered about the woman.

Her name was Stella and she welcomed them a bit breathlessly, thanked them for looking in on her and invited them in, and they made themselves comfortable in her living room. The woman admitted that she wasn't quite sure what to expect or how this all worked. The medium's partner spoke for them and was relieved to hear that she was home alone, although he didn't show it. Yes, it was he who'd been in touch with her by phone, he added after introducing her to Engilbert, the sought-after seer and philanthropist. He said that he himself was just his driver, and they had plenty of people to visit. 'Plenty,' he repeated. The woman was pleased to hear that, and she offered them coffee. 'Yes, there's naturally so much interest in these matters now,' she said, and he agreed with her wholeheartedly. Engilbert fiddled with his tie and took no part in the conversation. The woman was around sixty, with a cheerful face, wearing a beautiful blouse and a silver locket holding a photo of her husband around her neck. Every now and then, she smiled slightly nervously.

As she had mentioned on the phone, she'd been having bad dreams lately. She'd dreamed of her husband, Halldór; that he hadn't been feeling well, and twice she'd started from her sleep with his face before her eyes, full of rage and suffering.

'I've been having a lot of trouble sleeping because of it,' she said. 'His hair was all white. He had radiant white hair.'

'You two had a nice home,' said Konrád's father, looking around the sumptuous living room at the Kjarval paintings and porcelain figurines and the coffee table around which they sat. The room was dusky, as it was evening and the woman had drawn heavy, deep-red velvet curtains over the windows. She had lit a few candles.

'How would you like to do this?' she asked. 'Should we sit here, or maybe at the dining table?'

'It's fine here,' Konrád's father said, nudging Engilbert. 'He prefers to be on the move – don't you, Engilbert? You usually stand during séances.'

Engilbert grunted and he got up, walked over to the piano and stood there silently for a few moments before placing one finger on his temple, as if it was there that the connection would be made, should it come. He walked back and forth through the room and resumed his position at the piano, where he muttered something under his breath. It was as if he was having difficulties and wasn't hiding it. At one time, he'd been interested in acting and performed with an amateur theatre group; he could display dramatic flair when necessary and was sensitive to reading the room, as it was called, even if his audience was only a lonely woman who lived on Ægisíða Street. Suddenly, he hit the top of the piano with the palm of his hand.

'Damn it, it's not working,' he whispered. 'It's not working.'

'Is everything all right, Engilbert?' asked his assistant.

'No, I don't want this. It's not working. We should go.'

'What's wrong?' asked the woman.

'Shouldn't we give it a bit of time?' asked his partner. 'We're in no rush,' he added, smiling at the woman.

'No, it's hopeless,' said Engilbert. 'Hopeless. There are no currents here. None. There's nothing to be had here.'

'Currents?' the woman asked. 'Do you mean from beyond?'

'It's like a closed book to me,' said Engilbert. 'A closed book.'

'How sad,' said the woman, somewhat confused.

'Unfortunately,' said Engilbert, 'I'm not feeling up to it. It was a mistake to come here. I can't sense anything. Nothing. There's nothing here. We should go. It's useless. It was useless to come here.'

Konrád's father took careful note of the woman's reactions. On occasion, they'd gone too far when shifting the responsibility for lacklustre results over to the victim. People didn't want to disappoint them, and they were cunning in taking advantage of that.

'Is it me?' she asked hesitantly.

'Sometimes it happens,' he said apologetically, and as if in explanation, 'that people don't surrender themselves entirely to the seer. The connection is disrupted. It happens. No one's to blame. It just happens.'

'I'll do my best,' said the woman, worried about what this meant. 'I hope that I . . .'

'Yes,' Engilbert was heard to say. 'Yes, it's . . . I sense a man coming here . . .'

'Who?' asked the woman.

'Someone's coming to me here . . . a man . . . he says his name is Guðmundur. Is it someone you know?'

Engilbert suddenly seemed to have made contact with the other world.

'Yes, if it's that Guðmundur,' said the woman a bit hurriedly, longing so much for them to succeed in their efforts. She didn't want the seer to hit the piano any more and talk about a closed book. 'Guðmundur started a wholesale company with my husband.'

'Thanks for telling me.'

'But . . . but he's not dead,' said the woman. 'Doesn't he need to be dead . . . or . . . ?'

'No, this is another Guðmundur,' Engilbert said firmly, glancing at his partner. 'This is . . . he's . . . there's . . . such an aura of serenity.'

'My grandfather, maybe? His middle name was Guðmundur.'

'He's standing on green ground,' said Engilbert, 'and has such a deeply . . . deeply serene aura . . .'

'He was a farmer.'

'. . . it's all so serene and a woman is standing next to him,' said Engilbert, looking at a family photo on top of the piano. 'She's petite and her hair is plaited and she knows that you're worried. Do you understand what she means? Does it ring any bells? A petite woman? With a kindly expression. And there's a turf-and-stone farm and a hearth of stacked stone. There's a name . . . it starts with S. I see many S's.'

'It could be Grandma Sesselía.'

'Good.'

'She lived here with us the last few years of her life,' said the woman.

'She's telling you not to worry too much...'

'About Halldór?'

'She wants to tell you not to worry too much about your husband. He's in a good place. She knows that you're worried about him but is telling you to keep praying for him and then everything will be fine. She's telling you to pray for him and not forget to support those who are weaker, to support Christian organisations with...'

The assistant cleared his throat. Engilbert looked to him for guidance and was given a signal that he was going too fast.

'I sense her disappearing from my mind's eye, but here's another presence. A strong presence. It's a man and he seems to have an aura of excitement and fun.'

'Isn't it Halldór, then?' the woman whispered.

'He wants you to remember the happy times you had together. There's, um... I see something like a vast ocean and there's a passenger ship and music sounding over the deck and there are elegantly dressed people...'

'Probably the *Gullfoss*,' said the woman. 'Halldór and I sailed on it once a year.'

'I sense great joy. I hear singing and resonant music.'

'Yes, it was so wonderful. He was such a great singer. "The Castle Crags" – that was his song.'

Engilbert continued along these lines, and the woman sat up in her chair as all the good memories came back to her. It required no effort for Engilbert to hit the right notes. She was extremely receptive to everything he served up, and they remained in the light like that for a while, until the assistant thought it was time to step in.

He wanted to take the opportunity while there was something of a break in the séance to direct the seer back to their original purpose for coming there. He had gone to the cemetery on Suðurgata and taken a look at the magnificent tombstone that the wife had had made for her husband's grave, hewn from granite. Affixed to its front was a plate made of basalt, engraved with a gilded epitaph. Nothing had been spared to keep alive the man's memory, and that effort hadn't been solely intended for the deceased wholesaler, as there was another name on the tombstone.

The living room was silent. Engilbert acted as if he'd fallen into a trance. He slumped over the piano with his eyes closed and his chin hanging down to his chest, and there he stood, motionless apart from his head twitching at regular intervals. This behaviour was accompanied by an angry muttering, without any of the words being distinctive. The woman looked questioningly at the assistant, who smiled as if the medium's behaviour was completely subject to its own laws, which were as distant and incomprehensible to him as to her.

'No . . . I won't do it . . . there's something else going on here . . .'

Engilbert's muttering grew louder.

'What did he say?' the woman whispered.

'I don't know what's happening,' said his partner.

'. . . she's coming back. The old woman. Sesselía. She says that they're together. They've united. Do you know what I mean?'

The woman didn't answer.

'There's someone with her this time,' Engilbert continued. 'It's unclear what . . . it's all indistinct and hazy but . . . It's someone who's very close to you. Young. Does that ring any bells?'

Engilbert wiped his forehead with a handkerchief.

Stella stared at him with both hope and fear.

'It may not be your husband you've been dreaming of,' Konrád's father said. 'It may not be because of him that we've come together here?'

The woman hung her head.

'It's someone else, maybe?'

'I'm not sure I'm prepared to go any further with this,' the woman whispered. 'If you don't mind. I don't have much experience of such . . . such séances.'

'I hear . . . I hear something like a whisper,' said Engilbert, grabbing the piano tighter. 'No, it's maybe more than a whisper . . . is it crying? It's like a child crying, and it's coming from a great distance. Does that sound familiar?'

Konrád's father observed the woman's reactions and was pleased with what he saw. Engilbert was playing his role to the max and his body language appeared to have the desired effect on Stella. A few words about Christian youth work and quality religious associations should suffice. If she had the means to donate money to a good cause, they would gladly get it into the right hands. This was only their first séance. Konrád's father would see to it that there would be more.

The candle flames flickered in the dusky room and the thick curtains were like theatre drapes around the living and the dead. The woman looked up and gazed solemnly at the seer as she devoured every word that tumbled from his lips and nodded at his question.

'I feel a great warmth and light emanating from them,' said the medium.

The woman sat there motionless, staring at him.

'Is it him?' she stammered cautiously.

Engilbert didn't answer.

'Are they . . . together?' asked the woman. 'Can you ask Sesselía about our boy?'

'There's . . . there's a fog. A cold fog.'

'Yes.'

'And there's water.'

'Yes.'

'And there's a boy and he's freezing. It's as if he fell in the water.'

'Oh God.' Stella sighed.

'The old woman says that everything is fine now. He's with her and he feels fine and doesn't want you to worry.'

The woman fought back tears.

'The blessed boy,' she whispered.

'He was here a great deal,' said Engilbert, appearing to be completely under the power of the beyond. 'Here in the corner. I feel a strong presence at the piano. Did he play this instrument?'

Stella said that he did.

'Thank you,' said the medium.

'He was a very skilled pianist, despite his young age,' she said. 'He was studying music and they said he was one of the school's most promising students. We were so proud of him. No one has touched the instrument since he died. I don't even know if it's working properly.'

'I can perceive the light,' said Engilbert, running his hand over the piano. The keyboard lid was closed, and on a flimsy rack above it was a worn songbook. 'Right here in this place. The strong presence of this soul. The presence of the child. He has a good aura. Light and brightness and beauty.'

He had barely finished the sentence when from the instrument came a lonely sound, like a false note, before deathly silence fell over the room.

19

The man pulled open the garage door and Konrád saw what he meant when he said that the photograph collection was a mess and the garage cluttered. He hadn't lied when he said that the collection was extensive; after all, it spanned his father's nearly half-century career, and it would take many years to go through it, sort the photos and put them in order. He had applied for grants to do so after his father died, but had been denied every time. The garage was no storage space for historical relics of this sort. Some had even been damaged because the garage had leaked for a time, and water had twice flooded the floor where cardboard boxes held thousands of negatives and photographs. The man was most worried about it all catching fire, because as everyone knows, photographic film, which most people no longer used, was one of the most flammable materials imaginable.

His father had paid little attention to organising the photo collection. His great interest was taking photos, but he cared less about preserving them. For most of his life, he'd been a freelance newspaper and magazine photographer. Every now and then he'd taken a job with a newspaper, had worked for several years for an afternoon paper and a few more for one of the morning papers. In those days, numerous papers were published that were connected to political parties, and that had long since disappeared into oblivion. He'd never liked political journalism.

The man pushed a box that was up against the garage door and said that his father had witnessed numerous important events in the life of the nation. He'd also been there when celebrities visited the country: Lyndon B. Johnson, Reagan and Gorbachev, Benny Goodman, Helen Keller, Ella Fitzgerald and Louis Armstrong. He'd never said much about his work, although sometimes, if he was in high spirits, he recounted how Keller ran her hands over his face and said it was rough but kind.

'And he was always listening in on the police frequencies,' said the man. 'It's one of the very first memories I have of him. Sitting in his car with a couple of cameras and the radio buzzes and some notification is sent over the airwaves and he says he needs to pop out but will be right back.'

'He usually got there before us,' said Konrád, who remembered the photographer well, a rather serious man, thin and tall, with one camera around his neck and another in his hands. 'He always made sure not to get in the way or interfere with the work of the police, whether the subject was a car accident, a burglary or, on occasion, a murder scene.'

Konrád had explained to the man what he was after, without mentioning that he was personally connected to the case. He'd only said that he retired after working for many years on the police force and had little to occupy him, and this old case had been on his mind for a long time. He'd visited the descendants of another photographer who had showed up at the slaughterhouse that night, but to no avail. The man's earliest negatives and photos were lost. The paper that he'd been working for had merged with another, and then both were combined with yet another that finally went bankrupt. Its photo collection had been sold in several parts and some of it simply thrown away. Konrád hadn't felt like tracking down what remained.

'Listen,' said the man, looking over the garage, 'all the oldest stuff is in the boxes there in the back, with the material getting younger the closer you get to the door. Or at least that was the thinking. Some of it's in envelopes, labelled and dated, and some have been printed, but most of it's just loose negatives. Endless negatives. He was actually more organised the first years, so you could be lucky.'

'Did your dad ever talk about that incident, about what he saw at the slaughterhouse?' Konrád asked.

'No, I don't remember that,' the man said thoughtfully. 'He spoke very little about what he was working on, but my mother said he was sometimes saddened by what he saw through his lens. Especially when it was a serious car accident. That was long before seat belts were mandatory, of course. He found them the most difficult. The car accidents.'

They started at the back of the garage, where Konrád saw that there were photos and negatives in large brown envelopes that were dated to the start of the 1950s. One of them was dated 1954. It contained two developed rolls of film and three photographs of a new petrol station just outside Reykjavík, probably on its opening day. Cars at the pumps, men in hats and women in dresses with handbags on their arms sauntering in the sunshine.

After about an hour of searching, Konrád and the photographer's son had made it to the 1960s. There were strong fluorescent lights in the garage's ceiling, and they had straightened up and peered into the light through a myriad of negatives bearing images of long-forgotten people and events. Konrád was grateful for the man's patience, for being more than willing to help find the right negatives and showing this hunt of his a great deal of understanding. He had said that Konrád's visit would give him a welcome opportunity to get a grip on his father's photograph collection, which, for the most part, he'd left untouched until now.

After another hour they took a break and the man went and made coffee, returning with two cups of the steaming-hot beverage and a cruller for each of them. They chatted about this and that at the garage door, and it turned out that the man worked as a bricklayer and had to take it easy after minor surgery on his knee. He said he'd considered handing over his father's photographs to a museum; the National Museum, maybe. Much of the material they'd already looked at might seem useless, but it still had historical value. Konrád had been thinking the same thing when he looked through the photos and held the negatives up to the light. They showed Reykjavík's rapid development at the time when the city was spilling outwards into its modern-day suburbs. They showed fashion, entertainment, sports matches, the cars of the day, women and men at their daily tasks, human life that had disappeared into silence and oblivion.

The man finished his coffee, looked at his watch, and said he had to do a few things in the house, but invited Konrád to continue searching the collection. Konrád thanked him again for his understanding and carried on delving, while making sure to put everything back in its place. The sun was setting by the time he'd dug down to a cardboard box on the floor in one corner of the garage. The bottom of the box was damaged, clearly having been subjected to water, and tore apart easily when Konrád tried to lift it. The contents spilled onto the floor at his feet: loose negatives, a few empty film canisters and old, brittle paper sachets and envelopes holding more negatives and photographs. Konrád cursed silently. All of it was unmarked and he went conscientiously through the material, held negatives up to the garage's lights and tried to get a grasp of the subject. One envelope was bigger and thicker than the others and as soon as Konrád opened it and took out the photos he realised he'd finally hit on the right box.

The photos were black and white and some were dull and even out of focus, taken with flashbulbs, but Konrád immediately recognised the subject: the bleak surroundings, the walls of the slaughterhouse, the gate to the lot, Skúlagata, the shoreline below it. He saw the police officers and their cars and scattered bystanders watching from a reasonable distance. He didn't recognise any of these photos from the newspapers published at the time of the murder or from the police reports. This was new material for him, and when he went carefully through the photos, one by one, an old, uneasy feeling from a long-past night crept up on him.

At the bottom of the stack, Konrád found a photo of his father's body. It was taken a moment before the body was transported away from the scene, and over it hung a gloom, as if it were a war photo. The ambulance was parked close by, with its back doors open. Men were bent over the body, just about to lift it onto a stretcher. Lying there in the street, it was covered with a blanket apart from one hand that stuck out from beneath it, and Konrád stared at the cold hand that a few hours before had been his father's clenched fist, which he'd aimed at his son in a hateful rage.

20

Marta switched off her e-cigarette in the corridor and opened the door to the interrogation room. The man's name was Hallur and he sat up in his chair when he saw her. It was the day after he was arrested in his cousin's flat, and now he was more collected, almost clear-headed. He'd slept off his intoxication in a prison cell the night before, after attacking the police officers who'd come to pick him up. He'd appeared to be completely out of it and had managed to injure the hand of one of them by swinging a wheel wrench around before he was knocked to the floor, handcuffed and brought down to the station.

He was no stranger there at the station, although several years had passed since his last dealings with the police. Until now, when he'd been spotted in an unfortunate place at an unfortunate time.

'Glóey says hello,' Marta said, just to stir him up a bit.

'Why were you talking to her?' the man asked nervously. 'Can't you just leave her alone?'

'She asks about you constantly,' Marta replied. 'When you'll be free. What you were doing at her sister's place.'

'Fuck,' said Hallur.

Sitting beside him was his lawyer, who looked at Marta as if he didn't understand the purpose of this conversation with his client. Then he suggested that they get to the point, glanced at his expensive watch and seemed to be in a hurry to get to other, more important business. But he willingly took on cases such as these, especially if there was a chance they would be prominent in the media.

Marta looked through the papers she'd brought with her. Found in Hallur's possession were shoes that had traces of grass and dirt on them, similar to the soil behind Valborg's block of flats, where it was thought the assailant had come in. Hallur had already been asked about this, and he answered that he'd smoked a cigarette once or twice in his sister-in-law's back garden. He may have kicked at the grass a bit. Unfortunately, no one had seen him doing so, neither any of the building's residents nor any others in the neighbourhood. Quite a few cigarette butts were, however, found in the garden. It also appeared that residents smoked on their balconies and let the butts fall onto the grass. Dirt had been found in the stairwell and inside Valborg's flat, without any actual shoeprints being distinguishable, though.

Hallur was in considerable financial trouble. Glóey had been helpful with that part of the investigation, although she'd hardly been able to control her temper. She said that he was a serious addict and did business with certain individuals she didn't want to name and had started to owe them incredible sums of money that she had no idea how he was going to pay. He was constantly being threatened by them, but had told her that he'd found a way to solve this problem in one go. She blurted all this out before realising she may have said too much, let the cat out of the bag, got them into even more trouble. After that, hardly a word could be got out of her and she began contradicting various things she'd already let slip.

'Have you been in your sister-in-law's place often lately?' Marta asked after warming up with some general questions.

'Often? No.'

'Once a week? Twice?'

'Maybe,' Hallur said, scratching his upper arm. He was wearing a grey T-shirt and his arms were heavily tattooed, with pictures and symbols that Marta couldn't make out distinctly. One tattoo appeared to be the name Glóey, with a small red heart in place of the 'ó' in her name.

'Did you ever run into the woman who lived on the floor above your sister-in-law?'

'No.'

'Did you never see her on these trips of yours to the building?'

'No. I never saw her. I have no idea who she was and wouldn't have recognised her.'

'What about your sister-in-law? Did she ever say anything about her?'

'No. Nothing.'

'Nothing about money she kept in her flat?'

'No.'

'Am I correct in saying that you're in considerable trouble financially? That you owe a lot of money?'

'No, not at all,' said Hallur. 'I don't owe anyone anything.'

'And you've found a way to fix that problem?'

'No. I have no idea what you're talking about. These are just some bullshit lies. I did nothing to that old lady. Nothing.'

'We have a witness who said you left your sister-in-law's flat around the same time the woman upstairs was attacked. The witness didn't see you leave the building.'

'You think you can take such a pervert seriously?' asked Hallur. His sister-in-law slash lover had told him about the peeping Tom. 'I just went home. I don't know what that loser saw or didn't see.'

'So you left your sister-in-law's place, went down the stairs and out the front door of the building?'

'Absolutely. My car was parked on the street because there were no spaces free in the building's car park. I got into it and drove away.'

'Did someone see you, do you think?'

'No. But I did notice a woman in one of the windows. In one of the flats there.'

'What was she doing?'

'Nothing. She was just sitting by the window. Still, I felt . . . I had the feeling she wasn't well.'

'What do you mean?'

'I don't know. That's just what I felt.'

'OK,' said Marta. 'Let's go back to the building. When you left your sister-in-law's and stepped out onto the landing, did you notice anything unusual, a sound, even a smell? Did you notice anything that seemed out of place?'

'Are you starting to believe me?'

'I don't know,' said Marta. 'Should I believe you?'

'I didn't do anything to that woman,' said Hallur. 'I came out onto the landing and ran down those few steps and it seemed . . . to me like . . .'

'Yes?'

'Like, yes, there was an odour in the hallway.'

'An odour?'

'You know . . . as if someone had forgotten a garbage bag,' said Hallur. 'A kind of . . . smell of garbage or . . . I don't know how to describe it. An odour.'

Marta gave him a long look.

'I can't describe it any better,' said Hallur apologetically. 'That was what I smelled. And then I left.'

In all of her tribulations, Glóey had found time to varnish her toenails. She'd finally got hold of her sister, that immoral whore, and given her an earful, and got nothing but insults in return. They'd torn into each other over the phone and called each other awful names. Old frictions reaching all the way back to childhood had been kicked up, including, among other things, how Glóey had never wanted to take her little sister along to anything she did.

She sipped on a gin and tonic and lit a cigarette, inhaling the smoke and blowing it out of her nose while listening to American pop music on her phone. Then she dipped the little brush into the fiery red nail varnish. Her cast made things difficult, but not enough to keep her from varnishing her nails.

She had no interest in talking to her husband and was glad he had to rot in custody for a while because of the old lady in that building. She was adamant about never speaking to him again and had already decided that he would never again step through the door of her house. She'd had enough of his deceit and tricks. Fucking shitbags, both of them.

There was a knock on the door and she looked up from her nails. She wasn't expecting any visitors.

She opened the door. Standing there were two men she'd never seen before. Without warning, one of them hit her in the face with his clenched fist, before they both pushed their way in and shut the door behind them.

21

Konrád scrutinised the photographs, and took his time doing so. The photographer's son had given him permission to take the envelope that contained both negatives and photos from the scene at the slaughterhouse. He had spread them out on his dining table, fetched a strong lamp and found his magnifying glass, and now hunched over one photo after another, examining them carefully. The photographer had realised that it was a rare and newsworthy incident taking place there in the Shadow District and hadn't spared film on it.

Konrád tried to arrange the material in some sort of chronological order, starting from the first photos the photographer took when he arrived until the body had been driven away and the number of bystanders and police officers began to dwindle. Many of the first photos were dim and unclear, because the murder scene there at the gate was dark, as Helga had said, despite the photographer using flashbulbs. The cameras in those days were large and unwieldy and the bulb had to be replaced every time the flash was used, and he probably used all the ones he had with him. The later photos showed that the police had set up floodlights at the gate and that their vehicles' headlights were directed at the place, lighting the area better and consequently making the photos clearer.

In Konrád's mind, the photos had a strange, exotic feel to them, almost unreal when he considered that their subject was his father. They showed with the eye of the news photographer the brutal murder that had been committed at the slaughterhouse and was as if etched into the bleak environment: the bare stone walls, the imposing iron gate, the cold night. They showed shadowy figures hovering all around. Police officers standing there stiffly in the cold over the body, some in uniform, with white belts around their waists. The blank expressions of the people who had come out of their houses to watch what was going on and were shocked at the violence lying on display there in the street.

Konrád pored over the photos with the magnifying glass, taking a closer look at people's faces without being able to identify them. He did of course recognise one or two of the policemen, but none better than Pálmi, who was in several of the photos. He was a detective who would go on to lead the investigation of the case and was the one who informed Konrád of the murder. Konrád liked Pálmi. He'd been gentle and sympathetic in his approach when he made it clear to Konrád that his father was dead. Later, they would confront each other during tough interrogations, when the CID's eyes were focused for a time on the family, the divorce of Konrád's parents, the relationship between Konrád and his father and their argument the day his father was killed. Pálmi went hard at Konrád and for a time it looked as if the young man would be taken into custody, but that didn't happen.

Those were difficult days for Konrád. He continued to live alone in the basement in the Shadow District where he'd grown up, and sat there for long stretches of time with his hand on his cheek, staring into the strange void left by the death of his father. He hardly left the house for days and didn't talk to anyone. His emotions overwhelmed him when least expected and he burst into tears again and again as he sat there alone in the dark; numb, fearful, angry, sad. His mother had urged him to come east, where she lived with a new man and Konrád's sister Beta, but he couldn't see himself leaving Reykjavík, the neighbourhood, the basement flat. He couldn't imagine living in the countryside. Reykjavík was his place. He couldn't be anywhere else. He was a city kid and didn't want to be anything else.

He thought constantly of his father and how he'd met his death, and wondered whether he'd finally managed to go so far overboard with someone that it cost him his life. Konrád thought he'd known the man well, but he obviously didn't know about everything he'd been up to, and he didn't know all of those he'd associated with or had wronged over the years.

He knew, however, that one of them was a man named Svanbjörn. Konrád had watched his father assault the man over debts that hadn't been paid in a timely manner, and had had to step in and stop the violence. This Svanbjörn ran two restaurants and bought contraband booze from Konrád's father, but had a hard time paying what he owed him. A fire broke out in one of the restaurants shortly after their violent meeting. Konrád's father swore he had nothing to do with the fire. Not long after these incidents, he was stabbed. Svanbjörn produced witnesses who said that he'd been in Ólafsvík when it happened.

Konrád couldn't resist the temptation and one day, after

thinking long and hard about it, he went to Svanbjörn's restaurant to talk things over with him. Svanbjörn was doing something in the kitchen; he was short, slow in his movements, with dark circles under his eyes and always reminded Konrád of someone who was very ill. Svanbjörn was startled when he saw who had come to see him, and clearly hadn't been expecting him.

'What do you want with me?' he snapped.

'Was it you?'

'Was it me? Do you think I did that to your dad? I was in Ólafsvík.'

'You could have got someone to do it.'

'I wish I'd done it, but I didn't. Now scram.'

'Did you owe him?'

'Are you here to try to collect? I didn't owe him a single króna.'

'Do you know of anyone who did?'

'Why are you asking me that?'

'Do you know of anyone?'

'He owed people, too,' said Svanbjörn. 'It wasn't one-way, if that's what you think.'

'Who?'

'Leave me alone,' Svanbjörn said wearily. 'Get out of here and leave me alone. I can't help you, kid. Your dad was a loser. A fucking bastard and a loser and that's why this happened to him. You yourself probably know that best of all. If I knew who killed him, I wouldn't tell you. I wouldn't tell anyone.'

Konrád felt the anger rise within him. Svanbjörn was undeterred and walked up to him, grabbing a large kitchen knife as he did and letting it dangle at his side.

'Yeah, you want to come at me like your bastard father? You want to be just like him? Come on! Come on if you dare!'

Svanbjörn shoved him, and for a moment Konrád had to fight the urge to attack him, but then it passed, the tension was released and he retreated from the restaurateur and left the place.

Later, after Konrád was questioned by the police, along with his mother and many of his father's friends who were no strangers to law enforcement, and numerous leads had been followed without success, the weight of the investigation gradually lifted without it coming any closer to being solved. Around the time that Konrád started working for the police, the case had been more or less buried and filed with other unsolved ones.

Konrád continued to pore over the photographs, one after the other, and was on the verge of giving up and pushing them away when he spotted the window. It could be seen vaguely in several of the photos, but he hadn't really noticed it until he picked up a photo that showed it from a new angle. He held the magnifying glass up to the photo and compared it to other photos that showed the window, and as far as he could tell, it was tightly shut. The window was just over a metre above the street, and if Konrád remembered correctly, it was in that part of the slaughterhouse that housed the smoking kilns and the firewood used to fuel them.

Konrád knew that when Helga came upon his father lying in the street, only a short time had passed since he was stabbed. Yet she saw no one around. The assailant had disappeared as if the earth had swallowed him. Konrád had never seen this window mentioned in the police reports, or the possibility that the killer had hid by the smoking kilns, and he wondered if he could have slipped in there, gone through the Butchers' Association buildings and out onto Lindargata Street on the slope above.

22

Konrád put down the magnifying glass, rubbed his tired eyes, and thought of his father's enemies and how easily he seemed to have made them. He looked over the mess on the table. He'd taken from storage a few boxes of papers and small things that his father had left behind. Among them were some personal effects, such as a gold ring that the man always wore on his little finger, a Ronson lighter, faded on the sides from use, gold-plated cufflinks and a wristwatch missing its strap. Knick-knacks that didn't really matter, yet that reminded Konrád of his childhood, for better or worse. There was also an object or device or whatever it was that had been lying on the floor of the basement flat, and which Konrád had found when he was going through his father's belongings immediately after his death. For some reason, this peculiar thing had accompanied Konrád over the years, and on the rare occasions when he looked in the boxes, he took the thing out and wondered about it, trying to guess what role it played. The object wasn't remarkable-looking and fitted easily into a trouser pocket, was made of wood with a thin metal wire strung between two nails. A small spring was attached to the wood beneath the wire and had been loose at one time, but could no longer be moved at all.

Konrád recalled his father saying once that he'd never made as much money from anything else, and in his mind, he connected the object to a visit his father had one evening. Konrád hadn't got out of bed that day because he'd come down with something quite debilitating. He had a high fever and muscle aches and he was already haunted by hallucinations and nightmares as he dropped in and out of a sleepy haze, and sometimes felt that the visit never took place except in his own delirium. Through the fog of his illness, he noticed his father looking in on him every now and then without seeming particularly concerned, and suddenly he started from his stupor at the noise of the basement door being pounded violently.

His father sat in the kitchen drinking, as he did often. He could sit all day at the kitchen table by himself, drinking cheap brandy and either throwing dice or playing Solitaire. He had the radio on, but so low that it could barely be heard, and drank from a small shot glass to the muffled slapping of cards or the dice dancing along the tabletop. Fucking hell, he whispered to himself if it went badly.

Konrád heard his father get up from the table and go to the door. He heard him muttering, which turned into a clamour that carried into the flat. The door closed again.

'What's the meaning of this, storming in here? Get out of here! Out!'

Konrád didn't hear the response.

'I'm telling you, this is a misunderstanding,' he heard his father protest. 'I've never heard of this woman.'

'Fucking good-for-nothing, preying on a defenceless woman,' a man said. 'What kind of scumbag loser does such a thing?'

'This is just a misunderstanding,' Konrád's father repeated. 'I have no idea what you're talking about. I'm no medium. Do I look like a medium to you?'

'We want the money you took from her,' said another man.

'This is fucking bullshit! I didn't take any money, so get the fuck out of here!'

'Your friend said otherwise.'

Konrád's father hesitated.

'My friend?'

'It didn't take him long to point us here. Said you were the one behind it all. And what a hero! A pissant loser who uses fraud and deception to prey on defenceless widows. You should be ashamed of yourself, you bastard!'

'He's a liar and a drunk,' said Konrád's father. 'You're even stupider than you look if you believe anything he says.'

'Do you keep it here?'

'What?'

'The money? Is it here?'

Konrád had propped himself on his elbow, weak as he was, in order to hear better, and now he heard a commotion, chairs being pushed, drawers slammed, cupboard doors torn open, his father protesting. Suddenly a man appeared in his bedroom doorway and stared at him in astonishment.

'Who's this?' he asked.

'My son,' said Konrád's father. 'Leave him alone!'

The man was around forty, ugly and wearing a winter coat, it being December and cold outside. He looked around the little bedroom.

'Do you know what he's done with the money?' the man asked, but Konrád, completely bewildered, just stared at him. Konrád had no idea what prompted this visit and what money the men were asking about and why there was so much hostility between his father and them. The man barged into the room, and started looking under his mattress.

'Leave the boy alone!' his father shouted from the living room. 'He's sick as hell, can't you see that? Get out of here!'

The man backed out of the room and disappeared, and again Konrád heard a commotion and a tussle, until suddenly one of the men shouted that Konrád's father had a knife.

'You'd better watch out, you bastard,' said the man.

'Yeah, shut the fuck up!' Konrád's father exclaimed fearlessly. 'Get out.'

'You never know what might happen to a scumbag like you.'

'Get out. Out! Get out, I said! Get the fuck out of here right now or you'll pay!'

The tumult started up again. His father swore at the men and threatened to stick his knife in them, and they yelled that this wasn't over, they'd come back or jump him and he'd get what he deserved. The tussle continued like that all the way to the front door, but finally all fell silent.

'Dad?' shouted Konrád. 'Dad! Is everything OK?'

A good while passed before his father came to the bedroom door. He was still holding the knife.

'Who were they?' Konrád asked.

'No one,' said his father. 'No one! Just some scumbags. Go back to sleep, son.'

'What money did they want?

'They're fools. They think I stole some money. Don't worry about it. Try to sleep.'

Konrád lay back on his pillow and his father began tidying up after the scuffle, before sitting back down at the kitchen table. Soon the dice were heard dancing over the tabletop. Konrád dozed off into a disturbed sleep, and didn't know how much time had passed before he woke and found himself feeling a little better. Despite being weak, a bit sick to his stomach, and having a headache, he plodded to the kitchen to get himself a glass of water and saw his father sitting alone in the dark with that peculiar thing in his hands, entirely in his own world.

Konrád contemplated the object and thought about that strange visit in the past. He had no idea what role that simple, useless thing played. It was probably because of those mysterious visitors that he didn't throw it away when various other bits of junk belonging to his father went to the dump. He only knew that his father was fond of it, and that at some point he'd used it to make money that the strangers wanted him to return.

23

The woman was reluctant to invite Marta in and hesitated for some time until the detective gently urged her again, asking if she had anything she wanted to tell her; it always took a bit of time to recall these things. Memory was a peculiar phenomenon. Some things stuck so firmly with you that you couldn't get rid of them, no matter how hard you tried. Others vanished into thin air without you even realising it. The woman still wasn't convinced; she'd already spoken to a policeman and had nothing more to say. 'We'll see,' Marta said stubbornly. 'All testimony is relevant to such a police investigation, however insignificant it appears,' she added. That's why the police wanted to talk to her a little more and try to refresh her shaky memory.

Finally, the woman gave in. She was torpid, diffident, and spoke so softly that she could barely be heard. Marta noticed Lego blocks on the living-room floor and asked about the children, who were all at school. Then she chatted to the woman about this and that, until finally directing the conversation to the incident in the block of flats across the street. The woman said it had been very difficult, experiencing such a thing. The neighbourhood was so peaceful and the people that lived here so nice that she still had a hard time believing that such a tragedy could occur there on their street.

Marta agreed with everything she said and added that, fortunately, major crimes like this one were extremely rare in the city and that, therefore, great emphasis was laid on solving them quickly and conclusively so that people didn't have to live in fear. She said that the investigation wasn't going as well as it should, which made it important that everyone cooperate and help the police if possible.

'Do you work from home, by any chance?' asked Marta, sipping her steaming coffee.

'Yes, I have been for the past two years,' the woman said.

'Don't you miss being in the workplace?'

'Sometimes,' said the woman. 'My husband . . .'

'Yes?'

'No, it's nothing.'

Marta had been watching the woman discreetly. She was the one whom Hallur had seen in a window across the street from the block of flats, and who appeared to him to look unwell. The residents of that street, including her, had already been spoken to and their statements recorded. Nowhere in the reports did it say that the woman had seen Hallur go to his car and drive away.

Marta directed the conversation towards this without directly reminding the woman of it, and suddenly she vaguely recalled seeing a man get into a car and drive down the street. She apologised for this oversight, but she hadn't quite been herself that night. She had no idea if the man came out of the building, but the description could certainly fit Hallur. She hadn't seen him very clearly and hardly knew one car from another; she thought it had been a red car, which matched Hallur's.

From the living-room window, Marta looked down at the street. There was no view from there into the garden of the building opposite. She moved to the kitchen. From that window, one could easily see over the trees lining the garden and in through the window of the building's laundry room. She asked the woman if she'd noticed anyone in the garden that same evening, but she couldn't remember having done so. Then Marta asked if she'd noticed any unusual activity there in the garden or in the neighbourhood in the past few days, but the woman just shook her head and said she hadn't noticed anything out of the ordinary. Unfortunately.

Marta felt for her, and decided not to stop there. Deep down, she got the feeling that the woman longed to speak to someone but didn't have the strength to do so.

'Tell me one other thing,' she said. 'Do you want it to continue?'

'What?'

'This that you have to go through?'

'What do you mean?'

'I mean the violence.'

'The violence?'

'That he inflicts on you.'

The woman looked at Marta in surprise.

'Has it been going on for a long time?' Marta asked.

'I don't know what you're talking about,' the woman said hesitantly.

'I understand it isn't easy to talk about such things. Still, I really want to help you, if you'll let me. I have expertise in these matters because of my work with the police. I've helped numerous women who've been in the same situation as you and I know how difficult it is to take the first step. Almost unthinkable.'

The woman avoided looking Marta in the eye.

'It's time for you to think a little about yourself,' Marta said reassuringly. 'Not him. Not the children. Not anyone else in the family. Not your friends and acquaintances, if he allows you contact with them. You shouldn't think about anything but yourself for now. It's long overdue. You shouldn't sacrifice yourself for him any longer. For his will. His violence.'

Marta couldn't remain silent. She'd noticed faint bruises on the woman's neck, which the collar of her blouse couldn't cover completely. She also had an old bruise by her eye and favoured one arm when she was busy in the kitchen. She bore all the signs of being in a long-term abusive relationship. Marta had met many victims of domestic violence in her job, and recognised those signs. A posture that hid the pain. Shame that the eyes couldn't conceal.

'If you want, you can come with me,' said Marta. 'I have good friends at the shelter. I know they'll welcome you. We can go there now. If you feel up to it.'

'You should leave,' the woman said. 'My husband will be home soon. You don't want to meet him.'

'Why would you say that? I'd love to meet him,' said Marta. 'It's always interesting to hear what they have to say, these guys.'

The woman hung her head.

'Look,' said Marta, 'I realise you don't know me at all, and you feel as if I'm sticking my nose into things that aren't my business, but I'm going to let you have my phone number and you can call me any time, day or night. Don't hesitate to do so. I would appreciate hearing from you.'

Marta jotted down her number in a notebook that she kept in

her pocket, tore the page from it and held it out to the woman. She refused to accept it, so Marta put the piece of paper on the table and stood up to leave.

'So you didn't see anything there in the garden?' she asked before going. 'No one sneaking about in the dark?'

The woman shook her head.

'OK,' said Marta. 'I'm leaving, then, and . . .'

'Would you please not tell anyone about this?' whispered the woman. 'I don't know what you mean, saying the things you did. It's just a misunderstanding on your part . . . it's none of your business. None. Just leave me alone. For God's sake, just leave me alone.'

24

Valborg sat in the waiting room and grew more restless by the minute. She'd requested an antenatal check and was asked to come to the Women's Health Unit at this time to see a doctor. Three other women were waiting there for the same purpose, all at different stages of pregnancy. Two of them appeared to be close to delivery, but the third showed no such signs; she was quite stout and was reading a foreign fashion magazine, the very picture of serenity. Valborg was anything but calm. She flipped through several fairly worn issues of *Familie Journal* that were lying there on the table, but couldn't fix her mind on anything. She was deeply restless and worried about the meeting with the midwife. She was worried about the antenatal check-ups. About having to discuss her situation. She cursed everything the pregnancy had brought upon her.

Her worst fear had come true and she didn't know how to deal with it. The first thing that crossed her mind, as terrible as the thought seemed to her, was to have an abortion. She couldn't imagine having the baby. She wasn't used to such a feeling, such aversion, but she knew that the child would always be a reminder of what had happened and she wanted most of all to forget it and act as if it never had happened. She'd felt such dismay since then, and even, for a moment, contemplated taking her own life. It didn't help that she couldn't imagine talking to someone about what happened, and struggled with it in her loneliness and isolation through long sleepless nights.

One of the women in the waiting room was called in and Valborg knew that it would be her turn next. She tried to concentrate on what she was going to say. She'd practised it before coming to the waiting room and went over it in her mind again and again, left out some parts of it and changed others until she hardly knew what to say any more, deepening her anxiety. Then she calmed down. First and foremost, she'd come there for advice. She simply had to talk to someone about her situation, and feared she'd put it off too long.

She was startled when her name was finally called, and instead of following the woman who called her, she simply stood there and began to make excuses, then backed out of the room and left. She'd lost heart. There was no obligation to go for an antenatal check, but she wanted to know whether it was too late to ask to have an abortion. And she longed to talk to someone. Anyone. So a week later, she was back in the same waiting room, and when her name was called this time, she had enough strength to follow the secretary manning the reception desk into a small room where a midwife would soon come to see her. 'Have a seat,' said the secretary. 'She should be here any minute. Let me know if you need anything.'

The woman left her alone in the room, and shortly afterwards the midwife came in. They shook hands and it was as if the midwife sensed immediately that something was bothering her, so she asked if everything was all right. If she wanted a drink of water.

Valborg accepted the water. She felt like throwing up. The woman handed her a glass of water, and, speaking soothingly, asked if this was her first visit to a midwife, whether she'd ever had children, when she was due, if anyone had come with her. Every single question was like an attack on her, an accusation, a judgement. But she realised that these were only routine queries, and she knew she had to calm down if she was going to get the help she so desperately needed. The problem was that, on the one hand, she didn't know what she wanted, but on the other, she was adamant about what needed to be done. She was hesitant, yet at the same time determined. At a loss one day, but confident the next. All she knew for certain was that she didn't feel well and hadn't felt well since that terrible night just before Christmas.

'I don't want to know about this child,' Valborg blurted out. 'I want nothing to do with it. I know it's not a nice thing to say, but I have my reasons. Don't ask me what they are.'

'And the father?' the midwife asked sternly. 'Does he know about this? Is he of the same opinion?'

'No,' said Valborg. 'He doesn't know about it.'

'Are you planning on telling him?'

Valborg shook her head.

'No, I'm not going to.'

'May I ask why?'

Valborg shook her head again in silent anguish.

'Did he rape you?'

'I would appreciate it if you would stop asking me these

questions. I haven't talked about this with anyone. I don't want to talk about it.'

The midwife hesitated.

'Are you talking about abortion?'

'Yes. No. I don't know. Probably. Still, I don't want to . . . I'm afraid it may be too late.'

'How far along are you?'

'Almost three months.'

'So it was in December that . . . ?'

Valborg nodded.

'I'm afraid you're cutting it fine,' said the midwife, her expression even sterner. 'Are you sure you don't want the child? Sometimes a pregnancy can be difficult and stir up all sorts of ideas; it can lead to depression and the psyche becomes vulnerable. Abortion is a most serious matter and not permitted except under special circumstances. Strict conditions must be met. I'm afraid you can't get . . . just expect to get . . .'

'Are you refusing me?'

'It's complicated. You may have to accept the fact that what's done is done.'

'I don't want to see this child,' Valborg whispered. 'I feel bad enough having to admit that. Dear God, I can't do this, I just can't do this.'

She stood up and walked to the door.

'You can't refuse me. I'm sorry, but . . . you can't refuse me.'

Then she ran out.

Two days later, her phone rang. She didn't recognise the voice and even less the name when the woman introduced herself and said she'd heard she had a problem. Valborg didn't know what was going on, but the woman on the phone seemed to read her mind and had a strangely calming effect. She said she was a midwife and had got her number from a friend of hers, and she wanted to know if she could help. It was her understanding that the child might have been conceived under special circumstances without there being any need to go into any detail, and that Valborg had mentioned abortion.

'Yes,' said Valborg, 'I'm of the opinion that it's the best way for me but I'm not sure I can get . . .'

'And the child?' said the woman on the phone. 'Don't you think you should give a thought to the child?'

The woman didn't say this accusingly, and continued in the same calm tone.

'Naturally, it's your decision,' she said, 'but I wanted to know if you would consider finding the child a good foster home, instead.'

'I've also considered that,' said Valborg. 'At least I can't imagine keeping it.'

'I can help if you want. Of course, it's entirely up to you, but you shouldn't do anything rash. I've heard from women who have been in your position and know that you don't want to do anything you might end up regretting. I suggest we meet and see if we can find a good solution to this.'

This is what the woman said on the phone, and her words soothed Valborg and gave her the peace and comfort she'd sought for so long. She seemed to have a complete understanding of the situation and only wanted to offer Valborg her help.

'What did you say your name was?'

'Sunnefa.'

'And have you . . . have you done this before?' Valborg asked. 'Been in contact with women like me?'

'You're not entirely alone in the world,' said Sunnefa. 'It's bigger and more complex than you can imagine.'

'Do you know of others? Like me?'

'If you're asking if I've met women who've been in your shoes, I can't deny it. I understand you feel very bad about what happened. You're not the first and, sadly, you won't be the last either. I want to know if I can help you. If you'll let me. And if you think that abortion is the only answer for you.'

Valborg was silent for several long moments as she considered her words.

'If you want, I can place the child in a good home,' the woman continued. 'Naturally, it's for you to decide how we go about this, but we can make it so that no one needs to know anything.'

'No one needs to know anything?' Valborg repeated in surprise.

'If that's what you want. No one needs to know anything.'

No one.

25

It was raining; cold, dense and relentless. The man stood in the shelter of a work shed, smoking a Camel. He was white-haired, with stiff white stubble on his face. Small grey eyes peered out from under thick eyebrows into the rain, watching as Konrád made a wide arc around the building foundation and hurried towards him. Yet another hotel was rising from the ground up. It was the end of the working day and most of the crew had left, after building formwork. Tomorrow, concrete would be poured.

They shook hands and introduced themselves, and Konrád knew that he'd met the right man. His name was Flosi and he continued smoking his Camel nonchalantly, as if unsurprised by this visit. Konrád got the feeling that it would take quite a lot to upset him, and didn't expect that his business with him would, either.

Konrád's friend Eyþór hadn't sat idle after their meeting at the art gallery. He'd called people he knew from his Glaumbær years, not only employees he remembered, but also other individuals who'd been among the nightclub's most regular patrons and whom he knew from that time. There were quite a few of them. He enjoyed looking back on his years at the place, and some of the phone calls lasted quite a while. Some of those he'd known had passed away and others he'd forgotten, but in the end, he had a few names that he thought might be of use to Konrád, and asked him to let him know if his efforts were of any help.

'Fucking rain,' said Konrád, glad to be able to take shelter from it. He tried to shake off the water. He'd already talked to two old employees of Glaumbær. They vaguely remembered a woman named Valborg who had worked there, but not well enough for it to be of any use to him.

'It's all going underwater here,' said the man with the stubble, putting the butt of his Camel between his fingers and flicking it towards the foundation, at the bottom of which something of a pond had formed. His voice was hoarse from too many Camels. 'Are you this friend of Eyþór's?' he asked, looking Konrád over. His white hair stuck out in all directions from under a worn baseball cap.

'He said I could talk to you about Glaumbær. Said that you were a barman there. That you'd been working the night the place burned down.'

'I didn't think anyone was interested in Glaumbær any more,' the man said. 'I thought everyone had forgotten about it.'

'It was a fun place,' Konrád said, trying to imagine the man as many decades younger, serving him Chartreuse Green just before closing. 'I can't say I was a regular, but I did go there often.'

The man looked at him.

'I don't remember you. Eyþór said you worked with him on the force.'

'That's right. Do you remember a girl who worked at Glaumbær named Valborg? I'm sure Eyþór asked you about her.'

'And are you still a cop, or . . . ?'

'No, I retired from the police.'

'But not entirely?' said the man, still looking out into the rain.

'Well, I guess you can't shake it off so easily.'

'Eyþór mentioned that woman, but I can't place her,' said Flosi. 'I told him that, but he still thought I should talk to you, in case I recalled anything. A whole lot of people worked at Glaumbær when it was at its most popular, and there were bands and girls hanging around them and somehow it's all jumbled up in my memory. I told Eyþór that. Told him I wouldn't be of much use to you. I was only there for a couple of years.'

'I can imagine that Valborg was a very quiet girl who didn't draw much attention to herself. Did Eyþór tell you what happened to her?'

'Yeah. And no one knows anything?'

Konrád shook his head and said that the police were doing their best to catch the perpetrator, but had little to go on.

Flosi took out a crinkled pack of Camels and fished a cigarette out of it. He offered Konrád one, but he declined. Konrád hadn't touched a Camel in decades. He could just as well imagine smoking horse shit.

'I don't follow the news,' said Flosi, lighting the cigarette with an almost empty plastic lighter that he had to tap on his palm to get working. 'Still, I heard about that break-in and murder. Strange to hear too that it was a girl who worked at Glaumbær in the old days.'

'Yes, Valborg.'

'And what, you think it's connected to the nightclub? Is she a relative of yours? How did you know her?'

'I only met her very recently, in fact,' said Konrád. 'Before she died, she reached out to me and asked me to help her with something, and I feel like I owe her. Eyþór said you'd mentioned people who came to Glaumbær that weren't of the highest quality, so to speak.'

'Everyone went to Glaumbær,' Flosi said, 'including, of course, a few reprobates. People who'd been in prison or would end up in prison. Scum like that. The kind that went there just to start fights. Mess with another guy's woman and the like. Guys who were looking for trouble. We kept an eye on them. I'm sure you've seen a bit of that type yourself. Stuff like that, you know? The kind of stuff that always exists.'

Flosi had become philosophical in the cold downpour, and his stubble made a raspy sound as he scratched his cheeks.

'Anyone you remember in particular?'

'Did something happen to the girl at Glaumbær?'

'I don't know.'

'Why are we standing here?'

'I'm trying to figure out if something might have happened there,' Konrád admitted. 'Glaumbær was mentioned. She worked there around the time the place burned. Maybe she met another employee there? Or got into a relationship with someone who came there often?'

'So you're looking for a man in her life? At that time?'

'It's just something I'm pondering,' Konrád said. 'Whether she was in a relationship with someone from Glaumbær.'

'Too bad I can't help you,' said Flosi. 'I don't even remember the woman, let alone if she had a guy in her life.'

'But do you remember anyone who may have made advances

at her, and who she wouldn't want to have anything to do with? Someone who may have pestered her? Someone who didn't leave her alone? Someone the women complained to you about? Someone they feared? You know how men can be. Especially when they're out on the town.'

Flosi took a drag from his Camel. Then he looked silently down into the rapidly growing pond that had formed in the foundation.

'I don't remember anyone in particular,' he said after long consideration. 'Naturally, all sorts of issues came up, but nothing that I didn't forget about immediately. Arguments and fights and the kind of friction you can find at any nightclub or bar. Someone the women feared?'

Flosi stared out into the rain, trying to recall old stories from when he'd worked at Glaumbær.

'Yeah, I remember a man who came there quite regularly and had been charged with rape, if that's anything. My late sister told me about him. I don't remember how she knew it, but she pointed him out to me once and said he'd raped a girl in some town down on the Reykjanes peninsula, it may have been Keflavík, and that it had gone all the way to court but he'd been acquitted. My sister followed such cases. She was studying law in those years. So I started noticing him. Is that the sort of thing you're after? Are you fishing for examples like that?'

'Yes, maybe.'

'I think he was somehow connected to the Base,' Flosi continued. 'The soldiers kept a fairly low profile, for the most part, but they did occasionally come to Reykjavík to cut loose, and that fellow was sometimes with them. People didn't like the Yanks and I think they sensed it.'

'Your sister is deceased?'

'Yeah.'

'Do you remember anything else about this man? Or anyone like him? Guys who were talked about along these lines?'

'No. Nothing comes to mind besides this. I only vaguely remember it, to tell you the truth, and probably only because my sister mentioned it. Still, I think . . .'

'Yes?'

'It's like I recall her having said it happened at a dance.'

'What?'

'The rape. At a club. After closing.'

26

The story was well known within the family, even if it was mainly kept hush-hush out of consideration for the woman who was loved by all who knew her. Two men had taken advantage of Stella's weakness in her widowhood, besides playing on her most painful emotions due to the loss of her son, pretending to be in special contact with the beyond. After they'd earned her trust through séances, she began providing them with the funds that they promised to hand over to the various associations and charities they named. She trusted them completely and they pressed their advantage. The more goodwill she showed them, in proportion to her childish complacency, the worse they played her until almost all her savings were exhausted. It wasn't until she sought the advice of her brothers on how to get a new cheque book that everything was revealed. Then, the two men disappeared. She didn't even know their full names, because she was in denial and didn't want to believe anything bad about them. They'd opened a door to the afterlife, brought her comfort and helped her come to terms with her past, which was more than many others had managed to do. The fact that they were thieves and swindlers didn't seem to matter so much to her. It took a special effort to open her eyes to what had really happened in her home.

Although they occurred a long time ago, these events still made the woman's relatives shake their heads in astonishment.

'It was those fucking bastards,' Stella's great-nephew said after Konrád had introduced himself and Eygló and he realised that this man was the son of one of the swindlers, and with him was the daughter of the other. They hadn't called before going to see him, and the man, who was an accountant, was rather surprised by their visit initially, but quickly got over his surprise. He was used to meeting people who came to him with various concerns, and tried to make things easier for them.

'So you're the medium's daughter?' he said, looking at Eygló and making quotation marks with his fingers when he said the word 'medium'.

'He worked as a medium,' said Eygló. 'He was in bad company,' she added, looking at Konrád.

'Apparently your great-aunt wasn't the only one they swindled,' said Konrád. Neither he nor Eygló had heard of this case before. He believed what the man told them about Stella's interactions with the two men. Had no reason to disbelieve him. Konrád had heard many stories about his father and knew what he was capable of, especially when people who might be called gullible were involved.

'Yeah, we heard about that,' said the accountant. 'They seemed to know all the tricks in the book, and how to use them to take advantage of her weakness. Not just the losses she'd suffered. She didn't know how to handle things. And she trusted people.'

'It's actually a quality that's slowly disappearing,' said Eygló. After some hesitation and persuasion, the man told them all about his great-aunt's acquaintance with the two swindlers and how they had treated her. Her only son, a promising boy, had drowned in Elliðavatn Lake when his small boat overturned, just two years after she lost her husband. Somehow, the two scoundrels had got wind of this and dug up a few of the family's personal details, which they used in the scam. The police weren't notified. The matter was kept quiet. Stella's relatives were reluctant to go public with it, considering the publicity, police investigation and lawsuits that could potentially follow. They wanted to avoid such things as far as possible, keeping Stella's welfare in mind. Her reputation. However, two men had gone to see Konrád's father to try to recover some of Stella's money. She'd written a number of cheques and handed them over to the fraudsters. The money was gone. None of it was repaid.

'My father was one of them,' the man said. 'They wanted to try to get the money back. The one who played the medium, I understand, was just some loser. He blamed the other one for all of it and said that he'd taken the cheques and cashed them. He lived in a basement flat in the Shadow District and was drunk and threatened them with a knife.'

'Two men? In a basement flat in the Shadow District?' repeated Konrád, recalling the visit paid to his father one evening when he himself lay ill in bed.

'Yeah. Dad and his friend.'

Konrád's memory of that evening suddenly became clearer, more purposeful and significant.

'So that was your father?' the man asked.

'I think I vaguely recall that visit,' said Konrád, remembering the ugly man in the winter coat who'd looked for money under the mattress. 'I think they left our place empty-handed.'

'Yeah, as I say, the money was never returned.'

'So things were just left?'

'I think so, yeah.'

'You think so? What did your father do?' Konrád asked.

'He was an accountant. Here. In this office. Died about a decade ago.'

'And the one who was with him when they went to the Shadow District? His friend?'

'What about him?'

'Who was he? What did he do?'

'I don't see what that has to do with it,' said the man, looking alternately at Konrád and Eygló. They were sitting in an office surrounded by files and papers all relating to annual financial statements and tax returns and depreciations, assets and liabilities. The air in there was heavy; the windows were closed and there was no ventilation. The man had followed his father into the accounting business, and his shoulders were drooping from sitting at his desk for long periods of time. He was small of stature but had a strangely rough-hewn face, with bifocals perched on his wide nose, a big mouth and thick lips. This was in the city centre, a short distance from the cathedral, and through the closed windows, the sad chimes of the bells carried over to them.

'No,' Konrád said. 'But it would be nice to know.'

'He was just a family friend, a man my father knew.'

'Is he still alive?'

'Yes, actually. His name is Henning, and he's very old, but I don't know –'

'Did they make any more attempts to recover the money?' Konrád asked.

'More? No. I don't think so. What do you mean?'

'I remember them making threats,' Konrád said. Until now, he hadn't connected the visit with his father's fate. It had been too bizarre and unreal for that, more like a feverish nightmare than anything else.

'Are you suggesting they did something to him?' the man asked.

'My father was actually murdered, probably about a year after that visit,' Konrád said.

'Yes, I know.'

'So you heard about it?'

'I wasn't born then,' said the man, 'but this is all well known within the family. Though Dad never spoke about it. Mum didn't, either. Dad's friend, who went with him to the Shadow District, told me about the visit to the swindlers. I once tried to talk to my father about it, about how the man who treated Stella so badly was murdered, but he just shook his head. Said nothing. Didn't want to talk about it.'

'Didn't you find that strange? Why he was silent about these things?'

'No. I didn't really think about it. He was always a little . . . I don't know why I'm telling you this, but he wasn't a very cheerful man. He could be moody. For a time, he had mental issues and couldn't work. I learned early just to leave him alone.'

'But why do you think he never mentioned this?' Eygló asked. 'Or never wanted to talk about it?'

'I don't know. I'm trying to tell you how he was.'

'Wouldn't that have been normal?' Eygló said. 'The man who swindled his aunt is stabbed to death and the murderer isn't found. Shouldn't he have had something to say about it? Have had some opinions on it?'

'Are there any rules about that? What are you implying?' the man asked, clearly resenting the importunity of their questions. 'Are you . . . have you come here to blame him for the murder? Are you really trying to pin it on my father?'

'No, not at all, far from it,' Konrád said.

'Maybe you should go,' said the man, on the verge of standing up and showing them out. 'I don't like these insinuations.'

'We didn't mean to insinuate anything,' Konrád said calmly.

'No, but in any case, I don't have time for this. I can't help you any more.'

'But that friend of your father's?' Eygló asked. 'That Henning. Did he say anything about the murder? When you talked to him.'

'As I said, I don't like these questions.'

The man took off his glasses and began cleaning the lenses with a microfibre cloth. 'I have other things to take care of and am actually very busy. Besides, I was in my teens when I first heard about this, so a long time had passed since those incidents and I simply don't know enough about them to be of any help to you.'

'You know enough to call them bastards,' said Konrád.

Eygló gave him a sharp look. She wasn't there to end up in a fight with someone who'd suffered because of her father. The accountant looked at them in turn, then put his glasses back on.

'Sorry,' said the man, standing up. 'I didn't mean to offend you. I'm sure those two partners were exemplary in everything they undertook. Thank you for coming, but I'm quite busy and don't have time for this. Sorry for not being able to help you more.'

'Did he say something? This Henning, your dad's friend?' Eygló asked, smiling amiably to make up for Konrád's behaviour. The man was clearly angry at him.

'It doesn't matter because it didn't happen. Dad sometimes said things, without meaning anything.'

'What? What do you mean?'

The man looked at them through his bifocals. An unfathomable smile appeared on his thick lips. The ringing of the cathedral's bells could be heard from outside, and its doors opened to a funeral procession behind a white coffin.

'Henning said my father wanted to get rid of the swindler. Slit his throat like a mad dog's.'

27

Eygló asked if Konrád was interested in coming with her to the cemetery, but he said he didn't have time, so she headed there by herself after their meeting in the city centre. It was growing dark and the traffic was becoming heavier when she parked her car on a side street. The sky was overcast and a fine drizzle settled onto her clothes and face as she trod slowly between old graves and moss-grown memorials. She was careful not to step on any of the graves, but inched her way between them, reading the headstones and taking note of the dates. She came to the cemetery often and spent quiet time there, although its serenity was becoming rarer as more and more tourists spent less time downtown and started visiting it in their constant search for something different.

Eygló walked slowly around the cemetery. She'd often encountered people who believed firmly in the afterlife and felt they'd received confirmation of it in various ways. Engilbert was one of them and she grew up with that belief. Her father was convinced of the existence of a realm where souls of the deceased gathered when they escaped from their earthly bodies and could then, via special powers, come back into contact with the mortal world. He said he had plenty of evidence for it from his job. Eygló herself had experienced many things that were incomprehensible to her, even if she'd always had doubts about what her dad and the old mediums called the etheric realm. She had no fixed ideas about what forces were at work when her perception reached beyond the ordinary. They were as mysterious to her as when she began seeing the uncanny and unexplained as a child.

Eygló moved slowly past the Sturla tomb, which had been renovated recently, and, before long, stood at Málfríður's grave. The old woman lay next to her husband and was the only one who'd been buried in the cemetery this year, not counting the urns that were buried in older graves. The number of people who had reserved spaces in the city's oldest cemetery was decreasing greatly. Eygló would have liked to be buried there, but it was impossible. At one time she'd half jokingly offered to pay Málfríður for her burial plot. Her joke had fallen flat.

The few graves made nowadays in the cemetery were dug by hand, just as was done when the place was first put into use in 1838. Eygló inhaled the aroma of the fresh soil on top of Málfríður's grave and squeezed a handful of it in her palm. There was no memorial over the grave. That would come later.

'She's in a good place,' Eygló heard behind her, and when she turned to see who it was, she saw Málfríður's friend, the same one who'd been sitting at her bedside when Eygló visited her last. She remembered Málfríður calling the woman Hulda. She was wearing the same green coat, with a veil tied around her head. She had slipped up beside Eygló and was gazing at the new grave, her expression gentle as the drizzle.

'Could I have seen you with her the day she died?' Eygló asked.

'I wanted to be with her when she said goodbye.'

'I'm sure she appreciated it,' said Eygló.

The woman looked down at the dark soil.

'What she was looking for, she has now . . .'

Eygló didn't hear the end of the sentence. A man came walking down the cemetery path and called to her in English, asking if she knew where the grave of President Jón Sigurðsson could be found. Eygló didn't understand him at first. She thought his accent was Scandinavian, but replied in her broken English, directing him further east, in the direction of Suðurgata Road, to where the stone column rose over the president's grave. The man thanked her and went on his way and when Eygló returned to Málfríður's grave, the woman in the green coat was gone. Eygló looked around. She would have liked to say goodbye to her, but it was too late. The half-finished sentence hung in the air and Eygló wondered what she'd been going to say.

She stood at the grave for some time before continuing her walk through the cemetery. She had other business there. She generally felt good in the peacefulness of cemeteries, but not this time. She'd gone online and found directions to the plot and had no problem finding it. She was surprised that the headstone wasn't taken better care of. Grass and weeds grew wild inside a low stone wall that demarcated the three graves. The top of the wall had crumbled in places and the headstone was leaning back and to the side and was badly weathered. There was barely a trace of the gilding that had once lifted the names of the dead. The third name had been added many years after the other two, when the family was finally reunited in the soil.

STELLA BJARNADÓTTIR

Eygló read the names and dates before laying her hand on the stone and saying a short prayer. 'Forgive us our debts,' she whispered. Her father had taken advantage of Stella's plight. Although she could barely believe it, he appeared to have abused a gullible innocent in partnership with a criminal in order to get a few krónur off her. Eygló was filled with sadness when she thought of Stella and her son, and about her father. As a child, Eygló had a much closer relationship with Engilbert than with her mother. She and her father were of the same make, and when something was wrong, she turned to him and found warmth, comfort and above all understanding of her sensitivity. But everyone has his own demons. Eygló knew that he was a weak man and struggled with all sorts of problems. She didn't know all the stories, but feared that some were similar to the ones she'd heard from Stella's great-nephew.

And forgive us our debts. The headstone was cold and hard and coarse to the touch, and the ground had sagged beneath its weight, as if it could no longer bear the sorrow it harboured.

That evening, Eygló did something she hadn't done in a long time. She was distracted and had no idea why it happened, but suddenly she was sitting at the piano at home. It stood in a corner of the living room, a Danish heirloom from her father's family that had mainly been decoration. It had been in storage at her aunt's, and Eygló took it when her aunt died. Four sturdy, resourceful men had been needed to move it to its place in Fossvogur. They thought it weighed no less than three hundred kilos, and had never encountered anything like it.

Eygló didn't play the instrument, but at one point, when she took a few piano lessons, she summoned a piano tuner who said it was hardly worth his bother, its inner workings were in such bad shape. The piano tuner thought that it had been built in Denmark around the turn of the century, 1900, and said that it was a completely outdated, useless thing and went on about how seriously off-key it was. Eygló didn't understand what he was talking about. The instrument's wood was also badly damaged, making it utterly futile to tune it. On the other hand, its exterior was in decent shape and beautiful, with flowery decorations, and looked good in the living room. He said he knew that many people were proud of such heirlooms, but used them solely to adorn their living rooms.

And there she sat at the old piano, without knowing why. Maybe she'd heard a piano being played in one of the flats on Ljósavallagata Street, where she'd parked her car when visiting the cemetery. Maybe it was a piano concerto on the afternoon radio that she'd forgotten. She lifted the heavy lid and ran her fingers over the yellowed ivory, and noticed that one key was stuck. She tried to free it but couldn't, no matter what. She didn't remember the key being like that the last time she opened the piano, and wondered how this could have happened. She rarely had visitors and she knew for sure that none of them had touched the piano.

Nevertheless, it was as if someone had struck the key with such force that now it wouldn't come unstuck. Perplexed, Eygló shut the piano, but couldn't find any answers. Her pondering gave her a bad feeling that pursued her into sleep, and late in the night, Engilbert visited her in a dream. It was an ugly vision. He was hunched over the instrument, as drenched as when they found him and pulled him out of the harbour. The water dripped from him to the floor and seaweed was tangled in his salty hair. His back was turned to her and he didn't look up, but had opened the piano's lid and was playing the same false note over and over again, as if in a rage.

When Eygló woke up the next morning, she went hesitantly to the living room and knew that what she'd seen that night hadn't necessarily been a dream.

28

Konrád's meeting with the accountant made him somewhat late for his meeting in Reykjanes. He'd called Pálmi, who told Konrád that he was welcome if he didn't come too late, because he had things he needed to do that evening. Konrád drove as quickly as the traffic would allow southwards down Keflavíkurvegur Road, and when he pulled into Pálmi's driveway, it was dark.

They shook hands and Konrád came straight to the point – the trait of Konrád's that Pálmi liked best. Konrád told him that he'd finally, after all these years, sat down with the chief witness in his father's case, Helga, and that she'd told him the slaughterhouse's smoking kilns were running, although that hadn't been stated in the police reports.

'Weren't the kilns always running?' said Pálmi thoughtfully.

'No,' Konrád said. 'I grew up a short distance from there and sometimes the smell of smoke hung over the neighbourhood and sometimes it didn't. I played nearby and even wandered onto the lot and watched the men working.'

'But what does that change? This about the smoking kilns?'

'I remember that the kilns were fired up at the end of the working day and left running overnight, so there couldn't have been many people in the area when that was done.'

'We went through it all carefully,' Pálmi said. 'We talked to the slaughterhouse workers. We couldn't find any links to your father.'

'I saw that in the reports,' Konrád said, 'but we both know that not everything goes into the reports. Do you remember the smoking kilns coming up in the interviews?'

Pálmi nodded.

'As I said, I think we looked into all of it back then.'

'Dad was stabbed there right in front of them,' said Konrád. 'The kilns building was adjacent to the gate where he was found, and there was a small window in it.'

Konrád took the photo from the photojournalist's collection and handed it to Pálmi, who put on his reading glasses and looked at it. The image was dark and dull, but the window was clearly visible.

'It's big enough to climb through,' said Konrád.

'Yes, it certainly does appear so. It's closed.'

'Maybe it was easy to get in there unnoticed.'

Konrád told Pálmi what he'd started to consider since speaking to Helga, that only a short time must have passed between his father's stabbing and her finding him lying there. He was still alive and died before her eyes, and had tried to say something she didn't understand. She'd just missed the stabbing, and yet the murderer had vanished. Konrád wondered if the murderer had noticed her and the only way out of there was to slip through that window.

'I remember that we looked into it,' Pálmi said. 'This wasn't actually the only window that looked out onto Skúlagata, but was the only one that was possible to get in through. If I remember correctly, they'd meant to put bars in it, or they were replacing the bars at the time. We couldn't see any evidence that someone had broken into the place via that window. What's more, the door to the building holding the smoking kilns was locked from the outside.'

'He couldn't have hidden in there?'

'No,' said Pálmi. 'We searched the place thoroughly that same evening. Everywhere apart from in the kilns themselves, which were running. I remember it now, looking back.'

'You didn't open them?'

'No, you could hardly touch them, they were so hot.'

Pálmi recalled that the officers had quickly come up with three possible scenarios for the incident. First, Konrád's father had been summoned to Skúlagata with the intention of killing him, meaning the murder had been premeditated. Second, he had arranged to meet a man or men and an argument arose that ended in a bloody attack in front of the slaughterhouse, meaning the murder was accidental. Third, and also premeditated, he'd been watched and the decision was made to meet him at the slaughterhouse and assault him there. In all of these scenarios, the assumption was made that the victim knew his killer.

There was also a fourth possibility. Konrád's father had been walking on Skúlagata and met the murderer by complete coincidence in front of the slaughterhouse, something kicked off and it ended in murder. It had been committed without the murderer and the victim knowing each other in any way. When the investigation turned up nothing, the credibility of this fourth scenario grew, it being difficult to solve crimes that were committed by chance and for no apparent reason.

The two of them discussed the case back and forth like this without coming to any conclusion, as usual, until Pálmi said he had things to do.

'If he'd arranged to meet someone there, I think most likely that it was connected to the Butchers' Association in some way,' said Konrád. 'Maybe someone planned to smuggle him meat products or something like that through the gate.'

'But wouldn't that have been obvious to everyone on that street?' Pálmi asked. 'Isn't it hard to engage in clandestine business in the middle of Skúlagata? Besides, we didn't discover any links between your father and the company.'

'I realise that but, you know, people lie for less,' Konrád said.

'The person or persons who were behind this have probably passed over into the Great Beyond,' Pálmi said, walking with Konrád out to the driveway. It was pitch-dark outside, and the cold north wind played about them.

'Yes, of course. Still, I haven't heard of any deathbed confessions,' Konrád said. 'No one has wanted to relieve his conscience of the burden of this murder before going to meet his maker.'

'And probably ended up going straight down,' Pálmi said.

Konrád smiled.

'I'm not seeking revenge or punishment. I want to know what happened and why.'

'It was a big step for you to talk to Helga,' Pálmi said after a short silence. 'Was it OK, talking to her?'

'It was good to meet her,' Konrád said. 'I should probably have done it a long time ago.'

'Do you really think you can solve this case after all this time?'

Pálmi had asked this before, and the answer hadn't changed.

'I doubt it,' said Konrád. 'I highly doubt it. I've probably started far too late. And I'm aware of all the effort you put into it at the time, so...'

'It'll be fun to see if you get anywhere with it,' said Pálmi.

'None of this is any fun,' Konrád said listlessly. 'None of it.'

He hesitated.

'Tell me something else. I hadn't started as a detective at the time, but do you remember anything about a rape case here on Reykjanes sometime around 1970? A rape at a nightclub? After closing? It went to trial, but the accused was acquitted.'

Pálmi thought this over.

'1970? No, I can't say that I do. It could be...'

'What?'

'No,' said Pálmi. 'There was a troublemaker around here at that time, whom I know we picked up once on a rape charge. Fucking scumbag. Used a knife. That didn't happen often in those days. That's why I remember it now. I don't know if he's dead or not.'

'Can you check on it for me?'

'I'll see what I can find,' said Pálmi, telling Konrád to drive carefully back to town before hurrying in out of the cold.

29

The pain seemed as if it would never end, and was almost unbearable. Valborg tried to keep as quiet as possible and pushed until she thought she would pass out. Sunnefa spoke soothingly to her and encouraged her; it was all going as well as could be and would soon be over, she would have to be strong and push a little harder, now the baby's head is visible, it's almost over, just a few more minutes.

It had been three hours since she started having contractions. Her waters had broken shortly beforehand, and then Sunnefa took over. They were well prepared for what needed to be done and she was determined and very professional, filling Valborg with a sense of security. She didn't want anything to happen to the child. The disgust she felt about giving it up immediately was more than enough.

Late in her pregnancy, she'd gone east to Selfoss, where Sunnefa worked, to live with her. They'd talked about the risk involved in not having a doctor available if something went wrong. Sunnefa said she wouldn't hesitate to call an ambulance in that case. On the other hand, there was nothing to indicate the delivery would be anything but normal and go smoothly. Valborg was healthy and the pregnancy had gone well. Her sister wasn't in the country; she was working as an au pair in Copenhagen that summer and would continue to do so well into the autumn. Two years earlier, their mother had moved out east to Vík in Mýrdalur with a new partner and was only in intermittent telephone contact. Valborg had told her friends that she was going to Selfoss to work. She told no one what had happened to her, or her plans.

When it was all over, she was exhausted and fell asleep while Sunnefa attended to the child, washed it, and checked its vital signs. She rinsed out the sheets and towels and hung them on a clothes line in the bathroom. When Valborg stirred, she helped her clean up. Valborg didn't ask about the child and avoided looking towards where it slept soundly.

Sunnefa bent over her.

'I'm going to ask you one last time. Are you sure you want to take this route?'

Valborg looked into her eyes.

'I'm sure,' she whispered.

'Don't you want to see it?'

Valborg shook her head.

'No, never.'

'Are you sure?'

'You promised that I would have nothing to do with it.'

'OK. Do you want to know if it's a boy or a girl?'

'Don't say a thing. Take it,' ordered Valborg, shaking her head, more determined than ever. 'Take it and do what you're going to do and then leave me alone.'

30

When explaining her cracked lip and other facial injuries, Glóey said that it had been the car door, which had just blown open and hit her in the face, seriously injuring her. As if to prove it, she said that she'd experienced the same thing once before, quite a few years ago. As she was opening her car door, the same sort of gust, or whatever you'd call it, blew it smack into her face and split her lip. This time, the cast on her arm didn't help, she said.

Glóey was sitting in Marta's office, and had asked twice if she could smoke. Marta said no both times, but offered her her e-cigarette, which Glóey said was of no use. Marta had asked about her injuries and received that explanation, but otherwise Glóey said that she hadn't come down to the police station to talk about her interactions with car doors and wind gusts, but to point out that she hadn't been herself for the past few days, having drunk excessively and taken drugs and that everything she'd previously said about her husband had been greatly exaggerated. The truth was that she'd been practically out of her mind with anger at Hallur when she found out about his relationship with her sister, and started saying all sorts of things about him that had no basis in fact. She'd said all of it in a fit of rage and regretted it and wanted the police to know that. Hallur didn't owe anyone anything and hadn't been using drugs for a long time. No one had threatened him about anything. All of it had been said in order to hurt him and she didn't even know how she'd come up with that nonsense.

Marta listened to her calmly and tried to imagine how a person got their car door in their face when getting into the vehicle. It wasn't impossible. Even twice in a life as short as hers. She knew first-hand about such gusts. They were no joke. Once she'd lost her grip on her own car door in a gust of wind, and it was damaged. She'd been getting out of the vehicle at the JL building, where it was notoriously windy, and hadn't been careful.

Marta had heard far worse lies in her time, but it wasn't Glóey's story that caught her attention, despite it being a decent one. It was Glóey herself. She was no longer angry, but scared, squirming in her seat with her pretty face all messed up and the cast on her arm.

'What's wrong, Glóey?' she asked.

'My lip stings a little.'

'No, I mean, what are you afraid of?'

'Nothing. I'm not afraid of anything.'

'What about Hallur? Aren't you afraid of him?'

'No, why? Why should I be afraid of him?'

'What about his friends? Are you afraid of them?'

'No, I don't know . . . I don't know them.'

'Not the ones he owes money?'

'No. I mean, he doesn't owe anyone money. No one.'

'You told me he owed certain individuals, but didn't want to name them. Do you want to name them now?'

'I don't know –'

'Were they the ones who did that to you?'

'No, it was –'

'Yes, the car door, I'd forgotten that,' said Marta. 'Your husband owed them a lot of money, you told me last time we met. You had no idea how Hallur was going to pay them. I ask again, were they the ones who did this to you?'

Glóey didn't answer her.

'They threatened him,' Marta said, 'and he thought he'd found a way to pay them. That's what you said.'

'I wasn't in my right mind,' said Glóey. 'I was just making stuff up. All of it. Complete nonsense.'

'Were they the ones who did this to you?'

'I was just clumsy when I opened my car door,' said Glóey.

'Who are these people?'

'It was just clumsiness on my part.'

Hallur's interrogation hadn't yielded much. The only conceivable signs of his presence in Valborg's flat were traces of soil from the back garden found on his footwear and that he said had nothing to do with the case. He'd talked about the odour of garbage or an unclean smell in the stairwell when he left Glóey's sister's place, and no one knew what it could be until someone suggested the garbage chute in the wall of the hallway, which opened onto a wheelie bin.

The police had put some effort into obtaining data from the security cameras in the area around Valborg's home, in the hope of mapping Hallur's movements and comparing them with his testimony. The cameras, however, were few and far between, as in most residential areas, and their yield was proportional.

Marta had gone to see Emanúel. He said again that he'd only been testing a new spotting scope that he'd bought solely for use in amateur astronomy. The scope was an Acuter, on a sturdy tripod of the sort used by photographers, and took up quite a bit of space once Emanúel had set it up in his living room. For some reason, the astronomer had packed it away immediately after Konrád's visit.

The scope had a very good range, especially for those who wanted to explore something other and closer than the orbits of the planets. Marta tried to recreate with some accuracy the sequence of events that led to the murder of Valborg. Emanúel proved to be cooperative. Hallur not so much, but he let himself be persuaded. He was taken to the stairwell of Valborg's block of flats. A policewoman opened the door to the flat and Hallur pretended to attack her. She lay on the floor and Hallur entered the flat and went from one room to another. On his head he wore a black balaclava that had been found in his home, and he was dressed in the clothes he wore the night Valborg was attacked. Then he ran back out of the flat and the experiment was over.

Through it all, Emanúel stared into his spotting scope and followed Hallur's movements until he went back into the stairwell and out of sight. Marta stood next to him and made sure he stuck with it and finally asked what he thought. The question was simple. Was this the same man who attacked Valborg?

'I think it could be,' said Emanúel. 'But I'm not sure.'

Marta stood there silently, staring at the peeping Tom with a stern expression as if it might force a more categorical answer.

'I think so,' said Emanúel.

'Good,' said Marta.

'But I'm not sure.'

'Which one is it?'

'It could be. But I'm not sure.'

'Good Lord,' Marta groaned.

She'd spoken to Emanúel's son, who said his dad was a complete pervert who hung out at the window in the evenings with his spotting scope and spied on people when he thought he couldn't be seen. Yes, sometimes he went out on the balcony with the scope and looked at the stars. The other was more usual. He started it about a year ago, or soon after the divorce. The son was ashamed of his father's behaviour, and said he'd taken no part in it and was just waiting to move away from home. He and three friends of his were going to rent a place together in Breiðholt.

Marta didn't get much clearer answers from Emanúel about the experiment in the block of flats and let her colleagues know that it was finished. Hallur was taken back into custody. He maintained his innocence and didn't understand this ridiculous treatment. Marta continued to question Emanúel closely about what he saw through the telescope the evening Valborg was murdered. He stood miserably beside his spotting scope, waiting for the barrage of questions to subside and the policewoman to leave so he could get on with his daily business. She felt somewhat sorry for him, particularly when she thought about his son, who clearly resented his father.

'Why do you do this?' she asked towards the end.

'I don't know,' said Emanúel.

'Aren't you a little too old-fashioned? You know, these days, people spy on each other online. Isn't it simpler just to be on Facebook? No one peeps through scopes or binoculars from their living rooms nowadays.'

It was as if Emanúel sensed the slight sympathy that his son's resentment had sparked in Marta.

'What are you looking for?' she asked. 'Naked ladies?'

'No,' Emanúel was quick to answer.

'What, then?'

'Something else,' said Emanúel.

'What?'

'I don't know. Happiness.'

'Happiness? What the hell are you talking about?'

Emanúel said nothing, and Marta looked at the spotting scope and tripod and asked if he took photos. If he had a camera that he could mount on the tripod, and a strong telephoto lens to go with it. Emanúel was slow to reply, but admitted that he had a decent camera and went and got it.

'I was going to delete the photos,' he said apologetically.

He went to a special gallery that held his search for happiness, according to what he'd said, and allowed Marta to scroll through some of the photos. Most of them were taken on the street and showed people walking hand-in-hand, a family in front of an ice-cream parlour, young people kissing. A few were taken using the tripod in his living room and showed elderly people reading in their homes, children sitting at the kitchen table, a couple snuggling in front of the TV. All of the photos violated privacy laws, but none of them were indecent. Marta looked at one photo after another until she saw images of a woman she recognised. She was sitting alone in her living room and appeared to be crying.

'You've hardly found happiness there,' Marta said, showing Emanúel the photos of the woman she'd met and was convinced was the victim of chronic domestic violence.

'No,' said Emanúel. 'Her husband is awful. I saw him attack her that night. Saw how he . . . it was horrendous. Just horrendous.'

31

Konrád didn't know any midwives, but his wife Erna had been a doctor and worked in hospitals and knew plenty of nurses and doctors. Konrád had got to know some of those people over the years. One of them was a woman named Svanhildur, who in several instances handled autopsies and had worked with Konrád when he was in CID. They'd become good friends, and quite a bit more than that. After Erna died, Svanhildur had contacted him several times to find out how he was doing, but he'd responded coolly, preferring to act as if nothing had happened between them. However, he'd had to go to her for information he needed and she'd always been warm, welcoming and helpful to him without expecting anything in return. At most, she asked if they could maybe talk to each other about what was important, and told him that he had no reason to avoid her.

After much thought and a few glasses of wine to help work up his nerve, he called Svanhildur late in the evening after returning from his visit to Pálmi. He came straight to the point, as per usual, and said that he wanted to know if she could help him track down a midwife who'd been active around 1970 and who might have had a reputation for her opposition to abortions –

'Terminations of pregnancy,' said Svanhildur.

'Termi . . . ?'

'That's what it's called more often today.'

Svanhildur was immediately interested. If she was surprised to get a phone call from him so late in the evening, she didn't show it. Nor did she say anything about him mumbling a bit on the phone. She asked what he was up to these days that involved midwives and he told her about his acquaintance with Valborg, whom he'd denied his help, and said that it troubled him a bit that he hadn't helped her. He could certainly have done so, and shouldn't have been so peevish and difficult when she told him what she was looking for. The next thing he knew, she'd been murdered in her own home, and he could possibly have prevented it if he'd only bothered to help her.

He blurted this all out and she sensed that he wasn't feeling well, and had maybe lost control of his drinking.

'Is that the woman in the block of flats?' she asked. 'Valborg?'

'I could really have helped her,' Konrád said. 'I still don't understand why I didn't.'

'No, but you couldn't have prevented what happened,' Svanhildur said. 'You're not a cop. You're retired.'

'But if it was related?'

'What?'

'She'd made enquiries about her child before she came to me. What if that's what triggered all this?'

'Do you have some reason for thinking that?'

'No.'

'Did you say she was a midwife? Or what do midwives have to do with this?'

'Valborg was expecting a child that she wanted nothing to do with and got in touch with a midwife who delivered the baby and put it into someone else's hands. Got rid of it. She came to me for help finding her child. It's been almost fifty years since the child was born and the woman had no idea what became of it. She never saw it. It could have been a boy. Could have been a girl.'

'And what, are you trying to find that person now? Isn't it a bit too late?'

'Yes. It's damned late. But in any case, that midwife seemed to have known of foster parents who would provide a home for the child, and it was all done so that no one knew anything, apart, of course, from those who participated in it. She probably even forged the necessary papers. The foster parents could have said they'd adopted the child via the normal route or that it was their own. No one would have disputed that, certainly not at the time.'

'Do you know why the woman didn't want to have the baby?'

'No, I'm working on that,' Konrád said.

Both of them fell silent as they thought these things over, until Svanhildur couldn't take it any more.

'Did you call me just because of this, or . . . ?'

'It's good to be able to talk to you about it,' Konrád said. 'It's always been good to be able to talk to you.'

'So are you done avoiding me? It's been a long time. Ever since Erna died. It's not like I want to reopen an old can of worms, but I think you would benefit from talking about what happened. About us. I know it would do you good. And I know that you feel bad about how it all turned out. Because we went behind her back.

But I've told you before that she wouldn't have been any better off knowing about us. Not at all.'

'I would have liked it to have gone differently,' said Konrád. 'I shouldn't have listened to you.'

'You're not blaming me for it?'

'No, of course not, it's no one's fault when such things happen.'

'When such things . . . ?'

'Worst is that . . . sometimes I'm haunted by doubts. That she knew about us but didn't say anything. Knew about the adultery and was waiting for me to tell her everything. For me to come clean. I never did that, and it's not a good thought.'

'She knew nothing about us.'

'I'm not sure. And it hurts. Besides the fact that she should have been told. She had every right. She had a good sense for such things and it may well be that she put two and two together but said nothing. Waited for me to come clean and ask for her forgiveness.'

'You can't agonise over this.'

'No, but I do anyway.'

When they parted shortly afterwards, they said they should meet again soon, although without much conviction, and Svanhildur promised to enquire about midwives. Konrád opened a new bottle of red wine. It was called the Dead Arm. Erna had found it many years ago and given it to him because one of his arms was misshapen, weaker since birth, and withered; he didn't have full use of it. Konrád had got into the habit of keeping his hand in his pocket when he spoke with strangers, as if to hide his disability. Not that he was ashamed of being disabled; he just didn't want people to feel sorry for him. Didn't want them to see any signs of weakness in him. He couldn't stand the thought. Erna had never done so. Had never viewed the arm as anything but perfectly natural, and treated it with complete irreverence. In her mind, Konrád couldn't be anything other than who he was, and to celebrate that, Erna found him this fitting wine.

Konrád smiled to himself at the thought and looked at the old wooden object of his father's. He grabbed it and pondered it, as he'd done so many times before. He hardly remembered how the affair started. He was burned out at work after years of fruitless investigation into a disappearance that, much later, turned out to be a routine murder case. The body hadn't been found because it was buried on Langjökull Glacier, of all places, and was discovered only by coincidence three decades later, mainly thanks to global warming.

Konrád had rarely been so down. The investigation of the case had been halted and he felt that he'd failed, and then year after year passed without him being able to pull himself up out of his melancholy and depression. And once when Erna was at a conference abroad, he went downtown with a few other police officers and met Svanhildur and some of her friends at a nightclub. She'd been divorced for two years and lived alone. Svanhildur invited him to her place to call a taxi and one thing led to another. They had a drink, he looked at her, and they ended up sleeping together for the first time. The next morning, he slunk out without saying goodbye. As if he'd never been there. As if it had never happened. He was good at that.

But it did happen, and was so surprisingly effortless. It required no preparation or lead-up, which surprised him most of all. And it should have ended there because he could have told Erna that he'd made a mistake that one time, and it would never happen again.

He was prepared to do so and was waiting for Erna to come home when Svanhildur called him and asked if they could meet. Konrád refused at first, but then called her back and said he needed to talk to her. He was going to tell her that he had to come clean with Erna. They met at Svanhildur's place. It went exactly the same as the first time.

They kept seeing each other every now and then for the next few years, but stopped when Erna fell ill. Konrád never told Erna what happened. He and Svanhildur had easily found time for their dalliance. Erna worked a lot in those years and Konrád himself was always 'at work'. What was he looking for? What could he get from an affair with a divorced woman? What did it give him, when all was said and done? A change? Excitement? Did it take his mind off what was really eating away at him from the inside, which was that unsolvable case he had on his hands?

The thought that Erna had known about the lie without revealing that she did became unbearable to him over time.

Konrád knocked the wooden object against the edge of the table, and even harder the angrier he grew with himself. He knew that that peculiar object wasn't the only thing his father had left behind. One thing was indifference. Another was negligence. Anger, as well. Konrád had grown up with anything but honesty in dealing with other people. His childhood was spent in the close company of subterfuge and fraud. He knew that there was a great deal true and correct in what Erna said about his past. When his peers were learning the commandment 'thou shalt not steal', he was helping his father move what he'd stolen from one location to another.

He didn't always choose honesty if the other option was

more profitable for him, and lies were his constant companions. Not necessarily lies that he told others, but ones that he told himself.

Konrád suddenly felt as if this object of his father's was cursed. That everything that had gone wrong in his life was his father's fault, and he flung it away. It hit the wall with a strange hollow sound from the past.

32

The man was around Konrád's age and had lived in Reykjavík the past three decades. Pálmi had dug up information about him and knew where he lived, and Konrád decided to pay him a visit straight away. The man had worked in fish processing in various villages on the Reykjanes peninsula, as a labourer for Icelandic contractors hired by the US military at the Base in Keflavík, and had driven a taxi in the city. He'd been married for a time and had two children, but divorced many years ago and now lived alone in a basement flat in the Vogar neighbourhood.

He didn't have a registered phone number and wasn't at home when Konrád went to see him. So Konrád got back into his car and decided to wait and see if the man would show up. He'd brought a Thermos of coffee and a newspaper and tried to make himself comfortable in his car. He'd reached the obituaries when he noticed a man walk up to the house, take out a key chain, and go down three steps to the basement door. The man appeared to be the right age.

Konrád put down his coffee and newspaper, got out and walked towards the house. He saw that he hadn't closed the door behind him – which explained itself when he appeared holding a rubbish bag and took it to a bin in the back garden. He eyed Konrád but didn't greet him, and was heading back inside when Konrád decided to stop him.

'Ísleifur?'

The man turned and stared at Konrád.

'Yeah, that's me.'

When Pálmi called with the information, he said he'd dug up two rape cases that were more memorable to him than others from the past. He'd found out that the rapist in one of them had died quite a few years ago, a violent man who'd broken into the home of a woman in Grindavík, forced himself on her and nearly killed her, and been convicted for it. The other was a man named Ísleifur. Pálmi said he vaguely remembered Ísleifur as a young man, but he hadn't run into him since the early sixties, when a young woman accused him of raping her after a dance in Keflavík. It had happened in a popular nightclub after closing, when everyone had left. The woman worked at the place and had stayed behind to tidy and lock up following the night's entertainment. Ísleifur didn't deny having been there at the time, and said that he was there at the woman's invitation. They hadn't known each other previously, but had spoken earlier that evening and had got along quite well. She'd asked him to stay, saying that when she was done locking up, they could have some fun. And that's exactly what they did. They had sex on one of the couches there at the club before he headed home, not suspecting that he'd committed any crime, as he said.

The woman had a different story to tell. She'd interacted twice with Ísleifur earlier that evening, on his initiative, without knowing anything about him. The first time, he'd asked what time she finished work and what she was planning to do afterwards. She'd told him that she was going home and to bed. He'd been drinking, but wasn't particularly drunk. About an hour later, she ran into him again and they talked, and, as before, he asked her what time she finished, and she said she was going home after closing up the place, that she was dead tired after her shift and had no interest in anything but going home to bed.

When she was the only one left in the place, the band having packed their gear and gone and the barmen and other employees having left, and she was hurrying to finish everything up, she suddenly saw Ísleifur come out of the men's loo. She was startled, not expecting anyone else to be there. She asked what he was doing there and he said he fell asleep on the toilet. Her guard went up immediately and she asked him politely to leave; the place was already closed. He asked if there was any hurry, and if they shouldn't have a drink together.

She refused and when he made no move to go, she was torn between whether she should hurry out of there herself or find a phone and call the police.

She was terribly frightened and was about to run when he grabbed her, and now he was holding a knife.

Konrád regarded the man. Ísleifur looked as if he'd once been strongly built, as the woman had described him, even though he could hardly force himself on anyone any longer; his back was bent and he was slender, but there was a depraved look beneath his ragged eyebrows. Pálmi had mentioned the thin David Niven moustache that he still wore, as he had during the years when he tried to catch the eyes of women. Konrád looked at the thin moustache and got the feeling he still thought he was a pretty good catch.

'What do you want?' he snapped.

The woman's testimony was consistent from the first. She'd done as the man ordered after he threatened to slice her open and various things even worse. She was paralysed with fear and didn't resist. Although he'd threatened to find her and kill her if she pressed charges, she immediately called the police, who went and arrested Ísleifur and questioned him. A medical examination revealed that the woman had suffered injuries. However, she showed no signs of resisting the attack. Ísleifur had no criminal record. His testimony was deemed credible. It was a case of 'he said, she said'. Ísleifur was acquitted.

'I wondered if I could trouble you for a moment about something from the old days,' Konrád said. 'It shouldn't take long.'

Ísleifur stared piercingly at him.

'What . . . what are you talking about?' he asked.

'It concerns Glaumbær,' said Konrád.

'Glaumbær?' said the man, both ill-humoured and surprised. 'What's that?'

'What's that? You remember Glaumbær,' said Konrád. 'The nightclub.'

'And who are you?'

'I used to work for the police. My name's Konrád. Am I correct in saying that you used to hang out at Glaumbær in the old days?'

'That's none of your business,' said Ísleifur. 'What do you want from me?'

'I'd like to know if you did again what you once did to a woman in Keflavík.'

The man stared blankly at Konrád.

'If you had a knife on you at Glaumbær just before Christmas in 1971, around the time the place burned down,' Konrád continued. 'If you attacked a woman I knew. Attacked and raped her. As you did when you were in Keflavík.'

The man straightened up. This unexpected visit was becoming a bit more understandable to him. The connections were becoming clearer.

'I haven't heard about Keflavík for a long time,' he said after some thought, running a finger through his moustache. 'It was nothing but damned lies on that woman's part.'

'Why would she have told such lies about you?' Konrád asked. 'She didn't know you at all. Didn't know who you were. She could hardly have got anything out of it.'

'Everything those broads say is a lie. Fucking lying cunts.'

'And Glaumbær?' said Konrád. 'Nothing happened there, either?'

The man hesitated.

'No,' he said. 'I have no idea what you're talking about.'

'Her name was Valborg. The woman at Glaumbær. She was attacked the other day, and her life snuffed out. I'm sure you must have seen the news reports. Do you know anything about it?'

'No, I don't,' said Ísleifur. 'I'm going to ask you to get out of here. I've done nothing wrong. The woman in Keflavík lied about me and I don't understand any of this bullshit of yours about Glaumbær. Not a thing.'

The man headed back down the stairs to the basement.

'Did you use the knife there, too?'

Ísleifur didn't answer.

'You may have a child that you don't know about,' said Konrád, to shock him. 'Now wouldn't that liven up your existence?'

Ísleifur stopped.

'Valborg had a baby nine months after Glaumbær burned,' Konrád said. 'She never revealed who the father was. Kept it entirely to herself. Could it be you?'

Ísleifur turned towards Konrád and told him to go to hell, spat at him and then stormed down to the basement and slammed the door behind him.

33

Eygló had tried to get hold of the accountant, Stella's great-nephew, all day, but without success. She started calling him before noon but he didn't answer the phone, and didn't seem to have a secretary to take messages. The day passed, and Eygló decided to try one last time when it was nearing six o'clock. After several rings, the man finally answered. He remembered Eygló immediately, and she sensed his annoyance right away. In a petulant tone, he said he was busy and on his way to a meeting, and Eygló decided to get straight to the point before he could end the call abruptly. She'd racked her brain over something that had been bothering her ever since she and Konrád met the accountant, and she felt she had to get to the bottom of those speculations.

'Do you know how they managed to get her on their side?' she asked. 'What was the clincher? There must have been something.'

'Get her to what? Who?'

'Stella. On their side. My father and his partner. Do you know how they managed to deceive her?'

'Why are you bothering me with this?' the man said, and Eygló envisioned his thick lips and remembered the heavy air in his office. 'I told you I didn't want to talk about it. I have no interest in it. It's a family matter and no one else's business!'

'That's all I want to know, then I'll leave you alone,' said Eygló. 'I promise that –'

The man hung up on her. Eygló stared at the phone, entered the number again and waited. It was busy. She thought for a moment, then made her decision. A moment later she got into her car and drove as fast as she could towards the city centre. Questions had been gnawing at her non-stop since she woke up that morning and walked hesitantly into the living room, still with that sea-soaked figure in her mind's eye, her father Engilbert bending over the piano.

The accountant was stepping out of the office building when Eygló arrived. She'd had to park her car at a considerable distance and hurry to his place of work, and was somewhat short of breath when she called to him to wait. He looked around, and when he saw who it was, he quickened his pace. He was disappearing round the corner of the cathedral when she caught up with him and grabbed his arm.

'Wait a minute, for God's sake. Don't make me have to run after you,' she said breathlessly.

'What do you think you're doing?' the man said, tearing himself free. 'Can't you just leave me alone?'

'I need to ask you a few questions, and then I'll be done,' Eygló said.

'I'm not interested in talking to you about this. It's a family matter that we don't discuss with strangers!'

'Yes, I realise that, and excuse me for being so persistent, but I've been thinking a lot about this and it crossed my mind to ask you if there was something that tipped the scale. Sometimes that's the case. With people in that . . . that line of work.'

'Fraudulent mediums, you mean?'

'Yes,' Eygló said reluctantly, thinking of her father. 'If that's what you think.'

'They knew about her son,' the man said, continuing on his way but no longer trying to avoid her. 'How he died. I told you that.'

'Yes, I remember,' said Eygló.

'Naturally, it wasn't difficult to get hold of that information,' said the man. 'Why do you want to know this?'

'What do you think they did with that information?' asked Eygló. 'Did it have anything to do with music?'

'How do you know that?'

'Was that the case?'

'Her son was immersed in music,' said the man, stopping. He couldn't hide his surprise.

'What do you mean by that? Was he studying music? Did he play an instrument?'

'Yes. He was very skilled. A top student.'

'Was it the piano? The instrument he played?'

'Yes, how do you know . . . who told you that?'

'And what happened?' Eygló asked.

The man stared at her silently.

'What happened?' Eygló asked again.

'They made contact with her son,' the man said finally.

'Through the piano?'

Another long silence. Eygló waited breathlessly.

'This is a sensitive family matter and is really none of your business,' the man said again.

'I understand it's a sensitive issue,' said Eygló, 'but you can't say that it's none of my business. Was it through the piano? That they made contact with her son?'

'The boy supposedly gave them a sign via an old piano that he practised on,' said the man. 'Stella was adamant that she'd heard the same note played over and over without anyone touching the piano, and was convinced she could have communicated with her son in that way.'

It was evening when Eygló switched on the lights in her kitchen and living room and went to the piano, sat down and ran her hands over the keys. She remembered that when she went to bed the night before, the one key was still stuck and that she'd closed the lid carefully before retiring.

Eygló heard a knock on the door. She wasn't expecting any visitors and went and opened the door hesitantly. On the doorstep stood the raggedy woman who'd spoken to her in the car park of Fossvogur cemetery following Málfríður's funeral, and who'd said she'd known the old woman. She was just as raggedly dressed, like a beggar, of an uncertain age and with strong facial features.

'Has she made contact?' the woman asked unceremoniously. 'Our Málfríður? Has she made her presence known?'

'No,' said Eygló, not wanting to be impolite even if the woman was unusually pushy. She had known Málfríður, though.

'Did Málfríður say how she would do it? How she was going to go about it?'

'No,' said Eygló. 'And I don't know if –'

'Do you think she hasn't crossed over?'

'Sorry, I . . . it's late and I'm busy.'

'Is she dwelling in the realm of light?'

'Yes. Goodbye,' said Egyló. She wanted to get rid of the woman as quickly as possible.

'What are you afraid of?' asked the woman.

'I don't have time for this. I'm going to ask you not to bother me any more.'

'What is it you fear?' The woman took a step towards her.

Egyló hurriedly shut the door and waited for a minute or two in the hall, hoping the woman had left. When she thought the woman was gone, she sat back down at the piano, and after a few moments her mind wandered to the conversation she'd had with Stella's great-nephew and to how those two partners, Engilbert and Konrád's father, had convinced Stella that she could get in touch with her son via her piano. Egyló had heard such stories about resourceful, fraudulent mediums, and perhaps those stories had followed her into her sleep when Engilbert appeared to her in a dream.

If it was a dream. When she went into the living room the next morning, the piano's lid was open and the key, which she'd been absolutely unable to move the night before, was now loose and indistinguishable from the others.

Egyló ran her hand over the piano, seeing the ragged woman in her mind's eye and trying not to think too much about signs from the beyond.

34

The door quivered from the impact and Konrád stood there wondering if he could have approached Ísleifur in a friendlier manner. The man's reaction was understandable. He was undoubtedly justified in telling Konrád to go to hell. A complete stranger had appeared on his doorstep and started slandering him and making accusations about old sexual offences, and as if that wasn't enough, the stranger had suggested that he might have a child. Ísleifur had every reason to be angry. He had no criminal record. The rape at Glaumbær was an invention of Konrád's. He knew there was little to go on, but the ex-policeman felt that there was more to Valborg's story: that she'd suffered a major shock in life that was somehow connected with the child, and rape wasn't out of the picture. Maybe he was going too far. Ísleifur had once been charged with rape, but nothing could be proven against him and he was never convicted.

Konrád grimaced. At one time, he would have handled this

differently and better. His age was probably rearing its head. He no longer had the patience for tact and courtesy when it was needed most. Maybe that had always been a fault of his. He tried to convince himself that he hadn't said those things out of utter thoughtlessness, but had wanted to challenge the man and upset him and read his response. It did little good. He was worried about having overstepped the mark when he suggested that Ísleifur had raped Valborg and got her pregnant in the process.

Fuck it, Konrád thought to himself as he walked back to the car. There was no need for him to act like a policeman any more. He was retired. His mobile phone was lying on the dashboard, and he saw that Svanhildur had tried to reach him twice. He called her and found out that she hadn't been idle since the last time they talked.

Svanhildur had spent the better part of the day enquiring about midwives and abortions. She had connections in various hospital wards, but dug up nothing until she called a woman with whom she was vaguely familiar and who had studied midwifery before changing course and studying medicine. Svanhildur recalled that when she was at the Midwifery College, there'd been a young woman there who was known for her religious fervour. She belonged to a religious sect and had very strong views on abortion. She preached against it at every opportunity, had argued about that controversial issue with her fellow students, lost her temper several times, made threats and caused quite an uproar in general. The woman was reprimanded twice for inappropriate behaviour. What tipped the scales for the college authorities was a scene between her and a young woman who sought advice on the termination of her pregnancy. A midwife witnessed the incident, got into an argument with the student and ended up in a physical altercation with her. Afterwards, the student felt she no longer fitted in at the college and left it voluntarily. In another version of the story, she was asked to leave.

After telling Konrád everything she knew, which wasn't very much, Svanhildur gave him the phone number and address of a friend she thought was more familiar with the incident, having been a student at the college when it occurred. Konrád thanked Svanhildur for the favour. He decided not to put off paying the woman a visit. She lived on Goðheimar Street, a short distance from Ísleifur's home, where he was.

He didn't call ahead and the woman was quite surprised at this unusual visit. Konrád said that he was a friend of Svanhildur's, who had spoken to her earlier that day, and asked if he could talk to her about a certain woman who had studied midwifery but hadn't been able to complete her studies after running into trouble at the college.

'Are you that policeman?' said the woman, before inviting him in. 'Svanhildur called me earlier and said you might be in touch. Do you know anything about it?'

'I was hoping you did,' said Konrád.

'Why are you and Svanhildur wondering about this now? Sunnefa died many years ago.'

'Oh, is she dead? Her name was Sunnefa?'

'What do you want with her? Svanhildur said it was a police matter. That you're a police officer.'

'No, I was. I'm retired now. This is just something I'm looking into on my own. It's in connection with a woman I knew, but who died recently.'

'Svanhildur said it had something to do with the woman who was found murdered.'

'Yes, that's right. I wondered if she knew this Sunnefa. Whether they were in contact with each other in the old days. What can you tell me about her? I understand she got on the wrong side of the college administrators?'

'Her views got her kicked out. She was very uncompromising. People had started to think differently about these issues, and expressed far more liberal views, you see, and she was completely against it. Hated it all and wasn't shy about asserting her own views. She was insufferable in that respect. Couldn't leave it alone. Typical of those zealots. She preached to us as if she was the only one in the world who knew the truth.'

'More liberal views?'

'About abortion,' said the woman, as if she felt that Konrád should have his head more in the game. 'Free love and all that. Hippie attitudes. The point of view that women control their own bodies and have every right to do what they want with them. Those sorts of views.'

'But she had other ideas?'

'She did indeed. Never grew tired of making her opinions known.'

'So she left the college?'

'I'd actually gone into medicine by then, but I was told she'd lost it and bawled out a woman seeking an abortion, which is of course simply outrageous if it's true. She was a very promising student, actually. She really knew her stuff, but there was no way she could finish.'

'Do you think she never worked as a midwife, then?' Konrád asked.

'I can't imagine she did, but it's hard to say.'

'What were women supposed to do if . . . ?'

'They were just supposed to have their baby,' said the woman. 'God's will and all that. Whatever she could quote from the Bible. She knew it inside out.'

'But adoption? Wasn't that a possibility?'

'Yes, that was one way, and Sunnefa was a great advocate of it. Said that it was always possible to find a good home for the children.'

'Do you know if she helped any women in that way?'

'No. Did she?'

'I don't know,' said Konrád. 'If she didn't work as a midwife – or not at the Women's Health Unit anyway – can you imagine how she could have got information about women who requested an abortion or considered that possibility?'

'No, what –'

'Or how she could have got in touch with those women?'

'Why would she have wanted such information?' the woman asked in surprise.

'So she could turn women off that path. Something like that. I don't know.'

'Maybe she worked in a doctor's surgery. I have no idea. That poor woman who was found murdered – did she know Sunnefa?'

'I'd like to find out,' Konrád said.

'Was it related to something that happened in the past? Something to do with abortion?'

'I don't know,' said Konrád.

'Maybe she was attacked because of that?'

'No, I don't think so.'

'It's as if no one is safe any more,' said the woman wearily.

Konrád sensed that she'd had enough of his visit, but he still had a few questions for her, and pressed on, asking about the people whom Sunnefa socialised with during those years. The woman remembered few details. She suggested he speak with a friend of hers who'd started at the National Hospital around the same time as them, studying to become a medical laboratory technician, as they were then called. She thought that he and Sunnefa had seen each other once or twice.

'Which sect did Sunnefa belong to?' Konrád asked, entering the friend's name in his phone as he got up to go. The woman seemed relieved that this peculiar interrogation was at an end. 'Do you remember that?'

'Sect?' the woman asked.

'Didn't you say she belonged to a religious sect?'

'Oh, that. I have no idea. All I remember is that she was full of religious fervour and once said when she was railing against abortions that all God's children were welcome to join it.'

'The sect?'

'Yes. And she quoted the Bible, of course.'

'What passage?'

'Oh, what do you think?'

Konrád didn't have to think long.

'Let the children come to me . . . ?'

'That's right.'

When Konrád returned to his home in Árbær, he sat down at his computer and looked up something that had been on his mind ever since he met Valborg at the museum. She had mentioned a crag on a mountain to the west that sometimes came to mind when she sat in front of the sculptures in the museum – Tregasteinn, the Rock of Sorrow – and now he found its story. The crag was on Hólsfjall Mountain out west in the Dalir District, and the story went that once a woman had been outside with a baby when an eagle came and snatched the child and flew with it towards the mountain. The woman followed the bird to the crag and when she got there she saw a stream of blood running down the rock, and her heart burst from exhaustion and grief.

35

It had started raining again, heavily, when he went to pick up Eygló around noon the next day, and she hurried out to his car. She was unusually quiet, simply watching the windscreen wipers contend with the rain as Konrád drove up from Fossvogur. Konrád decided not to bother her and they drove westwards in silence, apart from the sound of the radio, which was tuned to an American rock station that Konrád liked. He'd turned down the volume when she got into the car and thought it best not to turn it up again.

'Is everything all right?' he asked at a red light.

Eygló sighed.

'Is it the etheric realm?' said Konrád.

'Go on, make fun of it,' said Eygló. 'There's some scruffy woman bothering me. One of the friends of old Málfríður, who died the other day, came to my house last night and claimed to have some message for me. It's unbearable. Why do people whom I've never seen in my life think they know me?'

'Incomprehensible.'

'And my piano is behaving strangely, too.'

'Your piano?'

'Yes, there's no point in talking to you about it,' Eygló said curtly.

Soon afterwards, they arrived at the home of the man they were planning on meeting. Konrád had spoken to him on the phone that morning and explained his business with him, and the man, whose name was Henning, was receptive to it. Henning lived alone and took care of himself, in the main, but wore a medical alert bracelet on his wrist and had help cleaning his place. He walked slowly, taking barely more than baby steps, staggered slightly and dragged his soft felt slippers along the floor. He took Konrád's measure, knowing that he was the son of the scumbag whom he'd once visited in the Shadow District with his friend, Stella's nephew.

'I've been recalling that visit since you rang,' he said as he invited them in. 'I'd forgotten it for the most part, and don't remember you at all.'

'No, it was a long time ago, of course,' Konrád said.

'I remember our visit to the Shadow District. I remember the man in the basement. I didn't like the look of him. Your dad was a real piece of work. Treating the widow like he did. It took a special kind of man. Not a trace of remorse in him.'

Konrád didn't know what to say. He'd long since grown tired of having to answer for his father's actions. He looked closely at the old man, but didn't know if he was one of the two who'd paid a visit to his father back in the day and threatened him; he hadn't seen them well enough, besides the fact that time and age had done their work on him.

The man smiled at Eygló.

'And you're the daughter of the seer?'

Eygló smiled back awkwardly and nodded.

'I never met him. Haukur – Stella's nephew – went to see him alone, and said he wasn't much of a man. He admitted his part in their game of deception, but pinned most of it on his partner. Said that they'd ratcheted up the drama when needed and had an easy time playing with her emotions. He regretted everything and had a great deal of remorse. He also said he'd genuinely tried to help the widow. He pretended to have some real ability as a medium. I have nothing else to offer you. Sorry.'

They told him not to worry about it, and Konrád added that they knew Haukur had been terribly angry at what the two men did to her.

'Yeah, he was furious. Not least because he was never able to recover the money.'

'And I understand he threatened my father. Said he was going to slit his throat like a mad dog's, or something like that. Which is interesting in light of what happened to my father.'

'Yes, but he would never have done that,' said Henning.

'Why not?'

'Haukur was a kind man, even if he had a temper. He could say something like that in a fit of rage, but he could never have done anything to anyone. It's out of the question. When photos of your dad appeared following the murder and we saw that it was the man who'd cheated money out of Stella, I asked if he had anything on his conscience. I asked him outright, because I knew what he thought of your father. I remember how surprised Haukur was that such a thought should ever have crossed my mind.'

'But it did cross your mind?' said Konrád.

'Yes, but not in any really serious way. It was said half-heartedly. I apologised to him for it.'

'Had he said anything that prompted you to ask him that?'

'No, apart from what you heard, but that was long before that, so –'

'We heard about the mental illness,' said Eygló.

'He had migraines. That's all I know.'

'Was he here in town at that time?'

'He was. He also said that your father had of course deserved what happened to him. Haukur never really beat about the bush.'

'Did he know much about knives?' asked Eygló.

'Not that I know of,' said Henning. 'On the other hand, he had a gun given to him by a friend of his in the British Army during the war.'

'Was he familiar with the Butchers' Association of the South?' Konrád asked. 'Its premises on Skúlagata? The people who worked there?'

'I really don't know. I don't remember him being so. He may well have been, though.'

The man fiddled with the alert bracelet on his wrist and Konrád wondered if he'd ever had to use it.

'Have you found out who that doctor was?' the man asked out of the blue, continuing to fiddle with the bracelet.

'What doctor?' said Konrád.

'Who owed him.'

'Owed who?'

'Your father. Haukur visited him again and then he was . . . more persuadable and promised to pay back some of what he took from Stella.'

'He visited him again?'

'Yes.'

'Why was he more persuadable then?'

The man hesitated.

'What happened?'

'It was some time before your father died. Haukur asked me not to tell anyone. Because of what happened afterwards. He threatened to kill your father if he didn't return the money. Your father took him seriously and he promised to get it. He told Haukur that he expected money from someone who owed him.'

'What for?' Konrád asked.

Henning continued to fiddle with the alert bracelet, then held the button up to his ear as if it were a watch.

'Haukur never found out what it was. Naturally, he didn't trust a thing your father said, but he mentioned a man here in town owing him money. I don't know why Haukur thought the man was from the medical profession; your dad probably said something along those lines. Maybe you should check on that. Since you're on this hunt.'

'Check on what?'

'Haukur thought your dad had something on the man. Perhaps he was even talking about blackmail, but then heard nothing more about it...'

'Oh?'

'Never got Stella's money, of course.'

'A doctor?'

'Yes. A doctor.'

36

Konrád and Eygló sat in the car in silence for some time after their visit. The man had no other information for them, and reiterated time and again that he knew nothing more about the interactions between Konrád's father and Haukur. He said he knew nothing about that doctor he'd mentioned and in fact backpedalled on it, more or less, stating, when they pressed him, that he wasn't sure those had been Haukur's exact words. He said that his memory was unreliable these days and he hadn't thought about those incidents for a long time, hardly at all until Konrád called out of the blue and asked if they could meet. Then various memories came back to him, but they were hazy, at best.

'That Haukur may well have attacked your father,' said Eygló. 'If he didn't get the money. Do you think he was crazy enough to do so?'

'What could Dad have had on some doctor?' Konrád whispered, as if to himself. 'Who the hell was he dealing with?'

'You haven't heard this before?'

'Never. I didn't know anything about it,' Konrád said, 'but he was so unpredictable and I heard so many bad things about him over the years that I stopped paying attention to them.'

'Do you think there's anything to it?'

'I simply have no idea,' said Konrád. 'There could be. It would be absurd to rule out anything when it comes to that man.'

They drove off towards Fossvogur, and Eygló told Konrád how she'd gone to see the accountant a second time to ask him what it was that made the widow trust their fathers so deeply.

'Do you really think Engilbert could have conjured up the boy?' Konrád asked distractedly.

'I've heard worse,' Eygló replied.

'Yes, I just have a hard time believing in such things. They were at it in order to make money, not to bring her into contact with anyone. They lied to the woman to get money off her.'

'Engilbert had abilities,' said Eygló. 'Real abilities.'

'I'm sure he did,' Konrád said, but his words lacked conviction. His mind was on his father and how he could still surprise him decades after his death.

'I really can't believe that he could have treated a defenceless woman like that,' said Eygló. 'A woman who'd suffered such loss.'

'Yes, they were really something,' Konrád said.

Eygló hesitated. So far, she'd met nothing but scepticism trying to convince Konrád that there might be other sides to existence, not just those that were visible and tangible and easily explained. So she didn't know if she should tell him about her father bending over the piano at her place and that she'd left the lid closed but found it open that morning, or about the key that was stuck and had come loose. That when this happened, she hadn't known what part Stella's piano had played when their fathers had lied to her and swindled her. So she'd proceeded with caution and decided to leave it alone for the time being. But then she couldn't resist.

'You don't have a high opinion of these abilities of mine and my father's,' she said.

'I don't believe in ghosts, if that's what you're asking,' said Konrád. 'You know that. We've gone over this before.'

'I wondered how they thought they'd made contact with the son and –'

'Thought they'd made contact? There was no contact, Eygló. They found out the boy was dead and then improvised.'

'Strange that you should word it like that. That accountant told me that Stella's son used the piano in the living room as a conduit. He was a promising student. It had stood there closed and silent ever since he died, but suddenly there was a sound from it. With its lid shut. She was adamant about it. The interaction was reminiscent of a Ouija board. One note for yes. Silence for no. In that way, the boy could communicate with his mother.'

'Eygló . . .'

'So what if Dad made contact? He wasn't a bad man. What if it was really like that? I've had stranger experiences. I myself have an old piano and . . .'

Konrád looked at her.

'They cheated money out of the widow in the most shameful way,' he said. 'The worst possible way imaginable, and we should leave it at that. Out of respect for her. Don't try to tell me they made contact with her son. Out of respect for him.'

'Dad told me about many such incidents. So was he lying to me?'

'I don't know. Maybe he said what his little girl wanted to hear.'

There was silence in the car until they reached Fossvogur and Konrád stopped in front of her terraced house. He sensed her dismay; how his words had hurt her.

'So about your piano?' he asked.

'Forget it,' said Eygló, and she got out of the car, slammed the door behind her and disappeared into the house.

Konrád cursed himself. He decided not to go in after her, but instead drove slowly up the street, accelerated and left Fossvogur for the Vogar neighbourhood, where Ísleifur lived. Maybe it was his strained interaction with Eygló that made him think he'd taken the wrong approach to the man when he encountered him the day before. So he decided to see if he could remedy that somehow, by speaking to him on a friendlier note. He'd just pulled up when Ísleifur suddenly came up the basement steps and headed towards the bus stop down the street. He stared at the ground and looked neither right nor left, but Konrád instinctively sank down in his seat. He decided to wait a bit and watch Ísleifur, even though he found such espionage lame and even akin to the type that Emanúel the peeping Tom engaged in.

Ísleifur was holding a plastic bag and walked slowly. He was wearing a tattered coat and a knitted cap on his head. He sat down at the bus stop and looked at his watch. Two young women were there waiting for the bus too, but he paid them no attention. He looked down the street, ran the back of his hand under his nose and waited. He scratched his head beneath his cap. Looked at his watch. Waited.

A few minutes later, the bus arrived and the two women and Ísleifur got on it. Ísleifur sat by the window. The bus set off and Konrád followed it from the Vogar neighbourhood towards the city centre. It was evening and traffic had died down after rush hour. The bus pulled over at every stop on its route, dropped off passengers and picked others up. Konrád followed. An old Icelandic song was playing on the radio, one that had been a favourite of Erna's, and he softly sang along about the eternal spring north in the dreamy Vaglaskógur Woods.

Ísleifur got off the bus a short distance from where the nightclub once stood and walked, shoulders hunched and holding his plastic bag, west down Borgartún Street. Before the economic crisis, new buildings of steel and glass rose there so aggressively and avariciously that they overshadowed even the old beacon in the tower of the Navigational College, as if no one on that Viking voyage for plunder and profit cared whether Iceland's ships and boats ran aground. Ísleifur walked slowly and stopped regularly. He didn't seem to be a daily visitor to these glass palaces. It was as if he were taking his bearings in unfamiliar parts. Eventually he stopped at one of the big buildings and looked up at it as far as his stiff body would allow.

Konrád had parked his car at the old nightclub and followed Ísleifur at a distance. A dense fog hung over the city and a drizzly mist wet his face. The street lights appeared dimmed, like a ship's lanterns in a fog. He stayed on the other side of the street and made sure that Ísleifur didn't notice him.

Konrád watched Ísleifur disappear into the building and crossed the street to try to see where he was headed. When he ventured nearer, he saw three lifts in the lobby. There was also an information board that showed what companies and what sorts of businesses operated on each floor.

For a moment, it occurred to Konrád that Ísleifur worked there in the building, as a nightwatchman. Ordinary office hours had ended some time ago, but people were still busily going in and out of the lifts and through the lobby. There was no front desk monitoring the comings and goings, although Konrád did notice surveillance cameras that had been set up in conspicuous places.

He walked in slowly, checked the information board, and saw that the building housed the offices of wholesalers, engineers and accountants. There were also dentists and architects, psychologists and physiotherapists and a few other businesses. At least two floors were occupied by legal firms, and the three top floors housed the offices of a well-known pharmaceutical company.

What the hell does the man want here? Konrád thought, studying the board and trying to imagine on what floor Ísleifur had stepped out of the lift.

About a quarter of an hour later, the lift doors opened and Ísleifur appeared in the lobby and walked, shoulders hunched, to the door in his tattered coat, plastic bag in hand. He was by himself, and as before, looked neither right nor left and didn't see Konrád until the retired policeman stopped him.

'Ísleifur?' Konrád said, as if they were meeting by chance.

Ísleifur was startled but remembered Konrád immediately, and his eyes wandered furtively to the lifts.

'What . . . foll . . . are you following me?' he stammered.

'Following? My accountant's office is upstairs,' Konrád said, as if he'd never told a lie in his life. 'What are you doing here?'

'Nothing,' said Ísleifur, continuing on his way towards the drizzle outside. 'Leave me alone.'

'Does it have anything to do with what we talked about yesterday?' Konrád asked, stopping him again.

Konrád didn't believe that for a moment. Still, he wanted to see if he could shake this guy up.

Ísleifur glanced again towards the lifts, so quickly that Konrád barely noticed it. Then he turned and disappeared out the door.

'Sorry, by the way, for how I acted yesterday,' said Konrád, following him out. 'I didn't mean to be rude. I had no business speaking to you like that and I'd like to apologise.'

Ísleifur didn't respond, but plodded out onto the street.

'Do you think I can meet you sometime in the next few days?' Konrád asked. 'I need to ask you about something I'm looking into. I would appreciate it if we . . .'

Ísleifur stopped and turned to him.

'Leave me alone,' he said furiously. 'Just leave me alone, for fuck's sake! Do you hear me? Leave me alone!'

Then he stormed off again and disappeared eastwards down Borgartún, the same way he'd come. Konrád watched him, then looked up along the building in all its glassy glory and wondered whether his visit to Ísleifur the day before did in fact have anything to do with the man's visit to these parts.

Konrád was still thinking about this when he called Marta late that evening. She finally answered after a few rings, and he hoped he hadn't disturbed her in the middle of something important, like a good night's sleep.

'Why now?' he said bluntly, as was usual in their conversations. Between themselves, they often sounded as if a previous conversation hadn't ended and the new one was just a continuation of it.

'What?'

'Why did Valborg start doing that? Cutting herself. Looking to me for help. Why now?'

'Wasn't she dying?'

'Sure, but that can't be the whole explanation. After all this time?

What was it that prompted her to start searching for her child? Was it something she heard? Something she saw? Why now?'

Marta had no answers for him.

'I need to get into her flat,' Konrád said.

'Out of the question,' said Marta. 'I'm in enough trouble because of you, having blathered everything to you like a moron.'

'Ten minutes, Marta. I need to get into her flat. I don't need much time. Ten minutes at most and I'll never ask you again for anything!'

'The chances of that happening,' Marta snorted.

As had happened the night before, Eygló heard a knock on her front door, and got up and went to the hall to see who wanted to speak to her so late at night. She hoped it wasn't the woman who'd bothered her yesterday.

She opened the door hesitantly but saw no one on her front steps. She stepped onto her doorstep and looked out into the autumn evening. Everything was quiet and the drizzle settled on her clothes. She called out, asking if anyone was there, having clearly and distinctly heard a knocking on her door, twice. The only answer was a wind that gusted down the street, and the thought ran through her mind that maybe she'd stopped distinguishing between the living and the dead.

Eygló waited a little longer, before finally going back inside and shutting the door carefully behind her. She knew that the woman had gone home and wouldn't be visiting her again.

37

Reykjavík was in the Christmas spirit. The city centre had been decorated with beautiful Christmas lights and evergreen branches that were fastened to the street lamps, and on Austurvöllur Square, the lights on the tree from Oslo had been lit. Valborg had walked down Laugavegur High Street towards Glaumbær and enjoyed seeing everything looking so Christmassy. The shops were open and full of gift items; some of the window displays were unusually elegant and she admired them as she passed by. She could smell apples and smoked lamb as she strolled past the Borg butcher shop. This was the only time of the year that she saw women in the workwear shop and men in the lingerie shop.

    Valborg stopped in at Kjörgarður. When she was younger, this first shopping centre in the city had a special attraction: an escalator. Such a marvellous machine had never before been seen in this country. Like other kids who came by to take an exhilarating escalator ride, she'd sometimes played on it if she happened to be on Laugavegur. By some magic that she didn't understand, the machine carried people up to the next floor and made it unnecessary to climb the steps. To her, it was a genuine adventure.

At Kjörgarður, there were shops of all sorts, and one of them was selling a green coat that Valborg wanted for Christmas but still hadn't persuaded herself to buy. It cost an exorbitant amount, but Valborg had tried it on several times and knew she had to have it. She was always hesitant about such purchases, going often to look at the thing she wanted and considering it from all angles. She rarely bought unnecessary things and didn't allow herself much. The saleswoman tried to budge her, saying the coat wouldn't be in the store much longer, and then asking if she should set the garment aside for her. Valborg could reserve the coat and fetch it the next day. A woman had come to the shop a short time ago and almost bought it, and said that she would come back again. It was as if the moment of truth had arrived.

When Valborg went back out onto Laugavegur, there was a slight spring in her step and her heart beat faster. The Christmas decorations were even more beautiful, if anything, the lights brighter, and as if that weren't enough, it had started to snow.

Nearing midnight, Glaumbær was packed with people, and out on the street, there was a line of partygoers waiting to get in. The dance floor on the ground level was crowded and the smoky fug stung the eyes. Alcohol flowed into dry throats and the throng of patrons streamed from one room to another. The noise was deafening. The babble of voices, the music from the different floors, the throng at the bars where people fought for the attention of the bar staff. Orders were simple and people drank pretty much the same thing. Brennivín and Coke, vodka and Canada Dry, and that bitter red Campari.

Valborg went from floor to floor but spent most of her time on the top one, and even though she was quite preoccupied with her work, she soon noticed the man who sat there watching her. Whenever she gave him an inconspicuous glance, it was as if he was staring back, and then he nodded at her. She replied in kind.

It was the same man who'd approached her around two weeks ago and asked if she had a light. He waved a cigarette in her face and she got him some matches. He made a decent first impression, was polite and affable, good-looking in his own way, dark-haired and thin, yet there was something in his comportment that made her a bit uncomfortable, that bothered her. Something in his glance. His smile. It wasn't exactly fake, but wasn't sincere, either. She had a hard time putting her finger on it, but there was something about him that didn't appeal to her.

'Have you been working here long?' he asked, inhaling the smoke and handing her back the matchbox, but she said he could have it. She herself didn't smoke.

'Just a few months,' she said.

She'd often had such conversations with the nightclub's clients. Young men. Older men. Drunk men. Sober men. Not all as polite as this one. They approached her, smooth and chatty, and she tried to be congenial because they were at least friendly. Others were coarse. Extremely rude. One or two grabbed her. Slapped her arse. Groped her breasts. She could handle it, and didn't worry about those men too much. She knew that the bouncers would throw them out if she gave them a signal. It actually happened once. The man was plastered and fought with the bouncers, and they finally had to call the police. This one was a smoothie.

'Do you like working in Glaumbær?' he'd asked. 'It's where it's at.'

'It's really fun,' she said, smiling. 'The people who work here are great.'

'And all the bands,' he said. 'It must be fun knowing those guys.'

'They're really just ordinary,' she said, trying not to be shy. She had a tendency to become awkward in such situations, when guys showed an interest in her. She tried to act normal. She wasn't especially self-confident, but didn't want it to show. 'No better or worse than others,' she added.

'Still, you have interesting working hours,' he said. 'Being at a nightclub. It's a special workplace.'

'Yeah,' she said. 'I like sleeping late.'

The man laughed.

'You must have to work well into the night,' he said. 'Tidying the place and closing up.'

'Sometimes,' she said.

They chatted a bit along those lines, and she hadn't seen him again until now when he smiled and nodded to her. She was busy, and spotted him again about two hours later, down on the dance floor. He wasn't dancing, though, but stood somewhat off to the side, listening to the band. Valborg watched him for a while until another waitress, somewhat older than her, passed by and noticed where she was looking.

'Is that someone you're interested in?' she asked, needing to shout in her ear.

'No, no,' Valborg said hastily, shaking her head.

'Don't you find him kind of cute? I've seen him here a few times before.'

'I don't know. Yeah, whatever. I chatted with him a bit the other day.'

'Did he hit on you?'

'No, nothing like that. Or, I don't think so.'

'Well, that's good.'

'Why do you say that?'

'Did he ask you when you get off work?'

'No, well, not exactly. He wanted to know if I had to stay after closing to tidy up and so on.'

'Did he say he would wait for you?'

'He didn't mention that. How do you know . . . ?'

'He asked me that the other day,' the woman said before hurrying off. 'I just told him I was married.'

38

Nothing in Valborg's flat had been moved following the murder. Her belongings were scattered across the floor. Cupboards were open and drawers had been pulled out, books had been torn from their shelves and simple ornaments broken during the incident. The murderer had trashed the flat in search of valuables, but it was hard to determine what had been stolen or what the murderer was after.

Marta had changed her mind. Maybe she didn't feel like listening to Konrád's nagging any longer. She called and told him that she might be able to let him into the flat if he promised not to stay longer than ten minutes. Konrád accepted her offer, with thanks. He had told Marta what he knew about Sunnefa, who had been forced to abandon her midwifery studies, been in some sort of contact with a religious sect and possibly delivered Valborg's child and placed it in foster care.

Marta had launched an investigation into the child's fate, but it was in the early stages. Sunnefa J. Ólafsdóttir was the name of a woman who had stopped studying at the Midwifery College in 1968. She died in the first decade of the new century, single and childless. She'd lived in a rented flat and it wasn't known what had become of her possessions, so no answers were to be found there that could help in the search for Valborg's child. Sunnefa seemed to have been completely on her own; she had no family around her, and no evidence was found of any links between her and Valborg or any other expectant mothers whom she might have known. Nor did anything come to light regarding the sect she belonged to or had worked for.

Looking over the flat, it appeared to Konrád that Valborg had lived a rather modest life. There was nothing flashy. An old radio that could well have been from the 1970s stood on a table in the living room. The television was hardly a recent model, either. Most of the books remaining on the shelves or lying on the floor were old. She'd collected the works of respected Icelandic poets and books on Icelandic culture and history. Thrillers and love stories were on the bottom shelf, almost invisible. It seemed to him a simple and uncomplicated life. No travel brochures about sun-kissed destinations. No family Christmas photos. Nothing that testified to exciting hobbies. It was more like stagnation. A life that had stood still.

He recalled once again how grateful Valborg had been when he finally agreed to meet her. How downcast she'd become when he refused her request at the Ásmundur Sveinsson Museum, amid all the beautiful works of art. Amid the mothers chiselled in stone. He imagined how she must have returned here after their meeting feeling more hopeless than ever. He thought he bore some responsibility for it. Instead of lifting her up out of the greyness, he'd pulled her down even further, and what was worse, he thought, was that he didn't know why he was so indifferent to her.

'Why are you doing this?' Marta asked as she watched Konrád rummaging through the desk in the living room, looking carefully at documents and papers belonging to the deceased. She immediately grew impatient and looked at her watch. 'What exactly are you looking for?'

The answer wasn't encouraging.

'I don't know,' Konrád said. 'What will happen to her flat?'

'We found a will that's probably valid,' said Marta. 'We spoke to the lawyer who helped her draft it. The flat will be sold and the proceeds will go to various charity organisations that Valborg designated. Mainly organisations connected with child welfare. She appears to have spent most of her disposable income on that cause.'

In the desk, Konrád found receipts going back many years. Old tax returns and Christmas cards from co-workers. Cinema and theatre tickets, an empty metal box that had once held sweets, a deck of cards, a glasses case.

'This lawyer, did he know about the child she had?'

'The lawyer is a she, and she didn't know anything about it. She didn't know Valborg at all.'

Konrád continued pulling out the desk's drawers.

'Valborg wasn't in a sect, was she?' Marta asked. 'Is that what you're looking for?'

'No, well, I could be. I don't know. I don't think so.'

'What about you? You're a heathen, aren't you?'

'Yes.'

'I was always sent to Sunday school,' Marta said, taking out her damp cig, as Konrád sometimes called it. 'I can't recall doing anything more boring. I think Mum and Dad just sent me there so they could . . . you know . . . on Sunday mornings . . .'

'What?'

'You know . . .'

'What?'

'Jesus, do I need to spell it out to you?'

'What?'

'Do it, get it?! Do it on Sunday mornings! God, you're thick.'

Konrád smiled to himself and continued rooting in Valborg's papers. Then he gave up on the desk and went to her bedroom, the bathroom, back to the living room, and then to the kitchen. As he'd sometimes felt before, when still a policeman, he was half ashamed going through Valborg's private life like this, but knew at the same time that it was just a part of the work of law enforcement. The kitchen cupboards and drawers had also been ransacked. Various packets of food lay scattered about, and even perishable items had been pulled from the fridge.

'We've looked over everything pretty closely here,' said Marta, who'd been following his travels through the flat.

'Yes, I know that,' Konrád said.

'If you could just tell me what you're looking for.'

On the table lay a worn plastic folder of recipes. Konrád took a look at it, and it appeared to him that Valborg had collected cake recipes from newspapers until the end. The latest clipping was from around a week before she died, and was of a delicious-sounding American apple cake.

'Have you seen this?' Konrád asked.

'Yeah, aren't those just recipes?'

Konrád was about to say yes when, among the recipes, he saw other types of newspaper clippings. Travel stories that Valborg had found curious. One told of a couple's trip to see the Egyptian Pyramids. Another clipping was from the business section. About a young woman who was starting a pharmaceutical company in partnership with foreigners. Her father, looking proud, appeared with her in a photo. The never-failing backer.

Konrád stared at the photo. Then went back to the narrative from the desert. The couple at the Pyramids. It was the same man. Konrád looked at the date. The articles had appeared eight years apart, around and after the turn of the century.

Konrád put the clippings back and took out other, more recent ones. They showed more cakes and pastries, making him wonder if Valborg had ever baked any of them. Then he found the third, most recent reference to the family: an article that was also about the man's daughter. Published two months ago or so. The woman was selling her and her father's shares in the pharmaceutical company to the foreign parties. The article focused on the large profit that they, as owners of the company, had made in just a few years. The daughter and her father. This time, though, he wasn't in the photo. Only she was. Dressed in an elegant, expensive woman's suit. A beige blouse. A modern woman holding all the threads, standing in front of a large desk and smiling at the world as if the world had always smiled at her. With her arms crossed. The perfect champion in business life. Her joy at the sale shone from her face.

'Did you find something?' Marta asked, blowing out vapour. At work, they'd started calling her 'the steam jet'. Konrád didn't know if he should tell her that.

'Do you know anything about these people?' he said, handing Marta the clippings.

Marta took them and looked at the photos, checked the dates and ran her eyes over the texts.

'No, no better than anyone else,' she said. She vaguely recalled a news report about the company over the years. The owners rarely appeared in the media. 'They didn't make a króna on that drug rubbish. Could that be the correct amount? Did Valborg know those people?'

'How old do you think the woman in the photo is? The man's daughter.'

'I don't know.'

'Born around 1970?'

'Yeah, possibly. Maybe. I don't know. Do you mean . . . no, do you think she's her child? Valborg's daughter?'

'She said she didn't know what became of the child,' Konrád answered.

'Do you think she found her in the papers?'

Konrád didn't answer. He was thinking about Ísleifur, in his basement flat.

'These clippings might have nothing to do with it,' said Marta. Nothing.

'But for some reason, she kept them,' Konrád said, taking back the clippings. 'Maybe it's something you should look into. The company is on Borgartún Street,' he added, seeing in his mind's eye the name of the pharmaceutical company whose offices were on the top three floors of the glass palace that Ísleifur had visited, wearing his coat and carrying a plastic bag.

39

Konrád had entered into his phone the name of the medical lab technician who had worked for years at the National Hospital and could possibly tell him something more about Sunnefa from her days at the Midwifery College. Upon leaving Valborg's flat, he found the name again and looked it up in the online phone directory. There were several other people with the same name, but one was listed as a lab technician which made it easy to pin down his phone number. Konrád called, but no one answered. He called again and let it ring, but to no avail.

It was evening when Marta said goodbye to him in the car park in front of the block of flats and said that she was going to contact the pharmaceutical company at the first opportunity. Although she had definite doubts, her curiosity was piqued. No newspaper clippings but those were found among Valborg's recipes for cakes and other dishes. Konrád decided not to tell Marta about Ísleifur and his trip to the glass building because he couldn't be sure if

Ísleifur had actually visited the pharmaceutical company, and he felt no need to mention it without first talking to the man.

He was on his way to the Vogar neighbourhood when his phone rang. Konrád recognised the number immediately.

'I was called from this number,' said a man's voice on the phone. 'Is that right? My name is Þorfinnur.'

Konrád thanked him for calling back, told him his name, and said he was looking for information about a midwifery student who was at the National Hospital half a century ago and whom Þorfinnur may have known. Sunnefa by name. His search was connected to a murder case, the so-called Valborg case.

The man was dumbfounded, hearing all of this over the phone, but Konrád just carried on and answered the man's questions as best he could. The man had seen the media reports on the murder case and found it odd to be dragged into it like this. He said he had no idea who he was actually talking to, why, or what the investigation of the case had to do with Sunnefa, but yes, he did in fact recall knowing her. Konrád understood his concerns and wondered whether all medical lab technicians, or biomedical scientists as they were called in modern parlance, were as cautious in their conversations with strangers.

In the end, the man agreed to meet him, saying he was coming from a meeting in the city centre and mentioned a restaurant where they could talk. He'd been planning on getting a bite to eat, anyway. Konrád thanked him for his flexibility, changed course and drove to the city centre, where he parked a short distance from Austurstræti Street. Walking into the restaurant, he stopped at the entrance and looked around, naturally unable to recognise the man by sight and having to trust that he himself looked awkward enough there at the door for Þorfinnur to make the connection.

The lab tech did, then signalled to Konrád to come over, and they shook hands and introduced themselves properly. They were of a similar age, but Þorfinnur was quite chubby and said in a great baritone voice that he'd already ordered a steak. A bottle of red wine was on the table. To Konrád, who considered himself something of a connoisseur of good wines, it appeared well chosen, even if it was from the New World.

'I remember you from the news,' said Þorfinnur, taking a drink of wine. 'Weren't you a cop?'

'Yes,' said Konrád.

'Strange case, that one with the glacier,' said Þorfinnur. 'How you guys were unable to solve it.'

'Do you come here often?' asked Konrád, who had no interest in discussing that topic.

'I got divorced recently, just so you know.' Þorfinnur sighed, as if to explain why he was staying out in the middle of the week. 'After almost forty years. I don't like cooking for myself, or can't, actually. I never really prepared food at home. One of the things the wife took care of. I can barely scramble an egg without burning myself.'

His throat rattled a bit as he laughed to himself. Konrád smiled. He didn't want to keep the man from his dinner, so turned to the subject and asked how he'd known Sunnefa in the old days.

'I had a bit of a crush on her,' said Þorfinnur. 'We went out together something like three or four times. Nothing happened. I remember kissing her once after a trip to the cinema. That was back in the day.'

'Was this after she left the college?'

'You've heard all about it,' said Þorfinnur. 'No, it was before. We'd both just started at the National Hospital and met through my friend Pála, who was a lab tech. She died recently – lovely woman, Pála.'

'I know this question might surprise you a bit, but did you know Sunnefa's position on abortion?'

'She was against it and was driven from the college because of it, I knew that, but it wasn't anything she talked about when we were together. I only heard later how she acted. I was a bit shocked because she seemed to me to be a very normal, well-balanced girl. I don't know, maybe the college overreacted.'

The food arrived and the waiter asked Konrád if he would like a menu, but Konrád said that he wasn't going to eat. Þorfinnur asked politely if Konrád minded if he tore into his steak; he was starving. He tucked a large white serviette into his shirt collar and smoothed it out.

'Did you talk to Sunnefa after it happened?' Konrád asked, before saying he should go right ahead and eat.

'I think she went abroad for some time,' Þorfinnur said. 'I never saw her again. I don't really know what she ended up doing. I haven't thought about her for years, so you can imagine how surprised I was at your call.'

'I understand she was very religious,' Konrád said.

'She was indeed. Devout. I wasn't at all, and wonder if that's what tipped the scales. I didn't like the look of it when I found out she believed every word in the Bible. And then she told me she was joining some congregation.'

'Do you remember what congregation it was?'

'No, it was something very religious, its name,' said Þorfinnur. 'She said she paid a tithe to it. A tithe. How medieval!'

Þorfinnur laughed to himself as if he'd never heard anything madder.

'Did they know each other?' he asked. 'This Valborg and Sunnefa?'

'Possibly,' Konrád said. 'A little later. In the early seventies. Valborg was pregnant with a baby she didn't want to have. Maybe Sunnefa got in touch with her.'

'And what?'

'Do you remember Sunnefa mentioning a foster home? People who adopted children? Friends or acquaintances of hers who held the same views as her about abortion? Even people from her congregation? People who'd adopted children?'

Þorfinnur thought this over. It had been a long time since he'd heard Sunnefa's name mentioned. He knitted his brow and Konrád could see how he was trying to recall memories that had long since grown cold.

'I don't remember anything like that,' Þorfinnur said. 'I don't remember any of her friends. But, as I say, I didn't know her very well.'

'No, and it's been a long time, of course. One other thing. I'm wondering how Sunnefa could have got access to women who were pregnant and considering abortion. She never graduated. She didn't work in the Women's Health Unit. How did she know about them? How did she know what they were thinking?'

'Sunnefa would never have considered an abortion,' Þorfinnur said.

'No, I know that. I'm asking you about something entirely different. Whether Sunnefa could have persuaded those pregnant women not to have an abortion, then helped them have their babies and then arranged to place them in foster care.'

Þorfinnur looked up from his meal. Put down his knife and fork. Wiped his mouth with the serviette and stared at Konrád.

'Persuaded women?'

'Yes.'

'This Valborg who died . . . what . . . ? Were they friends?'

'She got pregnant.'

'And had a child that Sunnefa delivered and then put into foster care?'

'That's basically the idea I'm working with,' said Konrád. 'I understand that Sunnefa was a very promising student.'

'She was. And truly hated terminations of pregnancy, as people might call them nowadays.' He smiled. 'That's how it is. Medical laboratory technician becomes biomedical scientist. New words for new times.'

'For religious reasons?' Konrád asked.

Þorfinnur nodded, and finally, it was as if a light came on in his head.

'Shouldn't it be registered somewhere?' he said. 'If a child was placed in foster care?'

'Well, it can be avoided if you want it to remain a secret. I'm sure there are some methods for going about it, although I don't really know how it's done. It was probably easier at that time, around 1970. Maybe today's strict monitoring system didn't exist then.'

'Now you mention it, I do remember that Sunnefa had a friend who worked at the hospital, but I don't know if she was in that congregation with her,' said Þorfinnur, grabbing his knife and fork and turning back to his steak.

'A nurse? Doctor?'

'No, a secretary,' said Þorfinnur. 'In the Women's Health Unit.'

'A secretary? Do you mean . . . ?'

'Yeah, she worked in the office. Would have seen all the reports.

Even met some of those mothers-to-be. If you're wondering about that. She and Sunnefa were good friends.'

'Do you remember her name?'

'No, it's completely gone,' said Þorfinnur. 'I'm no good at remembering names.'

40

A faint light shone from the basement flat in the Vogar neighbourhood as Konrád walked up to the house. The gleam of a television carried out into the darkness from the floor above. There was no bell at the basement door and no name on it. Konrád knocked on the single-glazed window inlaid in the door. The pane quivered at his rapping, and before Konrád knew it, Ísleifur stepped into the hall. He stared at Konrád through the glass and immediately recognised him.

'I wanted to apologise for how I've acted towards you,' Konrád said, knowing that the man could hear him quite well through the glass. 'I had no reason to behave as I did.'

Ísleifur looked at him blankly.

'I wonder if I could have a little chat with you,' Konrád continued. 'I promise to behave.'

'There's nothing for us to talk about,' said Ísleifur. 'Get out of here. I don't want to see you!'

He turned away.

'Do you rent from the people upstairs?' Konrád yelled.

Ísleifur stopped.

'Do you think they've gone to bed?' Konrád asked, and it seemed to him as if he may have hit the nail on the head. His plan about being careful in his approach to Ísleifur had gone out the window. 'It crossed my mind to go up and tell them about you. Do they know already, maybe? What the woman said you did to her in Keflavík? That there could even be others who got the same treatment from you? That a rapist lives in the basement?'

Ísleifur turned to him.

'I didn't do anything wrong,' he said through the thin glass.

'No, the woman you raped was just confused, naturally.'

'I didn't rape anyone.'

Konrád stared at him through the window.

'What do you want from me?' said Ísleifur. 'I've got nothing to say to you. Why don't you leave me alone? Get lost. Leave me alone!'

'Maybe I'll just talk to them,' said Konrád, looking up. 'Who knows, maybe they don't give a toss who rents from them. But they might. Do you think they have a daughter?'

They stared at each other like sworn enemies, with the window's fragile glass between them.

'I don't want you telling lies about me here at this house,' said Ísleifur, opening the door.

Konrád stepped into the hall. Ísleifur wouldn't let him go any further. Konrád shut the door behind him and they faced each other in the dark hall. Ísleifur, shoulders hunched, with his grizzled face and sniffling. Konrád in search of answers, despite hardly knowing the questions to them. He'd read part of the old complaint against Ísleifur and what the woman accused him of doing. It didn't make for pleasant reading.

'Can you tell me if you knew Valborg?' asked Konrád. 'If you ever ran into her?'

'The one who was murdered? I have no idea who she was. I never met her.'

'Did you go to Glaumbær before it burned down? Did you go there to have fun on the weekends?'

'I went to Glaumbær,' said Ísleifur, having lowered his voice so much that Konrád had a hard time hearing him. 'I wasn't the only one. Everyone went there.'

'She was a waitress there,' said Konrád. 'Did you know any of them?'

'No, none.'

'Did your friends?'

'My friends?'

'I assume you had friends.'

'I don't know what business that is of yours.'

'You worked at the Base in Keflavík. I'm guessing you made some friends there. Soldiers, even? Did they go with you to Glaumbær?'

'You're just spouting nonsense,' said Ísleifur, lowering his voice even more. 'Why don't you get to the point? Are you saying I killed that woman . . . that Valborg?'

'Did you?'

'No.'

'Did you have someone do it for you?'

Ísleifur shook his head.

'Do you know who might have done it?'

'I have no idea what you're talking about. I didn't go near that woman. I know nothing about it.'

'Do you know of anyone who may have lain in wait for her at Glaumbær at that time?'

Ísleifur didn't answer.

'Can you tell me that?'

'Can I tell you what?'

'Do you know of anyone who could have done it? Was it you, yourself? Did you rape Valborg like you raped the woman in Keflavík?'

'You're an idiot.'

'Did you rape Valborg?'

'Shut up!'

'She had a child,' said Konrád.

'Yeah, I know nothing about that.'

'Did you go to her place the other day? Did you attack her?'

'That has nothing to do with me,' said Ísleifur. 'It doesn't have a fucking thing to do with me!'

'Was it you?'

'Who what? Did what? What do you want from me? What do you want me to say?' Ísleifur hissed. 'What am I supposed to be telling you?'

'The truth.'

'The truth?! You're an arse. That's the truth. Anything else you want to know?'

'The truth about you.'

'You want to hear the truth about me? OK. Let's see. What can I tell you? I can tell you that that girl in Keflavík, the one who pressed charges against me, she was good. Damned good.'

Konrád didn't react.

'And not just her,' said Ísleifur, his voice becoming a soft whisper. 'There were others, but they weren't as stupid as that one in

Keflavík. They had the sense to keep their mouths shut. Keep their mouths shut, you understand?'

'Are you saying –'

'Listen to me, idiot!'

'Are you saying you raped her? Raped others?'

'No, I'm saying there was no rape. She asked for it,' Ísleifur hissed again, moving closer to Konrád. 'They asked for it. All of them. Begged me to drive it into them because they enjoyed it! They enjoyed getting it rammed in their pussies!'

He shoved Konrád, making him stumble back against the door with a heavy thud before regaining his balance. Konrád grabbed Ísleifur, pushed him against the wall and held him there tightly. Ísleifur didn't resist, but just smirked at him, revealing that he was missing a few teeth. In disgust, Konrád pushed him towards the hall door, which burst open, causing Ísleifur to lose his footing and nearly fall to the floor within.

'What were you doing at Borgartún?' Konrád asked.

Ísleifur straightened up and smoothed his clothes.

'Get out of here,' he yelled, but his voice cracked and became a strange shriek. 'Go to hell! Tell those people up there to go fuck themselves!' he shrieked, slamming the door on Konrád.

When Konrád got home a short time later and went to the dining-room cupboard for a bottle of red wine, he stepped on the strange wooden object that had belonged to his father and was still lying where it landed on the floor after he threw it against the wall. He picked it up and saw that the spring that was always nestled tightly under the strung wire was loose. He pondered the object for a few moments before placing it on the dining-room table, thinking that the spring had come loose either when the object hit the wall or when he stepped on it.

It was impossible to talk to Ísleifur without driving him mad with rage, he thought, taking a bottle of wine and pouring himself a glass, still somewhat upset and shaken after his visit to the basement flat. The little that Konrád could say about the man was that he was anything but congenial, and had even confessed to the rape in Keflavík. Hinted that there were other rapes. Konrád saw no reason to rule out Valborg being one of his victims.

He finished the glass of wine quickly, refilled it, then took the wooden object to the kitchen and opened the cupboard under the sink, where he kept a rubbish bin. As if on a hunch, he put tension on the spring with his thumb, and when he released it, the spring hit the wire strung between the two nails, making an odd sound, alien yet somehow familiar.

Konrád stood for a long time and stared at the thing, thinking that he must have misheard it.

Again he compressed the spring and released it, and finally understood what his father meant when he said he'd never made as much money on anything as this.

41

He hadn't been able to reach Eygló all day, and tried once more to call her on her mobile on his way to the Palliative Care Unit in Kópavogur. He'd learned that one of the women who worked in the office of the Women's Health Unit of the National Hospital in the early 1970s was close to death.

Again it was his friend Svanhildur who came to Konrád's aid when he needed to find out which of the National Hospital's office staff had handled appointments and record keeping. Svanhildur knew a man in the hospital's personnel department, and he looked up this woman for her. She was adamant that Konrád tell no one where she'd got the woman's name.

Konrád's enquiries about this woman revealed that she'd been transferred to the Palliative Care Unit quite some time ago. Konrád felt very uncomfortable about butting in during this difficult, sorrowful stage of the woman's life, but his curiosity proved stronger than reason, and not for the first time. He couldn't afford to worry too much about it. Time was too tight for that.

The woman's mobile number was listed, and when he called it, her son answered and told Konrád what state she was in. Konrád decided to come clean and explained that he was trying to find the child of a friend of his. She'd given it up, possibly at the urging of a woman whom his mother might remember, named Sunnefa. Konrád told the man that the year in question was 1972 – a long time ago. He also said that his friend's name was Valborg, and that she'd recently been killed.

The man was surprised at the call and promised he would call back soon. Konrád's enquiry had, as might have been expected, got her attention, and she agreed to meet Konrád for a short time.

The woman's son met the former policeman at the Palliative Care Unit and said he'd prepared his mother for the visit as best he could. He asked Konrád to keep it brief; he would be there with them and would intervene in their conversation if he felt it necessary. Konrád said he had nothing against that and thanked the man for his help, then apologised for the uncomfortable inconvenience his inquiry was causing them.

The woman had weakened significantly in the past few days and been bedridden, but she had asked to be dressed and placed in a wheelchair for this unusual visit. Despite being gravely ill, she wanted to meet the ex-policeman with the dignity she had remaining. She shook the man's hand as she sat upright in the wheelchair in her bright room, dressed in a beautiful blouse with a shawl around her neck, thin-voiced and weak. Her name was Fransiska. Her son sat down on the bed.

Konrád thanked her for agreeing to meet him and came straight to the point, asking if she remembered a midwife or a midwifery student by the name of Sunnefa.

'Yes, I remember her, but she stopped before 1970,' said Fransiska, looking at her son. The woman was quite clear-headed.

'Right,' said Konrád. 'She ran into trouble at the college and left it. Did you or any of you at the Women's Health Unit have any contact with her afterwards?'

'No,' said Fransiska. 'Not me, at least. She was unpredictable, as far as I recall, and not . . . not particularly well liked. Maybe I shouldn't say such a thing – but no student there had ever been forced out of their studies. It was always particularly fine girls who studied midwifery. Especially . . .'

'She was very religious, I understand,' said Konrád, sensing how weak the woman was. He tried to hurry. 'Did you know she was a member of a sect?'

'No,' Fransiska said wearily. 'I've never liked religion. I have no interest in it. Let alone life after death. When it's over, it's over. You told my son that the woman who died in that horrible way had given up . . . given up her child.'

Konrád said yes.

'Because Sunnefa persuaded her to?' asked Fransiska, with obvious interest.

'It's possible.'

'And then Sunnefa placed it in foster care?'

'That's also possible.'

'But how is that related to what happened to her? That woman? Valborg?'

'I don't know,' Konrád said, glancing at the son, who looked as if he may have misunderstood part of their conversation. 'I doubt it is. Valborg never knew what happened to the child and she wanted to find out. She came to me about it. I . . . I didn't help her.'

'And you want to make up for it now?'

'I want to find the child.'

'That's . . . nice of you.'

'I regret not helping her,' Konrád admitted.

The woman tried to smile. It was as if every little movement caused her pain.

'Do you remember anyone else you worked with, and who thought along the same lines as Sunnefa? Was against abortions? Was religious? Even in some sort of sect?'

Fransiska shook her head. Her son got up from the bed and looked at his watch, as a sign that Konrád would have to wrap this up.

'I understand that Sunnefa had a good friend who worked in the office.'

'Do you mean . . . Regína . . . ?'

'Regína?'

'I remember that they were good friends, Sunnefa and her. And now that you mention it, I seem to recall that Regína was . . . belonged to some . . . belonged to some congregation.'

'What congregation? Do you remember?'

Fransiska didn't answer him.

'Do you remember what congregation it was?'

The woman closed her eyes. She seemed to Konrád to be on the verge of passing away from fatigue. She reminded him of Erna in her final days of life. Erna absolutely refused to go to the Palliative Care Unit and Konrád supported her decision. She wanted to die at home.

Konrád looked at the son, who signalled to him that that was enough.

'We should stop now,' he said, bending over his mother.

'Of course,' said Konrád. 'Again, I'm sorry for disturbing you. You've been extremely helpful,' he added, taking Fransiska's hand.

She opened her eyes, stared at him, and whispered something that Konrád didn't hear. He leaned closer.

'The Creation,' said the woman.

'The Creation?'

'It was . . . her congregation . . .'

'No more of this,' ordered the son. 'That's enough. I have to ask you to leave!'

'All right,' said Konrád.

'My dear . . .' the woman whispered '. . . find . . . the child.'

As before, the incessant hum of the traffic on Hringbraut Road carried into the cemetery, where otherwise all was silent and peaceful. Once again, Eygló followed the rain-soaked path to Málfríður's grave, past the recently renovated tomb and the moss-covered headstones and crosses with their weathered sorrow. She'd brought some roses to lay on the grave, and looked around for Málfríður's friend, the woman in the coat and veil who stood there by the grave the last time Eygló came to the cemetery.

No one was there now but her.

Eygló had brought three white roses, which she placed on the grave. One for the Father, one for the Son, and one for the Holy Spirit. She thanked Málfríður for her friendship and prayed once again for a good end to her journey. There was a cool northerly breeze and Eygló was about to leave when the headstone at the top of Málfríður's grave caught her attention. It was standing straight up, with its back towards the head of her friend, so near that when it came time to set up Málfríður's headstone, they would almost touch.

Eygló walked carefully around to the front of that grave to see who was lying there beneath the soil, and as she read the stone, her heart skipped a beat and she saw in her mind's eye the woman in the green coat who'd been sitting at Málfríður's bedside in the hospital and later stood by her grave there in the cemetery.

She remembered the name when she saw it carved into the stone.

HULDA ÁRNADOTTIR
b. 9.7.1921 – d. 1.28.1984

42

Twenty minutes had passed since Marta was asked to wait a moment, and she was growing tired of the delay. After listening to Marta's explanation for her visit, the secretary had shown her into a meeting room. Marta hadn't made an appointment and the secretary, a woman of around thirty who acted as if she'd graduated from flight-attendant school, was taken aback slightly when she realised what Marta was. Visits from police detectives weren't a daily occurrence at the company, and Marta assumed that the woman in charge was trying to guess the reason for it.

Good luck with that, Marta thought. She looked around the sumptuous meeting room, which was adorned with two large paintings by Icelandic masters from the start of the last century. An Italian espresso machine stood on a table. A modern, stylish video projector hung from the ceiling. The room was on the top floor of three that the pharmaceutical company occupied in the high-rise on Borgartún Street, and now that the weather had cleared up, the view from it of Faxaflói Bay and the mountains Esja and Skarðsheiði was magnificent.

Finally, something happened. The tasteful secretary reappeared and asked Marta to wait a moment more; the CEO was particularly busy but had cleared space in her schedule to meet the detective. No sooner had the secretary made this announcement than the woman who ran the business appeared and made repeated apologies for the delay as she greeted Marta with a handshake. She was friendly and smiled warmly, but was clearly in a rush and wanted to deal with this unexpected interruption quickly. She was slim, dressed in a close-fitting skirt and matching blouse, with dark, short hair and beautiful brown eyes beneath well-groomed eyebrows. She was approaching fifty and Marta found her effortlessly sexy, needing little to accentuate that but to colour her hair every now and then. Her name was Klara.

Whether it was due to the investigation or not, Marta felt she could see Valborg in the woman's face.

'Please excuse me,' Klara said, smiling. 'Everything's a mess in here. The new owners will take over soon and we're a bit upside down. We're trying to make the transition go as smoothly as possible.'

'Unfortunately,' Marta said bluntly, 'I don't follow the business world.'

'Oh? Isn't that why you want to meet me? You're not from the Economic Crime Unit? We got your message two weeks ago. Our accountants have already answered it. The tax deduction that we calculated –'

'Hold on,' said Marta. 'Let me stop you right there. I have no interest in your business. I came to see you because of this here,' she continued, taking out photocopies of the newspaper clippings that Konrád found at Valborg's flat and laying them on the table in front of her. Klara looked over the articles.

'What . . . what is this?' she asked in surprise.

'You know these people, don't you?' said Marta.

'Of course. They're . . . they're my parents, when they took a trip to Egypt,' Klara replied. 'It was Mum's dream to see the Pyramids. I remember the article well. It was published in a travel magazine . . . and then this interview with me when we were starting up the business.'

'That's your father with you in the photo, right?'

'Yes. And then this here, the interview with me at the start of the process for selling the business. I have this photo of me framed. What are you doing with these? What are the police doing with these clippings?'

'We found them . . .'

The secretary came to the door and informed Klara that someone was waiting for her. Marta looked at Klara and wondered if this was a prearranged interruption designed to curtail their meeting. She smiled to herself.

'Yes, I'm coming,' Klara said, before turning back to Marta. 'Why are you showing me these?'

The secretary left and Marta took out a photograph of Valborg and placed it on the table next to the clippings. It was the same photo of her that had appeared in the media in the last few days.

'Do you know this woman?' she asked.

Klara stared at the photo.

'Isn't it . . . isn't it the woman who was attacked . . . the woman who was murdered?'

'We found these clippings at her home. Among cake recipes and the like. It took us a little time to find them. We didn't find any other newspaper clippings there. Only these. This one family. Your family. Your parents. You yourself. Do you know what brought that about? Do you have any idea why she had these?'

Klara looked at the photograph and Marta in turn, then picked up the clipping with the photo of herself smiling triumphantly at the readers. When she looked again at Marta, she appeared stunned.

'I have no idea,' she said. 'Isn't it just a coincidence? I didn't know her. We didn't know her. People clip all sorts of things out of the papers.'

'Of course. She isn't related to you?'

'No, not at all,' said Klara. 'Not that I know of. And I would know,' she added. 'I can't imagine why she collected these articles about us.'

The secretary came to the door again and looked at her watch. Before she could say anything, Klara told her to leave them alone.

'But –' began the secretary.

'Not now,' said Klara. 'I'm busy.'

After a slight hesitation, the secretary disappeared from the doorway and Klara asked Marta if there was anything else. She was somewhat upset, although she tried not to show it.

'Could your father have known her?'

'Are you connecting these clippings with what happened to her, that woman?' Klara asked.

'No, hardly,' said Marta.

'Hardly? What does that mean?'

'We can't see any connection,' said Marta. 'I just wanted to hear your opinion on all this. Find out if the woman was in contact with you at all. Is your father here in the building?'

'No, he's not.'

'Where can I find him?'

'Why do you need to do that?' Klara asked. 'You're going to bother him with this? We don't know that woman and have never known her. Believe me.'

She tried to appear composed, but Marta sensed how difficult she found this conversation, what an uncomfortable interruption it was to be visited by the police in a world she otherwise had under perfect control.

'Can you swear that your father never knew her?'

'We don't know who that woman is,' repeated Klara. 'Not at all.'

'So don't you find it even more surprising that she clipped these out and kept them?'

'I don't know what gets into people's heads,' Klara said, deciding that this meeting was over. She said goodbye to Marta with a handshake, resolutely and firmly, as she herself was by nature. 'Unfortunately, I don't have time for this. Hopefully I've made myself clear enough and you won't be troubling us any more about this . . . this blessed matter.'

Marta didn't let go of her hand. She wouldn't be finished until she asked about something that she didn't quite know how to bring up without upsetting the woman even more. The words were on her lips when she realised that she might be moving too quickly. That it might be better to wait a bit. Get more information, look at more evidence, before dropping such a bomb into her life.

So, letting it lie for now, Marta said goodbye to the woman and watched her hurry out of the meeting room.

43

Konrád found nothing online about a religious organisation or sect that called itself the Creation. There was enough material about the creation of the world, as it was described in various religions. The creation of life. The creation of man. Nothing about an organisation called Creation or The Creation. The sect had existed long before the days of the internet and social media, and when Konrád scrolled through the main newspapers from around 1970, he found nothing about it. Its members seemed to have a knack for keeping a low profile and staying out of the media. Gatherings weren't advertised. No address was given. Members weren't named. So Konrád assumed that it was a small group whose few members took pains to stay out of the limelight.

He was thinking about these things – sects, religious communities and religious issues, and how big a part they played in the lives of both individuals and the whole world – when he drove up to the dilapidated house in Grafarvogur and shut off his car's engine.

Personally, he'd never felt any need to believe in the existence of God or divine providence or the words of the Bible, or viewed any religious text or religious message as a guide for his life. He knew that his mother was religious in her own way, even though she never went to church, and he'd sensed in Erna a similar need to believe, especially after she fell ill. He understood them both, but remained the same atheist as before.

A small brass plate on the front door showed that he was at the right place, but no one seemed to be home. On a hunch, Konrád walked behind the house, where he noticed a woman who was probably several years younger than himself tidying up the garden. She was wearing good protective clothing and a wool cap and was holding a rake, which she was using to gather loose twigs into a little pile near the base of a tree. Konrád didn't want to interrupt her and possibly startle her, but just watched what she was doing. The woman appeared to enjoy her work, going at it slowly and leaning forward on the rake between gathering up broken branches and dead leaves and rubbish that had blown into the garden. She had a peaceful air, a product of the contentment she felt in her daily chores.

'Regína?' Konrád finally said, moving closer.

The woman turned round and seemed unfazed despite a stranger having suddenly shown up in her garden. She stopped what she was doing and regarded him for a moment before walking over to him.

'Naturally, if I'm in the garden, I can't hear when visitors come,' she said. 'I didn't realise you were here.'

'No, the garden needs to be taken care of like anything else,' Konrád said, just to say something.

'Thank you for such a quick response,' said the woman, as if she'd expected him, before shaking Konrád's hand. 'It certainly won't get fixed by itself.'

'What?' said Konrád.

'Oh, the silverfish,' said the woman, plodding past him towards the house.

'The silverfish?'

'Aren't you the exterminator?' she said, turning to him.

'Extermin . . . no, I'm afraid you've got the wrong person,' said Konrád. 'But are you Regína?' he asked in return.

'Oh, but . . . who are you, then?' said the woman. 'Yes. I'm Regína. Did you come here to find me?'

'I'm gathering information about a woman who I think was a friend of yours, named Sunnefa,' said Konrád. 'I was hoping that you could tell me a little about her.'

The woman stared at him.

'Sunnefa?'

'Didn't you know each other? From the time you both worked at the National Hospital? I understand you two were friends.'

'I haven't heard the name Sunnefa in many years,' said the woman.

'No. She died quite a while ago, of course,' Konrád said.

The woman had a hard time hiding her surprise as she asked who Konrád was and what his relationship with Sunnefa was and he replied that she'd delivered the child of a friend of his.

Just then, Konrád's mobile rang and he saw that it was Eygló. He excused himself and said he needed to answer it, and the woman went back to what she was doing. After their recent argument, Konrád hadn't expected to hear from Eygló any time soon. Eygló seemed to have forgotten about their disagreement; she didn't mention it at all, but came straight to the point and said she wanted to see him that evening – could he come to her place in Fossvogur? For his part, he said he'd been planning on calling her to tell her something he'd discovered about their fathers. Eygló was immediately curious, but he said he couldn't discuss it at the moment, and they agreed to meet that evening and finish their conversation.

Regína kept to herself in the meantime, but when Konrád put his phone back in his pocket he saw that her attitude had changed. She said she had nothing to say about Sunnefa and asked him to go and leave her alone.

'You were good friends, weren't you?' said Konrád.

'We knew each other, but I don't remember much about her and I'm afraid I can't help you. Sorry,' she said, holding out her hand as if to show him out of the garden. 'I'm expecting someone to come take care of some silverfish.'

'I'm sorry,' said Konrád, 'I don't want to bother you, but I think you can help me with the information that I need. It's a serious matter. Maybe more serious than you suspect.'

He saw that the woman was quite confused. He'd disrupted her years of peace there in the garden. He felt like the biblical serpent.

'What information?' Regína asked hesitantly.

'About the Creation.'

'The creation? What do you mean by that?'

'The congregation.'

'Congre . . . ? It's . . . I forgot about all that long ago.'

'Were you in it?'

'I don't see why that should concern you. I don't know who you are or what you're doing here asking these questions. I'd like you to go away and leave me alone.'

She walked up to the house, opened the back door, and watched to see whether Konrád would piss off out of her garden. He made no move to go.

'Do you want me to call the police?' she said.

'No,' Konrád said. 'There's no need. Though they may be calling *you* soon.'

'Me? The police?'

'I said that the matter is serious. It's possibly related to the woman who was murdered the other day at her home. I'm sure you've heard about it. Her name was Valborg. Do you recognise the name?'

The woman shook her head.

'I heard about the murder,' she said. 'Who are you?'

'A friend of hers,' Konrád said. 'Valborg came to me shortly before she died. She gave birth to a child she didn't want and gave it up right after it was born, without even seeing the baby. She asked me to find the person it grew up to be. It crossed my mind that you could tell me what became of it.'

'The child?'

'I'm pretty sure your friend delivered it,' Konrád said.

44

Regína looked out the window at the twigs she'd been raking into a pile. At the trees that had shed their leaves. For a moment, she'd been thinking about nothing but the autumn winds. She tried to take care of her garden, she told Konrád. Mow it regularly and sow the beds and weed it and rake the leaves in the autumn. And because of that, it came into beautiful bloom every summer and she sat for hours on a garden chair and admired the fruits of her labour. Tending her garden was really the only hobby she had.

She'd invited Konrád in and poured him a cup of coffee. Now they were sitting in the living room looking out at the garden, and she told him how much she enjoyed working in it. Before, she'd shown him where she'd found a dead silverfish in the kitchen. She said she hadn't seen such a creature in there for many years, and was worried she had damp.

Konrád listened and didn't press her on anything, but let her direct the conversation back to Sunnefa, the congregation and

Valborg when it suited her. He didn't have to wait long for her to pick up the thread.

Regína sipped her coffee.

'I didn't mean to be so rude to you,' she said apologetically. 'I wasn't really going to call the police.'

'I know that,' Konrád said.

'I was just a child,' she said. 'And those were different times. I was in some kind of strange opposition to them. All that freedom. Free love. You know how it was. The congregation was a kind of antidote to that. There were never many of us, as you might very well imagine. Maybe there would be more members today, I don't know,' she added, trying to smile.

'And Sunnefa was there, too?'

'She was the one who got me to join the congregation. We started at the hospital around the same time and immediately became good friends. She was interested in medicine and nursing, but was mainly interested in becoming a midwife. She felt it was somehow noble, and of course she was right. A midwife. There's something about the profession that just seems good and beautiful.'

'But then something changed in her temperament?' Konrád asked.

'Yes, she was at loggerheads with people on her course, at the hospital, the Women's Health Unit. She had these outdated views on abortion, when attitudes were changing a great deal and women started to talk about controlling their own bodies. Birth-control pills were poison to her. That harshness was one side of her. She could also be very sweet and funny and a good friend. She'd joined that congregation and got me to go along with her. It was founded by a couple. I think they'd spent some time in America, he'd been saved there, and they felt there wasn't enough stringency during those lax times. They rented a hall in the Ármúli area, I recall. She played the piano. He pontificated. Sunnefa, too. She was immersed in all that Christian stuff. Had been in the YWCA and a Christian youth group in secondary school.'

'So you agreed with her? About abortion?'

'Yes. I did. At the time.'

'Have your views changed since then?'

'Yes.'

'Did Sunnefa ask you to provide her with information about the mothers-to-be? After she left the hospital?'

'Yes. She did. But only some.'

'Those who mentioned the possibility of abortion? There were probably always a few of those?'

'Women who for some reason didn't want to have a child,' Regína said, nodding. 'Who were in difficult circumstances. They just couldn't. Didn't want to.'

'And you had access to that information?'

'I could get it,' Regína admitted. 'I know it was a breach of confidence, but I wasn't really thinking about that at the time.'

'Why did Sunnefa want to know about those women?'

'She told me she wanted to talk to them. Just meet them and talk to them and see if she could get them . . . oh, I don't know how I should word it . . . get them to see things differently.'

'Get them to give birth to their babies?'

'Yes. I didn't see anything wrong with it. We'd talked it over. Were of the same opinion.'

'Sunnefa seems to have done a lot more than that,' said Konrád.

'What do you mean?'

'I think she delivered some of those children.'

Regína stared at Konrád.

'No, that can't be,' she said.

'I've heard otherwise.'

'I didn't know that,' Regína said.

She looked out at the trees in the garden. At the bare twigs awaiting the winter. If she was overwhelmed by this news, she managed to hide it well.

'Was that Valborg one of them?' she asked. 'Did she get her to rethink things? To change her mind?'

Konrád said that that was probably the case.

'Does it have anything to do with her murder?' Regína asked hesitantly.

'I don't know,' Konrád said. 'I just don't know. But Sunnefa seems to have taken charge of the child. Could someone in the congregation have been able to foster a newborn child?'

'As I say, I know nothing about it. I remember that I only gave Sunnefa the names of three or four women. I only worked for a few years at the hospital, in the office. I hadn't even thought about this until you suddenly appeared, knowing much more than I do.'

'Do you think, if she delivered any babies herself and placed them in foster care, it was on her own initiative?'

'Sunnefa was very determined,' said Regína. 'She could bend a person to her will, or something like that, if you know what I mean. She had such strong opinions. I don't know. Maybe. Still, I think . . . I find it hard to believe that she would have done that. I hope she didn't. Then I would have been a participant in something I didn't want and never intended to be a part of. I feel sick thinking about it.'

'You don't remember Valborg in this context?'

'No, I've forgotten names. I didn't want to remember them, truth be told. I knew I wasn't allowed to use the files like that.

Knew I was breaking the rules. I've tried not to think about it since then.'

At that, the doorbell rang and they assumed the exterminator had arrived to look into the vermin problem. They got up and headed to the hall. On the way, he saw a framed picture on a dresser that had caught his eye when he entered the living room. It was of a girl of around seven years old, he guessed, taken many years ago, and it was as if something in her expression was familiar. Probably related to Regína, Konrád thought, but he wasn't sure.

'Is this . . . ?'

'My daughter,' said Regína.

'An only child?'

'Yes.'

'You don't have a husband?'

'We divorced.'

The exterminator was smiling, doubtless thinking that they were husband and wife. He looked at them in turn from the doorstep, noticed that they both seemed rather down and thought he knew the reason why.

'Silverfish . . . ?!'

45

A few printouts of material from the internet were scattered on top of the piano. Having opened the lid, Eygló tapped the key that had been stuck but was now free again. The note it made had a remarkably clean tone, considering the condition of the piano and how little it was used.

She was thinking about her friend Málfríður and the last time she saw her at the hospital. Eygló had tried to remember every detail of the visit from the moment she arrived in her room, their conversation and when they finally said goodbye. She could recall it quite well, she felt, but what she remembered most clearly was the woman who sat on the chair at Málfríður's bedside, who was called Hulda and was an old friend of hers, and believed more than most in life after death.

She tapped the key absent-mindedly with her index finger. When she was in her thirties, she'd wanted to learn to play the piano, so she could play the one that stood motionless in her living room. The piano teacher was a particularly congenial and patient woman who lived in a house on the Eastside of town, where Eygló went for her few lessons. The teacher went over some of the basics with her and one of the things Eygló learned was that the white notes were named after letters that repeated themselves across the keyboard. A was the note at the far left, and then came B C D E F G, followed by A again and so on. The key on her piano that had been stuck but came loose played a D.

She heard a knock on the door and was glad that Konrád had arranged to stop by, and she went and opened the door for him. It was somewhat late in the evening and she greeted him kindly, mindful of their last meeting when she rushed out of his car in a fit of anger. He stood hesitantly on the threshold, doubtless for the same reason, as if he weren't sure of the reception he'd be given. His worries were unnecessary. Eygló invited him in and asked if he would like some Parmesan crisps that she'd baked earlier that day. They were particularly good with white wine, she added, taking a bottle of wine from New Zealand out of the fridge and pouring him a glass. Being hungry, Konrád thanked her and helped himself to the crisps, and had to try hard not to stuff himself with them. They were tasty and did go well with the wine. Eygló poured herself a glass too, and they sat down in the kitchen, where Konrád told her all about the conversations he'd had about Valborg. Eygló said she knew nothing about any sects or religious associations. She'd never heard of the Creation except as a phenomenon in religious studies.

Gradually, she turned their conversation to the subject of their disagreement when he drove her home. She said she understood his position. That it seemed obvious to him that their fathers had treated Stella horribly with their lies and deceit, whereas she held on to the slightest hope that her father Engilbert had sensed something that had given the woman some relief. She showed Konrád into the living room, where the piano stood, and began telling him about the key that she'd happened to notice was stuck and wouldn't come free no matter what she tried. She had then closed the lid and gone to bed, then dreamed Engilbert looking like a zombie, standing at the piano and striking that key over and over again with his finger. Then, when she'd gone to the living room the next morning, the piano lid was open and the key had come unstuck.

'I know you don't find this remarkable and will have a rational explanation for it, but it certainly surprised me. I was shocked, in fact. The vision or dream was frightening. He stood here like a washed-up corpse banging on the piano, and had an aura of anger and hatred.'

'Isn't it because you've been thinking a lot about him lately?' Konrád said. 'Isn't that why you're sensing his presence?'

'I think it's all linked to Stella. I feel quite bad about all that.'

'Didn't you just go into the living room that night and do it yourself? While sleepwalking or whatever it's called? Open the lid and free that key?'

Eygló smiled.

'I'm not necessarily looking for a logical explanation,' she said.

'No, they're not needed in your world, of course,' Konrád said. 'It's the rest of us that have to deal with such trivialities.'

'I'm not your enemy, Konrád,' Eygló said. 'I also want to find out why your father died. And why my father died a few months later. What the nature of their partnership was at that time. Whether it played some part in what happened to them. I'm looking for answers just as much as you are.'

'I didn't mean to irk you.'

'I'm thinking about Stella, and maybe more about her son.'

'The one who supposedly spoke to his mother through the piano?'

Eygló nodded.

'Pianos play a considerable part in this story,' Konrád said.

'So it appears,' Eygló said. 'I went to the cemetery and found the boy's name, and the key that was stuck on this piano –'

'Eygló, it's clear that they lied to and betrayed an innocent woman who had suffered great loss. Your father was just as involved in it as mine. He was no better. I know how they –'

'You have your opinions on it and I respect that,' said Eygló. 'You need to let me have my opinions, and show them just as much respect.'

'I know how they did it.'

'I already know your views,' continued Eygló. 'But I believe the powers that some of us perceive may be at work in our lives and can even influence them. Sounds. Smells. Sights. However that may be. Whether they're figments of the imagination and it's a complete coincidence that they fit the circumstances each time, or whether they're messages from elsewhere. The stuck key in this piano plays a D. Stella's son was named Davíð. Doesn't that tell us something? Isn't it the same note that the boy used at Stella's to get in touch . . . ?'

From his pocket, Konrád took the object that had belonged to his father, with the wire and spring.

'Dad kept this piece of junk and was quite fond of it for some reason,' he said. 'I just said that I thought pianos play a prominent part in these ghost stories. Stella's piano. This one here at your place. I think I know now what happened at Stella's when they said they could communicate with her son through the instrument.'

'What's that you've got there?'

'Some gadget I found among my dad's belongings when he died,' Konrád said. 'I've kept it ever since, along with one or two other little things of his. I don't know why. Probably because it's a kind of tie to my youth, just like everyone has. To my father. Even if he was rotten. I don't know. My father wasn't the kind of man you remember with much warmth.'

He handed Eygló the object and she rolled it between her fingers without understanding what it was or the role it played.

'Dad once told me that he never made as much money with anything as he did with this cheap piece of crap. I think he made it out of bits from a broken music box. It would be just like him, to take such a thing to a séance.'

'I don't understand what you're getting at,' said Eygló. 'What are you saying?'

'You think Engilbert was in contact with the boy?' said Konrád.

Eygló didn't answer him.

'That they communicated through the piano?'

'I said I didn't want to rule anything out. Did you come here to belittle me?'

Konrád shook his head.

'I would never do that. Maybe I brought it to show you that Engilbert was no better than my father.'

Eygló, taken aback, stared at him in bewilderment.

'He was just as much of a swindler and scumbag,' Konrád said. 'They were the same. Both were equally guilty of taking advantage of poor Stella's grief. The Great Beyond had nothing to do with it! Nothing. This thing here, this piece of junk you're holding – it's the entire Great Beyond! You should keep that in mind next time you talk about –'

'What are you on about? Why do you say –'

'They played Stella like an old music box!' Konrád exclaimed. 'Literally!'

Feeling that he'd gone too far, Konrád stopped. He hadn't meant to hurt Eygló. People were entitled to their own opinions without him sticking his nose in. They could believe what they wanted – it wasn't his business.

'Forgive me,' he said. 'I didn't mean to come across like that. I just don't like hearing you say . . . Your dad was no angel.'

'What is this?' Eygló asked. 'What do you do with it?'

'You put tension on the spring and release it,' Konrád said, showing her how the gadget worked.

'How . . . like this . . . ?'

Eygló hesitated for a moment. Then she did as he said and when she released the spring, they heard a faint, lonely sound, like a note from a piano.

46

It was as if the bottom had dropped out of their conversation, and after a slight hesitation, Konrád said he should be going. It was late and he didn't want to keep her up. Eygló was still holding the gadget, distractedly pressing and releasing the spring, completely in her own world. Konrád looked over the printouts lying on top of the piano. They seemed to be obituaries.

'Thanks for coming,' Eygló finally said. 'That's right. It's late.'

'I hope I haven't . . . haven't been too brusque. That wasn't my intention.'

'No, of course not,' said Eygló. 'It's late,' she repeated. 'You should go.'

Konrád made no move to go. He didn't want to leave her in such a sad state.

'Of course, I'm familiar with such swindles,' said Eygló, handing him back the object. 'That's what they were known for, pretty much.'

'I'm sure it was my father who decided how they'd go about it,' Konrád said.

'No, they were clearly both immersed in this,' said Eygló. 'I don't know why I thought Engilbert had been any better. I was hoping maybe it had all been in your dad's hands and Engilbert tried to counterbalance the fraud. Tried to be a bit more honest. He had the gift of clairvoyance. I know he did. I felt as if he always tried to be honest. But maybe that was just with me. I don't know. He instilled those views in me. Knew what I had in me, that I resembled him, and he taught me not to fear it. Told me to be honest with myself, and then everything would be all right.'

Konrád didn't know what to say.

'I thought he was speaking from the heart,' she continued. 'Poor Stella,' she then said. 'It's no surprise that she shovelled her money at them.'

'I didn't mean to . . . I'm sorry that this should bring you so much disappointment,' Konrád said. 'If I'd known . . .'

'No, it's good to have this all out in the open. Anything else would have been impossible,' said Eygló. 'He'd started to drink heavily around that time. I don't know if that's an excuse. Stella. Hansína. God knows how many others.'

'They didn't make any friends, doing what they did. That's quite clear. Are you collecting obituaries?' Konrád asked, pointing at the papers on top of the piano. 'Who's she?' he asked, taking one and skimming it. 'Did you know this Hulda?'

'No, and she'll be of no interest to you,' Eygló replied.

'Anything to do with séances?' Konrád asked.

'She was a friend of Málfríður's. They were both in the Society for Psychical Research. I never met her, but I found an obituary online that Málfríður wrote about her. Others wrote about her, too. I was just collecting them all.'

'Why?'

'I wanted to see what was said about her. That's all. You have no interest in such matters.'

'Are you going to be all right?' Konrád asked.

'Don't worry about me,' said Eygló.

They said their goodbyes and she sat at the piano for some time after he'd gone. Before he arrived, she'd planned to tell him what she experienced in the cemetery and the promise she gave Málfríður about being open to messages. Now, however, she knew better than ever that it was useless to talk to Konrád about such matters. At the moment, he'd have the upper hand in any such discussions.

She'd tried to open his mind a bit with her stories, the ones that were important to her. He'd listened to them and tried to show interest, but the realist in him didn't allow him to go any further than that. From the way he responded, she could read his opinion, that what she saw, heard and felt were just her own fantasies, but they were so powerful that she believed, *knew*, them to be real.

Eygló reached for the obituaries and ran her eyes over them. The one by Málfríður had appeared in *Stories of Icelanders*, a supplement to one of the morning newspapers in the old days, which only published obituaries. Eygló remembered people making fun of it, calling it by the Danish term 'Dödens magasin' – Death's magazine. She smiled to herself. She liked the old tradition of saying goodbye to one's loved ones by publishing words of remembrance in the papers. For many, it was part of the grieving process.

Málfríður wrote that she and Hulda had been childhood friends who had grown up together on Laufásvegur Road, not far from where the old Teachers' College stood. They were Reykjavík girls to their fingertips, she wrote proudly. They'd stuck together through life, both with an unwavering interest in ghosts and ghost stories and accounts of the afterlife, and both were members of the Society for Psychical Research, attended countless séances and experienced many things that could never be explained. They'd talked a lot about life after death, and both were convinced of its existence. Málfríður said she was confident that Hulda would be waiting for her when it came to her final days, and that she had a place next to her in the cemetery on Suðurgata Road. So they would stick together through all eternity.

Eygló regarded the photograph of Hulda that accompanied the obituary and had no doubt that she was the same woman she'd seen in the cemetery, standing at Málfríður's grave. They'd even exchanged words, and Eygló tried to remember something that Hulda said. Eygló hadn't heard her very well because a tourist had walked by at that moment and asked her for directions. When she turned back to the grave, the woman was gone and the sentence hung half finished in the air: What she was looking for . . .

'. . . she has now found,' whispered Eygló.

She shook her head and stood up, picked up a jacket tossed over a chair and took it to the coat cupboard in the hall. She grabbed a hanger and hung it up, then noticed the sea-green coat she'd bought around Christmas 1971, but had never worn. It was in a clear plastic garment bag and was as spanking new as the day it was purchased. Eygló hadn't liked the garment, after all. It was beautiful and fitted her, but Eygló didn't feel comfortable in the coat for reasons she was at a loss to explain. She'd bought it at the Kjörgarður shopping centre on Laugavegur High Street, where there'd once been shops of all sorts, and when she was on her way out of the shop with it, she'd heard one of the girls working there say that the coat was an unclaimed order.

Eygló shut the cupboard door. Sometimes, it crossed her mind that the reason she'd never worn the coat was because of the unease that came over her the few times she tried to wear it, a feeling that she wasn't its rightful owner.

47

The only properly God-fearing man Konrád knew was a hospital chaplain whom he met when Erna was ill. The man didn't take his job too seriously despite being a true believer, and made no attempt to win over the atheist Konrád when they spoke together in the hospital corridor about Erna's final days and hours. The chaplain mainly talked about what would happen afterwards, in particular the funeral, which Erna herself had actually organised down to the smallest detail. The chaplain had also performed the ceremony, and Konrád had subsequently met him and they'd got on well. It turned out that the chaplain knew a bit about sects and religious associations, including, among other things, the association called the Creation that was active at one time in town.

He was able to tell Konrád that its founder had been a drinker and had gone to the United States when it was common for Icelandic alcoholics to go there to sober up. While there, the man had met a televangelist, started attending religious meetings, claimed to have seen the light and testified to having experienced visions. He was saved by the Lord God Almighty, was baptised and returned to Iceland thirstier for God's word than anything else.

He took an active part in Icelandic religious organisations but was never very influential until he founded his own congregation. He was thought a fiery preacher, spoke a lot about man's weaknesses, and declared his devotion and that of the entire congregation to the Lord Jesus, laid hands on people and claimed to possess the gift of healing by the power of God, Jesus Christ and the Holy Spirit. His church's office was located on Álfheimar Street and he was immediately nicknamed Álfheimar Jesus by those positioned on the opposite side of the Scriptures.

The chaplain told Konrád that the man had been thought a real womaniser; he'd been so during his drinking years and hadn't slackened in that regard despite becoming an expert in everything connected with forbidden fruits. All his devoutness didn't prevent him from having affairs with married women in his congregation. A few grumbles were heard from his flock after its cuckolded members discovered the truth, but otherwise, everything went well and the congregation flourished.

Until he fell off the wagon.

The chaplain, Konrád's friend, didn't know the details, but the man did one scandalous thing or another while the demon alcohol had its way. It turned out that he'd engaged in fraud, tax evasion and forgery in order to profit as much as possible from the congregation and its members, among other things finagling an older couple out of the ownership of their home. He was convicted and went to prison. Yet God hadn't completely abandoned his sheep, because while he was inside, the founder was redeemed a second time, had more water poured over him and rediscovered his healing powers, and had hardly stepped out of the prison onto Skólavörðustígur Street before he founded a new movement. It was the Creation.

Something had changed. Rakishness was a thing of the past. The man had dried himself up for the last time and, having become a strict ascetic, devoted himself with all his heart to his congregation. He didn't preach much about forgiveness now, and had stopped chasing after women. On the other hand, now he thundered about rampant licentiousness, what with free love being practised on every corner. He warned against women's liberation and was a great opponent of abortion, which was increasing in frequency and went, of course, hand in glove with the liberality of the times.

Although the chaplain told Konráð all of these things in a rather serious tone, he pointed out that the man, whom he'd met several times, was a colourful character and had been highly influential as a church leader during this second phase of redemption. He'd been adroit at reading his community and a skilful orator when appealing to their displeasure and frustration. He'd scraped together more followers than ever before. His congregation had grown and prospered and been quite prominent among the ones that happened to show these matters any interest. All until the founder died unexpectedly and suddenly of a heart attack at his home, two years shy of seventy.

He'd been such an autocrat that there was no one, really, who might naturally step up and take the torch following his death. Some attempts were made to find the congregation's next leader, mainly at the instigation of the man's widow, but the congregation itself dissolved slowly but surely. Over the months following their leader's death, various members trickled over to other religious organisations, until nothing was left of what was once called the Creation and had come into being in the prison on Skólavörðustígur Street.

Konrád was thinking about all of this on his way to the Faxafen business district, where one of the founder's sons ran a travel agency specialising in golf and football trips. The chaplain knew him because he'd gone on golf trips through that agency twice, and the trips had gone exactly as planned and agreed upon. The chaplain suggested Konrád contact that son if he needed further information about the founder, and even offered to talk to the man and set up a meeting. Konrád accepted his offer.

So the man was expecting Konrád, and couldn't hide his curiosity because the chaplain had told him all about Konrád's search. It wasn't every day that an ex-policeman asked about his father, let alone that it was related in some way to something so tragic as the murder of the woman in the block of flats.

'Was she in the congregation?' asked the man, whose name was Einar. He was in his fifties and his face was tanned, as if he himself had just returned from one of the golf trips he sold.

'No, she wasn't,' Konrád said. 'I don't know if she knew your father. Were you active in the congregation? Did you follow its activities?'

'No, sorry. Naturally, I grew up with all that religious fervour but had no interest in it. Dad dragged us to the meetings, but I just wanted to play football. He made us kids sing for the congregation and so on, and used us to help spread his message, if necessary. As soon as I was old enough and mature enough to rise up against him, I did. Let's just say that I left home at an early age.'

The man smiled and asked pro forma whether Konrád had any interest in football or golf trips. There was a huge number to choose from, maybe more than he realised. Konrád said he had no interest in golf, but followed English football closely, and now he knew where to turn if he wanted to take a football trip.

'Just visit us online,' said the man, smiling. 'Everything's online now. Not a single soul comes here any more, as you can see,' he added, looking over the empty room. 'It's a bit strange.'

'Did the congregation have any children's programmes?' Konrád asked, bringing them back to the subject.

The man had to think about it. His father's congregational work clearly hadn't touched him much. He apologised and said it had been a long time since he stood before the congregation and sang hymns with his siblings. But yes, he vaguely remembered the children's activities, especially around holidays like Christmas and Easter, and he'd met the children of congregation members back in the day, but, no, he hadn't kept in contact with any of them. To tell the truth, he hadn't thought much about those times, and mentioned in passing that his father had had two children with his first wife but divorced and soon remarried, and had had four children with his second wife.

'Would that be your mother?' Konrád asked.

The man said yes.

'Did your mother help run the congregation, or did she focus more on looking after the home, as was customary in those days?'

'She took an active part in the congregation,' said Einar. 'She was very energetic. She took care of more or less everything, us kids and her husband, and was a prime mover in that organisation. She baked, prepared food, made coffee and served it. A powerhouse and true Christian, through and through. Prayed and did so much to keep it all going.'

'Do you remember what congregation members thought about abortion?'

'They condemned it,' Einar replied. 'Absolutely. My mother found abortions truly abhorrent. I think she was a huge influence on my father in that regard. It was probably her more than anyone who gave him material for the pulpit.'

'Do you remember whether people who weren't entirely sure about the issue of abortion looked to her or your father? Even mothers who were pregnant but had doubts about having children?'

'I'm sure of it,' said Einar. 'Absolutely sure, even though I don't remember any specific examples. I know that people came to them, and especially to Mum, for advice, people who were in financial trouble, yes, definitely young mothers, drinkers. People looking for spiritual guidance.'

'Do you remember a woman named Sunnefa . . . ?'

'Sunnefa?'

'I think she was in the congregation.'

'Was she a nurse or something like that?'

'Trained as a midwife.'

'I remember a friend of my mother's by that name. She was in the congregation and looked after us sometimes when we were little. Sunnefa? It must have been her. I wonder what happened to her. I haven't heard anything about her for many, many years.'

'She died quite a while ago,' Konrád said. 'She was studying midwifery but came up against the college and its administrators with her views. She was a virulent opponent of abortion, like your mother. They had that in common.'

'But, wait, I don't understand this, what does all this have to do with the woman who died?' Einar asked. 'That Valborg? How does she come into this? You said she hadn't been in the congregation.'

'She knew this Sunnefa,' Konrád said. 'In the early 1970s. Valborg was pregnant. Sunnefa may have delivered the baby and placed it in foster care. It was done in secret. Sunnefa was in the congregation.'

'Do you mean that someone in the congregation took the child in?'

'That's a possibility.'

'And you . . . ?'

'I want to find the child,' said Konrád.

Einar had been leaning back in the chair at his desk, surrounded by posters of foreign football teams and sun-drenched golf courses. Now he straightened up and looked seriously at Konrád.

'I . . . I remember a boy . . .' he said. 'Was it a boy or a girl? That she had?'

'I don't know,' Konrád said.

'You should talk to my sister. She might remember it better. But I remember a boy who hung around Dad and we never really knew where he came from. He stayed with us sometimes and once I remember he came with us to our summer cottage, but he didn't talk much and I never really got to know him, and then we stopped seeing him altogether. It was, like, at the end of the seventies. He was the same age as my sister and they actually kind of became friends.'

'How old was he?'

'He was around six,' said Einar, leaning forward in the seat. 'Once I asked my dad about him and I remember him saying that the boy was having a hard time and we should be nice to him. And then Dad said something that I didn't understand.'

'What was that?'

'"Nobody wants him." He kind of whispered it to me. "Nobody wants him."'

48

The band on the ground floor played their last song, a bitter-sweet melody perfect for slow dancing. The dance floor was packed with people. Others were lining up at the bar now that the dance was coming to an end. Soon the place would be closed. There were whispers of after-parties here and there. It wasn't long before the lights came on and the patrons started streaming towards the exit. Couples and some who were apparently hooking up led each other out into the darkness of the night. Some were unsteadier on their feet than others. Some slipped on the ice behind the church and toppled over. Friends who tried to come to the rescue slipped and fell on their bums, too.

There were always a few individuals lying abandoned in the booths or slumped over the tables, smashed out of their minds or asleep from sheer exhaustion. Valborg went around the club and woke up those who'd dozed off and tried to revive others who were sloshed. It usually went OK, even if now and then some idiots gave her a hard time once they'd regained consciousness, at which point the bouncers and bar staff would deal with them. Once or twice, a fight broke out, and the police needed to be called.

The bands had packed up and gone and the staff trickled out as well. Care was taken to ensure that no one remained after the evening's entertainment was over, and Valborg was delayed on the top floor when she came across a young woman who was out cold. She'd puked on the floor and the stench blended with the odour of alcohol and smoke that permeated the place. Sometimes the smell of smoke was so strong in there that Valborg, who didn't smoke herself, put her clothes in the wash as soon as she got home following her shift. She had a hard time waking the woman, although she did eventually manage it. The woman was confused when she came to and started swinging her fists and swearing, but Valborg was able to calm her down and was about to help her down the stairs when one of her co-workers, wearing a coat, suddenly turned up and said he was on his way home and could walk her out.

Valborg thanked him. She was exhausted and sat down on a comfortable chair to rest a bit, and before she knew it, she woke with a start, having dozed off for a short time.

'You're still here?' she heard someone say behind her. 'Isn't everyone gone?'

She turned and saw the man who'd asked her if she found it fun working there. At the place where it's at.

'We're closed,' she said immediately, as if to let him know that she wasn't going to engage in any friendly conversation with him. 'You shouldn't be here. I need to ask you to leave.'

'Yeah, no, I fell asleep in the toilet,' the man said apologetically, with a smile.

Relaxed as could be, he lit a cigarette.

'I drank too much, that must have been it. It doesn't happen often.'

'I'll walk you out,' said Valborg.

She was heading towards the stairs when he grabbed her.

'Where are you going?' he said.

'Downstairs,' she said. 'You can't be here.'

'How about just being cosy up here?' he said. 'The two of us.'

'Cosy?' she said, breaking free.

'Are you in a rush?' he asked, positioning himself between her and the stairs.

'I'm going to ask you to get out of here,' said Valborg firmly. 'If you don't, I'll have to call for help.'

She was wearing a rather short skirt and a light blouse and his eyes wandered over her, as if checking her out. He took a drag on his cigarette, then flicked it casually away with two fingers. As he did, he stared at Valborg and didn't see it when the cigarette landed on a plush sofa nearby and rolled between its cushions. At the same time, Valborg backed away from him and he leaped at her just as she was about to shout for help, clamped his hand over her mouth and knocked her to the floor.

He was strong and had no difficulty keeping her down, shoving his hand under her skirt, tearing off her pants and groping her. At the same time, he held his other hand over her mouth. She tried to scream for help, but her screams were stifled by his hand, and it was as if it excited him even more when she tried to break free. She was quickly overwhelmed with fear, and he slowly released his hand from her mouth and nose and whispered that he would strangle her if she made a sound. He clenched his fingers around her neck and tightened his grasp to show that he was serious. He was like a wild animal on top of her, and she didn't dare move. Didn't dare shout for help. He'd wrenched up her skirt and she felt his hand on her breasts, then felt it as he unbuttoned his trousers. She cried and whispered to him to stop. Begged him. To leave her alone. Not to do this. She wouldn't tell anyone. If he only stopped now.

'I'll kill you if you say a word about this,' he growled. 'I'll come and kill you, you fucking cunt! I'll find you and kill you! I'll say that you wanted this. That you're a dirty cunt who wanted to do it up here!'

She gasped in pain as the man drove it into her and clamped his hand back over her mouth when she started to scream. He slapped her and grabbed her by the neck and tightened his grasp and pounded her, whispering 'dirty cunt' again and again until he slumped over her.

She wanted to die.

Sick with disgust, she'd started to squirm her way out from under him when he stirred and pushed her down even harder.

'Let me go,' she begged. 'It's over. You're done.'

'Shut up,' he grunted.

Valborg lay dead still and to her unbearable horror, before she knew it, he started again.

49

The phone rang that night. Eygló was fast asleep, exhausted after being upset almost all day because of her visit with the psychic healer to the girl with kidney disease. As she stirred from sleep and heard the phone, she had the feeling it heralded nothing good.

She shuffled over to the phone on its table in the hall. The ringing was deafening in the silence of the night. She didn't turn on the light, but hesitated in the darkness. Then lifted the handset.

It was Málfríður.

'Did I wake you, dear?' she said as soon as Eygló answered. 'Maybe I shouldn't be calling like this in the middle of the night.'

'What time is it?' asked Eygló.

'It's going on four. I thought you should hear about it right away,' said Málfríður. 'Kristleifur was anxious and called the hospital again and spoke to the mother. She was still there. The poor woman.'

Eygló didn't want to hear what came next, but knew that it was unavoidable. She'd accompanied Kristleifur on a few house calls in order to learn from him, but didn't expect that one of those visits would turn out to be so fateful. That the patient would be in such dire straits. She'd done what she could to help the girl. She was the one who had them call an ambulance and rush her to the hospital.

Eygló envisioned the girl lying in her mother's bed in the tiny bedroom and the boy lying asleep on the sofa in the living room, not moving a muscle. The mother being so worried about her daughter that she'd rung up not only a doctor on call that night, but also a psychic healer, to see if by any chance it could help her.

'What happened?' asked Eygló.

'The girl died,' said Málfríður.

Eygló had hoped beyond hope that she wouldn't have to hear this. She'd felt better that evening when she heard that everything seemed to be going well. Now, grief weighed heavily upon her.

'She'd got a bit better,' said Málfríður, 'but then she went downhill again and there was apparently nothing that could be done.'

'The poor girl,' Eygló sighed.

'You did your best,' said Málfríður. 'That's how it goes sometimes, and there's nothing anyone can do about it. I wanted you to hear it right away,' she repeated.

'Thank you,' said Eygló. 'How . . . how is the mother doing?'

'She's devastated, of course, the blessed woman. Kristleifur couldn't really talk to her, but will probably try to meet her in the next few days. He wanted to know if you'd like to go with him.'

'I think I'll skip it,' said Eygló.

'He has a high opinion of you,' said Málfríður, 'and thinks you can be of use. If you choose to go this route. He said you expressed an interest in it.'

'I felt more like I was getting on his nerves. Not that it mattered.'

'Well, no, he got over it quickly. He had nothing but good to say about you.'

'I'm afraid this isn't for me,' said Eygló. 'I've been thinking about it all day. The poor girl. Her mother. I don't think this is something I want to put myself through. I don't think I have what it takes.'

She was about to mention false hopes, but decided not to. She felt it unnecessary to stir up animosity over such tragic news. Kristleifur was only trying to do his best. As she was, too. As the day passed and then the evening, and now in the middle of the night, she'd realised that she didn't have the psychological stamina to deal with such visits. An incident like this one cut too closely. She never wanted to live through another day like it.

'Maybe we can discuss it better later,' Málfríður continued, after a long silence. 'Try to go back to sleep.'

'That's probably impossible,' said Eygló. 'Will you ask Kristleifur to give my condolences to the mother?'

'I'll do that.'

'Now I've forgotten her name,' Eygló said so softly that it could barely be heard.

'What did you say?'

'The mother. What's her name? I've forgotten.'

'Regína, I think,' said Málfríður. 'Yes, her name is Regína, poor woman.'

50

Konrád made the mistake of driving through the city centre on his way to the university. He'd been avoiding that area lately. He didn't want to have to look at the hideous high-rises that had been erected there one after another and shoved aside everything that recalled Reykjavík of the past. He felt that those glitzy glass buildings had no business in this place, and bore witness to the city's flagrant mismanagement and subservience to the power of money. The new city centre reminded him of his old neighbourhood, the so-called Shadow District, where the ugliest blocks of flats in the country had been built like brick walls in front of the friendly residential streets that ran up the hill. Now he avoided the city centre at all costs, and especially avoided going through his old neighbourhood.

After circling the university campus for a while, he saw a car back out of a parking space in front of the main building and pulled into it. He rarely had business at the university. Once or twice he'd gone to watch an English football match at the Student Cellar bar with his son, and that was about it. After he retired, he'd wondered several times whether he ought to enrol in an academic programme, maybe law or something. He'd become interested in law after his years as a police officer and could spend entire evenings watching legal dramas on TV, much more than police dramas, all of which he found utterly ridiculous.

He asked for Soffía at the main office and was told where her office was located on campus, and had no trouble finding it. She had a student with her, and Konrád waited patiently outside her office in the meantime. Soffía was Einar's sister, and despite being the children of the director of the Creation, they hadn't trodden the narrow path of Christianity, but had turned their back on all of that and gone their own way. Not necessarily in opposition to their parents, according to Einar, but more to declare their own independence, besides the fact that the congregation's message had never really appealed to them.

Soffía was a counsellor, and after the student left, she welcomed Konrád with a smile. The working day was at an end, so no students in need of advice were gnawing her threshold that day. She had a coffee maker in her office and asked if he would like a cup. Said that her brother Einar had called and told her about Konrád's visit, so she knew a little of what was going on.

'I'm just so surprised,' she said. 'Einar said that it was about that murder. I made him repeat it. About the woman in the block of flats?'

Konrád didn't know how much Einar had told her and was worried he'd said too much about Valborg and her child; that it may have been fostered by someone from their parents' congregation. Still, he didn't know how he could have avoided saying that.

'Einar mentioned a child she'd had,' said Soffía.

'Your brother remembered a boy you knew and who sometimes spent time with your family,' Konrád said. 'He said you might be able to remember him better. Do you recall his name?'

'You mean Daníel?'

'Daníel? Was that the boy's name?'

'He was a little younger than me,' Soffía said, nodding. 'I was born in 1970. We always called him Danni. I just assume his name was Daníel.'

'Did you know anything about his parents?'

'No, I knew nothing about that. I didn't think about such things at the time. I mostly thought about playing. And we didn't spend much time with him. I remember him at our summer cottage, and sometimes he would eat with us. It was like we were looking after him for someone. I never knew who it was. I think Mum took care of it. I mean took care of him. From what I recall, she seemed to have looked after that boy extremely well.'

'Your father told Einar that no one wanted the boy. Do you know anything about that? What he meant by it?'

Soffía shook her head.

'He said all sorts of things you couldn't understand, especially when the evangelical spirit took hold of him. The congregation sometimes had special children's and youth activities, but I don't remember that boy participating in any of them.'

'It sounds as if the boy had no fixed home,' Konrád said. 'That he was something of a stray. Can that be?'

'I couldn't say. But I think he came from somewhere in the countryside. I went once with my mum to pick him up at the long-distance bus terminal.'

'Do you remember Sunnefa, whom I understand was a friend of your mother?'

'I remember her well. She believed every word in the Bible. Had that in common with Mum, and they were good friends. Sunnefa was often at our place, helping with the work of the congregation. A lovely lady, as I remember her. Truly lovely.'

'Another woman from the congregation that I know of is Regína,' said Konrád. 'She was a friend of Sunnefa's and initially knew her from the National Hospital. Do you remember if she ever came to your house?'

'Regína?'

'Yes.'

'That's a really sad story.'

51

Some of the video footage was unclear, but here and there it was easier to make out the faces. It showed a lot of the same people, coming to work or leaving, going for lunch or returning from coffee breaks. To that were added people who had business in the building, which was no small number, given the various companies housed there. The surveillance cameras in the lobby by the lifts showed clearer images than those near the entrance, which had something to do with the different lighting conditions. The footage reached back to the time when Valborg looked to Konrád for help. Marta had assigned an officer to go through the footage and compare the people in it with photographs of Valborg found in her home. That was two days ago.

The detention order for Hallur had expired without renewal, and he was released from custody but placed under a travel ban. Glóey had met him on his release and it appeared to Marta that the two of them got on quite well. Hallur had adamantly denied involvement in Valborg's death; none of his DNA was found on her body or in her flat, and Emanúel couldn't say for certain if it had been him who forced his way into the woman's flat. So it was difficult to justify a two-week extension on the detention order, as Marta would have preferred. She had trouble admitting that the police were back at square one.

She went and got herself a coffee, e-cigarette in hand, and started sucking and blowing. A young policeman in the break room said hello, then took his mug out into the corridor, as smoking got on his nerves. There he met a colleague who wanted to know if there was any coffee left. The young man nodded in the direction of the break room.

'Ask the volcano.'

Just then, Marta appeared in the corridor. She was about to go back into her office with her coffee when she heard someone calling her. It was the officer she'd assigned to view the surveillance tapes. He said he'd found something that he wanted to show her.

Marta followed him into a room where three computer screens displayed the footage from Borgartún. The man asked Marta to sit down beside him, then started the video on one of the screens. Marta inhaled the nicotine and tried not to miss anything, until the image froze on a woman standing in front of the high-rise.

'Is that her?' the officer asked, handing Marta a photo of Valborg.

Marta stopped vaping, compared the photo with the woman on the screen and saw immediately that it was Valborg. She nodded and the recording continued from the point when Valborg first appeared. She walked determinedly towards the building from the east, but just before she reached the door she hesitated and then stopped. People walked past her in and out of the building, while she stood there looking up at the tall glass facade, staring straight into the camera for a moment without seeming to realise it and then fixing her gaze on the door, which opened and closed automatically. People continued to go in and out of the building, but she stood there, uncertain and hesitant. A short while passed like that before Valborg turned and disappeared from the view of the cameras.

'That's her,' Marta said.

The officer rewound and the footage froze on Valborg's face as she stared at the automatic door, and Marta felt from her expression that this wasn't just some ordinary reluctance or diffidence on the woman's part.

It was as if Valborg didn't dare step into the building.

There was a knock on the door and the young man stuck his head in the doorway and said that someone out front was asking for Marta.

'Who is it?' Marta asked.

'A woman in sunglasses,' said the man.

When Marta came to the front desk, she saw the woman she'd urged to contact her if she wanted to report domestic violence. She was sitting dejectedly on a chair, but got up when she saw Marta and took off her sunglasses. She and Marta looked into each other's eyes before Marta took her by the arm and walked her to her office.

52

Having second thoughts, Soffía looked intently at Konrád. She wanted him to know that she wasn't inclined to gossip and spread rumours about people. Konrád said that he was the same. He had no interest in spreading stories about people. He'd made it his mission to find Valborg's child, and he would continue that mission whether Soffía helped him or not. Soffía said that she was very willing to contribute, but just wasn't used to talking to strangers about her family and childhood and didn't know where the line was between what she felt up to revealing about her parents' friends and what was important to him. Konrád assured her that everything she said was confidential, and he would make sure it didn't go any further.

'Have you met Regína?' she asked.

'Yes, actually, I went to her house,' said Konrád.

'Why did you go –'

'She was the one who let Sunnefa have the names of expectant mothers who were hesitant about having children or choosing abortion. She admitted it. Valborg happened to be one of them.'

Soffía sat quietly for several moments.

'Regína is the friend of my mother who had it hardest,' she said. 'I don't know the whole story, and don't know what you . . . what you're looking for.'

'Anything can help.'

Soffía said that they'd become friends in secondary school, had both been involved in Christian youth organisations and were religious, except that Regína hadn't been quite as immersed in all that as Soffía's mother. She mainly remembered her mother saying that Regína had been more drawn towards mysticism and musings about the afterlife. In any case, she did manage to drag her mum with her to a few séances. Regína got married early, and later it turned out that her husband was a brute who beat her, and two or three times, Soffía's father had to come to her rescue. In between, the man promised he'd mend his ways, and everything went fine until he started beating his wife again. Along with the violence came isolation, as the man was both jealous and suspicious and didn't want her to associate with anyone except those he approved of, and they were few in number. Several years passed like that until Regína managed to divorce him, despite her husband's constant death threats, and she moved away from him, taking their daughter with her. She rented an attic flat a short distance from the city centre and was living under straitened circumstances when tragedy struck. Her daughter fell ill with what was initially thought to be an ordinary flu; she was taken to hospital but the girl died shortly afterwards.

'Regína was in shock,' said Soffía. 'She'd put up with that bastard for so long, and then that devastation was laid on top of it. She lost her grip on reality and was admitted to a psychiatric ward, and was there for almost a year. Gradually, she managed to work through her tragedy, though she never really recovered from the loss of her daughter, of course.'

'Do people in such circumstances ever recover?'

'My mother told me about this sometime after, when Regína came up in conversation. I was so young in those years that I didn't get the whole story until much later. I often thought about the girl.'

'Did Regína only have that one child?'

'Yes.'

'Did you ever hear them talk about adoptions?' Konrád asked. 'Your mum and Regína?'

'No. Never.'

'Did you ever hear them talk about that Danni or Daníel, as far as you can remember?'

'No, I don't remember that. On the other hand, Regína did attend Sunnefa's funeral. I don't know how many years ago that was. It was in Fossvogur Church and quite a lot of people came to pay their final respects. I said hello to Regína and she was as nice as always, and . . . no, I don't think I've seen her since. Those sorts of relationships unravel over time. When Mum died, her friends disappeared, too. But I do remember, I saw Regína talking to a man who somehow really reminded me of Danni, but by the time I got over to them, he was gone.'

'Did you ask Regína about him?'

'No. But it could have been him, and he didn't look particularly good.'

'What do you mean?'

'He just looked a bit unhealthy, and was dressed rather shabbily. It was as if life hadn't treated him well.'

'You don't know what went on between them?'

'No. I just noticed them talking, and it seemed like they were good friends. They seemed quite close, the way they greeted each other; she hugged him and he held her hand. It was beautiful. It was like old friends meeting after a long separation.'

53

The operation by the police and customs authorities was considered a success – and in any case, the criminals' plan wasn't really worth its salt. Customs employees had received a fairly reliable tip that a crew member on board one of the cargo ships was smuggling a considerable amount of steroids and ecstasy into the country, along with cocaine. The tip came from the ship itself. A particular man was named and, following the ordinary customs inspection, he was watched as he disembarked and then tailed as he headed home, to see if he had accomplices.

Shortly afterwards, he was visited by two men known to law enforcement for their involvement in a large-scale drug importation scheme a few years earlier. They usually worked together, and both had done time for smuggling. All three were arrested right away at the sailor's home. In a sports bag taken from the house, the drugs in question were found.

The men were cooperative. They'd been through all this before, pretty much, besides the fact that they were caught red-handed.

One of them named Hallur as an accomplice. He had said he'd make a contribution, and thereby would gain a share in the profits from the smuggling. He didn't put his money where his mouth was, though, and when the other partners heard he'd been arrested and brought in for questioning in connection with an entirely different matter, they paid a visit to Glóey to deliver her the message that it would be best for the two of them if he kept his mouth shut about their scheme.

They immediately suspected Hallur of treachery. That, despite everything, he'd blabbed to the police about the smuggling. The men were absolutely convinced of it. They talked openly about murdering the fucking bastard.

Marta was quickly notified of this. The reason was that the men had quite an interesting story to tell about their friend Hallur and the old lady in the block of flats.

'What about her?' Marta asked as she sat down in front of one of the men who'd gone to see Glóey and attacked her.

'The old lady?' said the man.

He had a tattoo that ran up his neck and behind one ear. Marta couldn't make out what the tattoo was supposed to be. A dragon, maybe. Typical.

'What did Hallur say?'

'He said she had a shitload of money, that old bird. He just needed to go and get it.'

54

Regína was sitting in her garden chair behind her house, looking at the trees that stretched up into the dullish-grey sky. She was wearing a winter coat and a hat, it being cold outside and winter round the corner. She didn't answer when Konrád knocked on the door, and it crossed his mind that she was in the garden.

'Oh, is that you?' she said when she noticed him, as if she'd expected him again, whether today or tomorrow or sometime later. 'I've always wanted to plant a proper vegetable garden here,' she went on. 'With swedes and lettuce. I've always felt the garden was a bit too small for such a thing, but that's probably just foolishness.'

'It doesn't really need to take up too much space,' said Konrád.

'No, exactly, I'm thinking of a few carrots and swedes and potatoes that I can dig up in the autumn. I like working in the garden. Did I tell you that already? I like watching it come to life in the spring.'

'I don't have a green thumb myself,' said Konrád. 'And besides, I'm lazy.'

She pointed him to a garden chair by the wall and he went and got it and sat down beside her, and together they gazed at the garden. Konrád looked up at the sky. He thought it might rain, but hoped it wouldn't. They sat there silently for several moments, until Konrád cleared his throat.

'I'm not sure you told me the whole truth when we met last,' Konrád said.

'Oh?'

'I'm sure you have your reasons for it, and I can understand that, but it would help me a great deal if you could tell me what you know.'

Regína stared at him, silent and questioningly.

'Do you know a man named Daníel?' Konrád asked.

'Daníel?'

'Yes. A foster child, as far as I understand.'

Regína didn't answer him.

'Could he be Valborg's son?' Konrád asked, watching a blackbird settle onto a branch high above them.

Regína cleared her throat, but didn't answer.

'Can you tell me anything about him?'

Regína looked up at the blackbird.

'Regína?'

Finally, her head seemed to clear.

'I couldn't be with him any more after she died,' she said. 'I didn't have the strength for it.'

'Daníel?'

'Yes.'

'After your daughter died?'

Regína looked at him and Konrád told her that he'd spoken to the daughter of an old friend of hers in the congregation. She'd told him about Regína's loss of her daughter and that she'd suffered greatly for a long time afterwards.

'Were you gossiping about me?' Regína said.

'No, not at all. On the contrary, she was very reluctant to tell me the little she knew.'

'Did she tell you about my husband?'

'Yes. She did.'

'He's dead now. Our daughter was the only light in all that darkness. I finally managed to break free from him. It wasn't easy. I rented a place and looked after us as well as I could, and then Sunnefa came to me and asked if I could take the boy.'

'Why?'

Regína didn't answer him. Konrád waited patiently. He sensed that she hadn't spoken of such things in a long time, if ever.

'It turned out,' she said eventually, 'that the people who took in the boy were . . . very disorderly, and then the woman had an accident. She was hit by a car and ended up dying in the hospital. The man went on drinking and . . . he didn't treat the boy well, let's say. Sunnefa spoke of neglect. They were friends of hers and had taken the boy in at her encouragement, but then he simply couldn't stay there any longer. They were registered as his parents, and I don't know how she did it, but Sunnefa had had it specified on the documents that they were his blood parents.'

'Did they belong to the congregation?'

'Yes, as far as I understand. Otherwise, I wanted nothing to do with the whole thing and didn't ask. I didn't want too much information. She asked if I could take the boy in, which I did, with no problem. He was lovely, though of course a bit wary at first. They got on well together, him and my daughter, and it all went fine until . . . until my daughter came down with the flu. Just an ordinary old flu.'

Regína got to her feet and picked up a branch that had broken off one of the trees. She was alone with her thoughts for a short time, until Konrád went to her and asked if everything was all right.

'It's difficult to speak of these things,' she said. 'Forgive me.'

'Of course,' he said, and just then, his phone started ringing. Konrád was going to switch it off quickly, but saw who it was and knew he had to answer. He excused himself and stepped away. Regína seemed not to care at all about the interruption.

55

On the phone was a colleague of Konrád's who had once worked for the police in Keflavík. He'd left many years ago and worked now at the Keflavík town hall, but at one time had tried his hand in CID, where he worked alongside Konrád and they became good friends. Konrád knew the man had connections with all sorts of non-profit organisations and knew everything and everyone on the Suðurnes peninsula, and it had occurred to Konrád to ask him if he could look up information on the employees of contractors who did construction projects for the military at the Base in Keflavík decades ago. The man had been more than willing to help and found the information that Konrád was looking for, and which didn't particularly surprise him.

'Is this of use?' his friend in Keflavík asked.

'It may be,' Konrád said.

'You're not going to tell me what it's about?'

'No. Not right now. I can't. I'll talk to you later.'

He said a hasty goodbye and walked back over to Regína, who was still standing by the tree, holding the branch.

'Sorry,' Konrád said. 'I know this is hard for you to recount.'

'I haven't done so in years. No one should have to experience such a thing,' Regína said. 'Such loss.'

'No, of course not.'

'I've always been religious,' said Regína, holding on to the branch as if it were her sole support in life. 'And I've always believed in life after death. In those years, I was fairly involved in such matters and went to séances and the like and got a well-known psychic healer to come and see Emma. A young woman came with him, and she must have sensed something because she had us call an ambulance immediately. But it was just too late. Emma died that night. She had an infection in her organs and nothing could be done. I was too late to react. I should have already taken her to the hospital. I should have done something. I lost faith in myself. In life. In God. In everything. I was admitted to a psych ward and . . .'

'Sunnefa took the boy back?'

Regína nodded.

'She eventually placed him in a good home up north. I was in no condition to take care of him after Emma left, so the boy . . . was sort of passed from place to place for a time after he left me and until he moved north. That was around 1980. Sunnefa was always very concerned about the boy and I think she stayed in contact with the people there.'

'Are you in touch with Daníel at all now?' Konrád asked.

Regína hesitated.

'I understand you met him at Sunnefa's funeral, at least.'

'I guess that was more than a decade ago. He didn't look well, the poor thing. He'd moved back to Reykjavík quite some time before that, and it was my understanding that he wasn't in much contact with the people up north. He'd gone astray and scrounged some money off me. I asked how he was doing and he said he had no complaints. We talked a little about Emma. He remembered her. I told him to come and see me if I could do anything for him, but he never came. He looked like a tramp, to tell you the truth.'

'Do you know where I can find him?'

'No,' said Regína. 'I can't help you with that.'

'This was the only child that Sunnefa delivered and made such arrangements for?' Konrád asked.

'Yes.'

'Are you sure?'

'Yes. Yes, I'm sure of it. She told me that. Said it had been a mistake to take that route. She'd wanted to help the woman keep it a secret, and without terminating the pregnancy, but Sunnefa didn't do it again. Not that I know of. If she did, she didn't tell me. It was most unusual, what happened.'

'Did you know why Valborg didn't want to have the baby?' Konrád asked. 'Did she ever tell Sunnefa?'

'I think it's because she was raped. If I remember, she told Sunnefa that it happened at Glaumbær. Sunnefa said she'd tried to get her to press charges, but she refused, saying she couldn't imagine meeting that man again in court and recounting what he did to her.'

'And you . . . ?'

'I found it understandable, pretty much. That she should have chosen that path.'

'Did she mention to Sunnefa who it was who raped her?'

'I gather that she'd never seen him before in her life.'

'Did the boy ever know the truth about his birth? About Valborg? Did you ever tell him?'

Regína shook her head.

'I . . . I just couldn't bring myself to,' she whispered. 'I felt like I'd done something to him and . . . it was all so hard and . . . no, I couldn't, couldn't do it.'

56

Somehow she made it back to her house through the snow and all the Christmas decorations, determined to act normal. Act as if nothing had happened. She was going to forget this and never think about it again. She slunk out the back door of Glaumbær and disappeared into the night. She didn't ask for help, didn't scream in despair that she'd been raped. She hid it all inside.

The man had been quick to vanish when he was done, spat a few horrible words at her and left her lying on the floor, paralysed with terror and disgust. Added to that were shame and anger and strange self-recrimination. All of those emotions started festering in her mind, and she would struggle with them for a long time.

She didn't feel the cold on the way home. Twice she had to stop to puke. She took busy, well-lit streets and was constantly looking around, fearing that the man was following her and would ambush her and do her even more harm. She sped up and started running, and finally ran as fast as her legs would carry her, and when she got home, she locked the door carefully behind her and pulled a chest of drawers in front of it just to be sure. But she still didn't feel safe. She would never feel completely safe again.

She had bruises on her neck and her entire body was sore, and she was in a great deal of pain where he'd had his way. She felt her body up and down and had no sooner stepped out of the shower than she stepped back into it and washed herself again, as if she could wash off her disgust with soap and water.

Knowing she wouldn't be able to sleep, she sat down in her small kitchen and stared out the window at the neighbours' Christmas decorations, red and yellow lights on their balconies and poinsettias in their windows, and tried to clear her mind of what had happened. It was utterly impossible. She could only throw a thin cloak around the burning pain for a brief moment at a time before it pushed its way forward again, absolutely relentless.

The first thing she heard when she turned on the radio the next day was that there had been a huge fire in Reykjavík that night, and that the nightclub Glaumbær had burned to the ground.

57

A song from the 1960s was playing on the radio, reminding Konrád of Erna, and he sat there in the car after shutting off the engine and listened to those sweet tones. Húgó had called again from the States and told him all was well. They would be coming home in a few days and asked if Konrád felt like driving to the airport to pick them up. 'That goes entirely without saying,' Konrád said. They'd invited him to go with them, but he didn't much like flying these days, and it was a long journey, besides the fact that they were staying with friends and he didn't want to get in the way of their fun. They shouldn't have to carry him along wherever they went.

Marta called shortly afterwards and asked how he was doing. She told him the Narcotics Unit had apprehended Hallur's partners, two known offenders, when they received a shipment from one of the cargo ships. They'd been quick to finger Hallur as an accomplice and actually thought he'd blabbed all their plans to the police. 'One of them said he'd heard Hallur talking about some old lady who had shitloads of money. He just had to go and get it.'

'And did he?'

'Hallur denies having done so, but it does seem possible,' said Marta. 'He was in dire straits and thought that Valborg had money and went up to her place.'

'What does his lover in that building have to say?'

'His sister-in-law? We can't find her. She's gone. Glóey claims not to know where she is.'

Marta asked if he'd uncovered any more details of Valborg's story. Konrád was still hesitant to divulge the information he'd gathered. He thought he needed more time and said he would talk to Marta again soon.

The part from the music box was in his car, and he picked it up. He considered calling Eygló. She believed in her father, which was respectable. He himself had no such feelings for his father. He knew the man was capable of cheating people out of their money, especially innocent widows, with lies and cheap music-box tricks.

Konrád had had trouble telling Húgó about him. Growing up, the boy had no grandfather, because Erna's father had died soon after Húgó was born. Konrád and Erna had told the boy a lot about his maternal grandfather, who'd been a deck officer with the Coast Guard and accepted Konrád with a few reservations. He was orderly and disciplined and enjoyed people's respect far beyond the Coast Guard. His paternal grandfather, however, was always shrouded in a kind of mist whenever he came up in conversation, until Konrád decided to tell his son the truth before the boy discovered it himself. Húgó listened as his father told him about the murder at the slaughterhouse and asked a lot of questions, which Konrád tried to answer as best he could. He became a bit tongue-tied when Húgó wanted to know if it was because his grandfather was a bad man that he'd suffered that fate.

The song on the radio ended and Konrád saw Ísleifur come out of the basement, carrying four bags full of empty beer cans. He walked a bit awkwardly towards the bus stop and past it, and didn't notice Konrád getting out of the car and following him at a distance. Holding the bags in both hands, Ísleifur looked neither left nor right, but just stared at the pavement as he walked at a fairly brisk pace for a man his age. Before long, a recycling centre appeared, towards which Ísleifur headed. Konrád saw him go straight into the cans area, where he had to wait in a short queue before emptying the bags.

Konrád stood at a reasonable distance, and when Ísleifur came back out, he decided to go for it. As soon as Ísleifur saw Konrád heading towards him, he sped up to try and avoid him. When he saw that he wouldn't get far, he slowed back down and finally stopped, now behind the recycling centre.

'What do you think you're doing, spying on me like this?' he shouted at Konrád. 'I can't get you off my back!'

'I saw you heading this way. I just want to –'

'Leave me alone!' Ísleifur spat. 'I'm not talking to you! I have nothing more to say to you!'

'I have just a few questions and then I'll be gone,' Konrád promised, grabbing Ísleifur's arm when he tried to dash away. 'I want to ask you about a person you worked with once at the Base. I know it was a long time ago, but I suspect you remember him.'

'Stop this bullshit!' Ísleifur said, trying to break free. 'Leave me alone!'

'It was during the hippie years,' Konrád said, glancing around. No one seemed to notice them as they stood facing each other behind the recycling centre, amid empty skips. He didn't have any idea how he might handle it if Ísleifur started getting violent. He didn't want to get into a fight with the man and attract unwanted attention or interference.

'I have nothing to talk to you about,' said Ísleifur. 'Leave me alone!'

'His name is Bernódus,' said Konrád. 'Your friend from the Base. Is that right?'

Ísleifur stared at Konrád, who let go of him.

'The Base? Why do you say that?' Ísleifur asked in surprise.

'Didn't you two work for contractors who did construction for the US military?'

'Who says that?'

'Old personnel files,' Konrád said. 'Ones covering the years 1968 to 1971. You worked for the same company and stayed in workers' quarters up at the Base but went to Reykjavík on weekends. Like most of the other workers there at the time. You'd been at that company for a year when he started working with you. You were ordinary labourers, both of you.'

'What the hell do you care?'

'Right now, one of you is counting his coins at the recycling centre while the other is rolling in dough. Founded a pharmaceutical company with his daughter and became filthy rich.'

'What about it? What bullshit is this?'

'Have you kept in touch since working at the Base?'

Ísleifur didn't answer him.

'Didn't you go and see him the night I ran into you at Borgartún?'

Ísleifur sniffled and avoided looking at Konrád.

'Do you meet regularly? Reminisce about old times?'

Ísleifur didn't answer him.

'Weren't you on your way to see him before I asked you about the rape at Glaumbær?'

Ísleifur shook his head.

'Was that something that stirred up your old memories?'

'Leave me alone.'

'You said that what happened to Valborg had nothing to do with you.'

'For fuck's sake, leave me alone!'

'What about him? Your old friend? Did he know Valborg?'

'Shut up.'

'I can't quite figure this out. Did you go to Valborg's to shut her up? Did you go to her place with those damned plastic bags of yours? Was that it? Was she going to tell what –'

'Bullshit!' spat Ísleifur. 'You know fuck all, you fucking idiot!'

'Tell me what happened.'

'Shut up! Leave me alone!'

'Why would you want to silence Valborg after all these years? What could she do to you? You're just a bum. No one gives a shit about you. It's another matter with . . .'

Konrád stared at the man, his filthy coat, a plastic bag sticking out of one pocket, the hand that wiped his dripping nose.

'Valborg collected newspaper clippings about your friend at Borgartún. Was it because . . . ?'

Ísleifur started smirking at him.

'Was it . . . ?'

Konrád grabbed Ísleifur's arm.

'It was him . . . ?!'

58

Valborg couldn't work up the nerve to go into the building. She made two attempts over the space of a few days, but couldn't bring herself to walk through the door. Something held her back. The thought of seeing him again. Of facing him after all those years. The thought of it horrified her. Since that horrendous night, she'd seen him only in the news and intended never to have any contact with him, yet the thoughts never left her. Thoughts about the child that was theirs. Thoughts about the wealth he'd earned.

The second time she went to Borgartún, she wandered in a kind of restless agitation in the vicinity of the building, trying to work up her courage. She'd come there by bus and walked the short distance from the bus stop to the door of the tall glass building, but as on the previous attempt, she stopped there and finally turned away. Still, she had no desire to go home immediately, but found a cafe nearby, went in and sat down. From her table, she could see the entrance to the building that housed the pharmaceutical company and could watch the people who flocked to it and came out of it again to go about their business or run errands in the hustle and bustle of the day.

Valborg recognised him immediately from the photos in the newspaper. It was the first time she'd seen him since the horrific incident at Glaumbær. She'd been flipping through the morning paper one day and was shocked when she saw an article about him, but later she cut it out and put it with her recipes. She didn't actually know why. Didn't know what she was planning on doing with that clipping. The article was about his trip with his wife to the Pyramids in Egypt. The woman seemed quite sweet, judging by the photos, with a beautiful smile and thick blonde hair. She told the reporter how she'd travelled a lot with her husband, and that she'd long dreamed of seeing the wonders of Egypt. Finally, they'd decided to make the dream come true, and their trip didn't disappoint. It had been magnificent. Like a fairy tale, literally.

Sometime later, more articles appeared. They told of the man's business through the years, and how his daughter joined him when she was old enough. They'd invested wisely and eventually established a pharmaceutical company, which, according to the latest reports, was in the process of being sold. The papers evaluated the company's capital gains over the past two decades. How enormous they'd been. How much they would possibly make from the sale. The man's daughter was featured in the newspaper business pages in this connection. An extensive interview with her was published, in which she pointed out her father's merits and their excellent collaboration.

Valborg finished her coffee, got up to pay, and was on her way back towards the building when she suddenly saw him walking out the glass door and then round the building to the parking spaces behind it. Her heart skipped a beat and she instinctively followed him at a distance. By the time she rounded the corner, he'd opened the boot of his black Mercedes, put his briefcase in it, and taken out what appeared to her to be a golf club.

Valborg walked hesitantly up to him. She had no idea what she would say. How she should act. Her heart pounded in her chest and she could barely catch her breath, she was in such a state.

'You . . . ?' she said.

He turned round, golf club in hand.

'Yes?' he said.

The memories of that night long ago assailed her mind, but she tried to push them aside. She didn't want to show this man any sign of weakness.

'You don't remember me, do you?' she said, struggling to breathe. A sickening feeling nearly overwhelmed her.

'Can I help you?' he asked. 'Do we know each other?'

'Yes,' she said. 'We do know each other, though you may have forgotten it.'

'Sorry,' he said, 'I can't place you. Do you work for me?'

'No,' she said, trying to control her breathing and the heat she felt spreading through her whole body. Meeting him after all these years had immediately made her agitated, even though she tried to ward it off. 'I don't work for you. I collect clippings about you from the papers. I'm saving them for a better time. Until I tell the whole story.'

'Are you all right?' he asked when he saw how upset she clearly was, and apparently not entirely in her right mind.

'I want you to find the child,' she blurted out.

'The child?'

'It's also entitled to that money of yours. I want you to find it and admit it.'

'What are you talking about? Admit what?'

'That it's your child! I'm talking about your child! I want you to find it, admit it's yours, and let it have its share. There are tests that can reveal the paternity, and the child can have –'

'What rubbish is this?' exclaimed the man, bewildered. 'I don't have time for this,' he said, putting the golf club in the boot. 'I don't recall having seen you before. This is a misunderstanding.'

He closed the boot.

'You don't remember me?' Valborg stepped closer to him and felt her courage grow stronger. 'You don't remember what you did to me? You don't remember what you did to me the night Glaumbær burned down? It was as if the Almighty took control and turned the place into an inferno after what you did to me!'

The man looked at her in astonishment, until a light finally went on in his head. His eyes widened as if seeing a zombie that had risen from a long-cold grave. He stared at the woman, whose face, like his, showed the passage of the years, at the coat that had seen better days, and knew that it was she whom he'd once disgraced.

'You?' he stammered.

'Yes, me!!' shouted Valborg.

59

The meeting was short. No lawyer was present. Marta had pretty much expected that. It took place in the meeting room at the headquarters of the pharmaceutical company. Marta came alone. They wanted it that way, and she saw no reason to object. She was only gathering information about Valborg. There was no other purpose to the meeting.

The father and daughter sat opposite her. Klara, dressed impeccably in a black suit with a white pearl necklace, had met Marta at the secretary's desk and shown her to the meeting room. They waited in awkward silence, and finally the father appeared and shook Marta's hand in a serious manner. He was over seventy but bore his age well, slim and tanned, staying, as Marta understood it, half the year or more in southerly countries and enjoying his retirement years. He was wearing a beautiful dark blue suit that she couldn't imagine as being anything other than tailor-made and on his ring finger was a gold ring with a black, square stone and a tiny diamond in one corner. He fiddled with the ring every now and then during their conversation. Impatient. Resentful. The man, Bernódus, greeted his daughter with a kiss.

'Can we put a quick end to this nonsense?' he said after sitting down. 'I understand you want to connect us and this company to a murder.'

Klara smiled apologetically and touched her father's arm, as if trying to keep him from getting too worked up. They needed to be cooperative for a short time, and then this would be over. Marta imagined what must have been an unhappy look on the man's face when his daughter told him about the visit the police paid to his company with regard to Valborg's case.

'Hardly,' said Marta. 'As I explained to your daughter, we found clippings of newspaper articles about you and your wife and Klara at the home of the deceased, and we're following up on that. Can I ask if you knew the woman?'

'No, I didn't,' the man said. 'I understand that Klara has answered all your questions regarding that woman.'

'Can you imagine why she collected clippings about your family? We found no articles about other business people. Only about you.'

'I have no idea. Naturally, we're . . . we're running a big company here that's talked about around town, but we can't say why people cut out articles about us. I'm sure you can see that.'

'Yes, of course. Was she in any contact with you or your company in the past few weeks or months?'

'No,' said Klara, 'I think I can safely say that she wasn't.'

Marta took a copy of Valborg's phone record from her bag and placed it on the table in front of them. The man put on gilt-edged reading glasses. Klara ran her eyes over the record.

'She called the company three times in the weeks before she died,' Marta said. 'Did she talk to either of you? Any of your employees?'

'No,' said Klara, 'not to me. I can't answer for our employees. I'd need to check on that.'

'Countless numbers of people call here every day,' said Bernódus, taking off his reading glasses and putting them back in the breast pocket of his jacket.

'Of course,' Marta said, digging for another folder in her bag. She placed three photographs from the surveillance cameras on the table.

'Could she have come to meet with you?'

The father and daughter pored over the photos.

'Is that the woman?' Klara asked. 'Outside this building?'

'What is this? Are we under investigation?!' the man exclaimed excitedly, pushing the photos away. 'What's the meaning of this?'

His daughter grasped his arm again as a sign that he should calm down.

'Did she meet with you?' Marta asked again.

'No,' said Klara.

'Certainly not,' the man said, twisting the gold ring on his finger. 'There are dozens of businesses in this building. Who knows, she may have been going to the dentist.'

'Unless she called here,' Marta said calmly. 'Called you.'

'I don't know,' Klara said. 'Maybe she knew someone here in the company. Lots of people work here. I'll look into it.'

'But then there are the clippings,' Marta said, smiling. 'They're not about any employees of the company. They're about you.'

'We didn't know that woman,' said Klara. 'I've never seen her before. I've never spoken to her on the phone. I've never met with her.'

She looked at her father.

'This is ridiculous,' said Bernódus. 'We have no idea who this woman is.'

'She had a child in 1972,' said Marta. 'We know that she gave it up after it was born. She didn't want to have it, for some reason. We have no idea why, but before she died, she looked for the child. We don't know if it was a boy or a girl. She asked a man in the police to track down the child for her. She had incurable cancer and wanted to find out what had become of the child she'd given up. The question is whether that search led her here.'

Marta looked at Klara and her father in turn, but they remained stone-faced. It was as if neither of them knew what she was getting at with this interrogation of hers.

'The search for her child?' Klara said finally, glancing at her father. 'I don't know what –'

'What's the meaning of these questions?' said Bernódus, now seriously knitting his brow. 'Where is this headed? We didn't know that woman. How often do we have to tell you that? We didn't know her at all. Not at all!'

Marta tapped her finger on a copy of the newspaper clipping about Klara alone, in which she was smiling confidently at the readers.

'What did she find here?' she said.

Klara was bewildered. Marta watched her silently.

'I . . . that I was born in 1974?' Klara said hesitantly. She looked in turn at her father and Marta, her expression full of astonishment and disbelief.

'Yes, I looked that up,' said Marta. 'You're not –'

'Klara isn't a foster child!' Bernódus spat, no longer able to restrain his anger. 'How can you spout such nonsense?! Such bullshit?!'

He stared at Marta.

'What crap is this, anyway? This is ridiculous! I agreed to meet you because I thought we could help you with this tragic case, and this is what I get thrown at me. You're mad! You must be mad!' he cried, getting up. 'I'm not going to sit here and take this! This . . . this stupidity! Klara . . . you . . . I've never heard such bullshit! I'm not taking this. I'm not going to sit here and take this!'

He glared at Marta and stormed out of the room, leaving Klara and Marta alone with the clippings, the photos from the surveillance cameras and the printout of Valborg's phone record. Klara looked it all over and stood up.

'So this is over,' she said. 'Goodbye.'

60

Most of them were the same, the houses in the neighbourhood by the sea, big square boxes with expansive windows, dark-tinted panes in some, and columns at the front as if the Greeks had come ashore there at some point.

Konrád drove further down the street until he came to the end of the cul-de-sac. There stood one of the finest detached houses in the neighbourhood, built more or less like a ship's hull, with its prow facing Faxaflói Bay and tall picture windows on both sides.

Konrád rarely passed this way, but he remembered Sunday drives with Erna and Húgó through some of these streets once upon a time. The neighbourhood was well established and properties came up for sale only every now and then, and were then fought over.

He hadn't been in touch with Marta, but was putting it off until he'd spoken to the man he'd come to meet. Ísleifur had been a little more helpful after Konrád threatened to call the police, and recalled for Konrád a few things from the past that could possibly be useful. Konrád was still full of conjectures and suspicions, which he was going to try to get answers to there in the house by the sea. He was doing this primarily for himself. And for Valborg, even though it was too late. Maybe he was off course. Yet he thought it more likely that he was right. He had the feeling that he was reaching the end.

He'd called Regína and told her who he was going to meet, explained his suspicions and asked if she knew the man at all. Whether Sunnefa had ever mentioned him. Regína couldn't be of any help to him, but had difficulty hiding her curiosity. Konrád said he would be in touch again when things had become clearer.

As he approached the house, he heard what sounded like a muffled clack come from it. He stopped and listened, and shortly afterwards, heard the same sound again. He felt like it was coming from the other side of the house, the one facing the sea. After a moment's hesitation, he slunk into the garden. The evening was mild and it was still bright enough for a fight, as the old books said, the setting sun casting a red glow on the sky. Konrád made it unimpeded through the large garden and up onto a sun deck that faced the sea and was huge, with a storage shed, a hot tub, and an outdoor barbecue in one corner. Near the front edge of the deck was a gadget used on golf-driving ranges, loaded with golf balls that almost magically appeared one by one on top of a plastic tee sticking out of a green mat. That's where the sound came from. Bernódus stood there on the plastic mat and swung a golf club that hit the ball with a little clack, making it soar into the air and land in the sea around two hundred metres away. As soon as he'd hit one golf ball, the plastic tee sank down and picked up a new one that Bernódus knocked out to sea.

He didn't notice Konrád, who watched him from the deck and tried to imagine how many balls this practice of Bernódus's left lying on the seabed. A fine white golf bag stood upright near the device, and Bernódus seemed to be no stranger to the sport, hitting every ball flawlessly. He took a break from practising to switch clubs and rekindle a stout cigar sitting in an ashtray on top of the ball machine. Next to the cigar was a half-full glass of cognac.

'Isn't there enough trash in the ocean already?' Konrád asked. Bernódus didn't seem surprised by the interruption. Holding the cigar over the lighter's flame, he turned round while inhaling the smoke.

'Sorry,' he said. 'I've been meaning to look in on you.'

He noticed Konrád's hesitation when he didn't respond to his greeting.

'Aren't you the one who moved in next door to us?'

'No. I don't live in this neighbourhood. My name is Konrád.'

'Konrád? And . . . ?'

'And I knew a woman named Valborg. And I'm getting to know Ísleifur better and better all the time. And I think you're a scumbag.'

'Who are they? Am I supposed to know these people?'

'I'm afraid so.'

'Well, how about you just piss off, my friend? You have no right to intrude like this.'

'Ísleifur still denies it, but I think you sent him to Valborg's the other day, which ended with her death. Suffocated in a plastic bag he used to take beer cans to the recycling. Not a very exciting death, but then again, Ísleifur is nothing special, either. Though you once found him to be so. Do you remember that?'

'I don't know what the hell you're on about,' said Bernódus, tossing his cigar off the deck. 'I'll have to ask you to get out of here before I call the police.'

He was about to go into the house, but Konrád stopped him.

'Do you know what I think happened? I think Ísleifur told you what he did once in Keflavík. I think he told you about it sometime when you were working together at the Base. Do you remember that? That he went out to have some fun and asked the women who worked the club what they were doing after the place closed for the night. That he hid inside the club and pretended to have fallen asleep. That he raped a woman. I think he told you all about it one time when you were drunk at the Base, blowing off steam at the Officers' Club and pretending to be big men. Is that right?'

'What fucking bullshit is this?'

'He made out it was easy to get away with because it's not all women who have what it takes to recount such a horrendous experience to others, but are just tormented by it in silence for years. Yet there was one woman who pressed charges against him. The woman in Keflavík. But he was lucky that the judge didn't find her credible enough. For some reason, though, Ísleifur was. Not her. "Really?" someone who knows Ísleifur might say. Someone like you.'

Bernódus pushed Konrád away.

'You decided to imitate him and Valborg ended up in your clutches. Maybe other women, too. I don't know. Ísleifur didn't tell me everything, but he did tell me one or two things. That you'd told him what you did at Glaumbær. And that you came to him recently and said she was pestering you and upsetting everything, the woman you raped, and you asked if he could do something about it. You wanted Ísleifur to go to her and teach her a lesson, so she'd stop bothering you. He said he'd refused to do so, which made you furious. Maybe he's lying. He lies a lot. Maybe he did as you asked and went to Valborg with his plastic bags. Maybe you went there yourself after he refused.'

Bernódus went to the golf bag, took one of the clubs from it, and stepped menacingly towards Konrád.

'Why don't you just piss off!' he said.

'You're not concerned about the child?' said Konrád, without moving. 'You and Valborg's child?'

'She was lying,' said Bernódus.

'So she was in touch with you?'

'She ambushed me and accused me with some bloody rubbish. It was a lie, like everything she's said to you.'

'I haven't confirmed it, but I think she had a boy who was given the name Daníel. It was some religious drunks who took him in. It's my understanding that he hasn't had a good life, but that's going to change. When he's handed all this money. All this wealth. By his dad. Wasn't that Valborg's business with you? Before you sent Ísleifur to her place? Before you went to her place?'

Konrád saw that the man was trying to control his anger.

'You and Ísleifur have always kept in touch, haven't you? Ever since the old days?'

Bernódus swung the club at him, but Konrád dodged and grabbed it, yanked it from his hands and flung it towards the hot tub and the big Texas grill. The club hit the grill with a clang.

'Have you told your wife about this?' said Konrád, acting as if nothing had happened. 'How Daníel came into existence? Have you told your daughter about it?'

At that, the door to the house opened and a woman of Konrád's age stepped out onto the deck. He thought he recognised her from the clippings. It was Bernódus's wife.

'Told his daughter about what?' she asked, looking in surprise at Konrád and her husband, then at the golf club lying by the grill. 'What's all this commotion?'

'Nothing,' said Bernódus. 'Go inside!'

'Bernódus?'

'Get back inside!' the man ordered. His aggression didn't go unnoticed by Konrád. He didn't think the man's behaviour towards her now was something new.

'There was a woman in town who accused your husband of raping her decades ago,' said Konrád. 'She never pressed charges, but the rape resulted in a child she didn't want to keep, and gave up. She contacted me and asked me to find the child.'

The woman stared at her husband.

'What is he saying?'

'Nothing, don't worry about it. Get back in the house, woman!'

'Is this true?'

'It's a lie. I told you to get the hell back inside!'

'Bernódus . . . is this true?!'

'Inside, you airhead! You're so fucking stupid! I've never seen this man before – don't let him lie to you!'

'The woman's name was Valborg and I think she asked me to track down the child so that he can have his share in all of this,' said Konrád, looking over their splendid house. 'She's the one who was murdered the other day – I'm sure you've seen the news reports. I'm trying to find out if your husband had something to do with that.'

The woman stared thunderstruck at her husband. No sooner had Konrád said those words than his mobile rang. He pulled the phone from his pocket and saw that it was Regína, and thought it best not to wait to answer. He heard straight away that she was extremely upset.

'He's here,' she whispered fearfully as soon as Konrád answered. 'Here in the house . . . he's so angry, I hardly dare . . . Daníel is –'

Just then, the call ended. Konrád's phone battery had died.

61

After leaving Bernódus and his wife on their deck by the sea, Konrád drove as fast as he could to Regína's home. He had told the couple that they could expect a visit from the police very soon, to answer questions about Bernódus's interactions with Valborg in years past and again in the days leading up to her murder. He would have called Marta immediately if his phone hadn't died.

About ten minutes after he got the call, he parked his car at Regína's house but saw no light in any of its windows, no signs of life. He ran up to the house, rang the bell and knocked on the door, which he found to be locked. He called out to Regína but got no response, so he hurried behind the house and tried the garden door, which opened. He made his way slowly inside and called out to her again.

'Regína! Are you here? The police are on their way,' he lied. 'They'll be here soon. Are you all right?'

There was a crunching noise as he stepped on a piece of glass, and when his eyes had adjusted to the darkness inside, he saw that someone had trashed the place. Light bulbs had been broken, chairs knocked over, and books thrown on the floor.

He saw a shadowy figure emerge from the kitchen, and Regína came into view. She'd been crying and was clearly in shock.

'Are you all right?' Konrád asked, hurrying to her. Her forehead was cut and bleeding.

'I think I was knocked out,' she said.

'I'm going to call for an ambulance,' Konrád said, helping her sit down.

'Daníel attacked me,' Regína said. 'He was so angry. I think my head hit the door frame over there,' she said, pointing at the kitchen door. 'I lost consciousness . . .'

'Don't move,' Konrád said, before going to her phone and calling the Emergency Response number. 'You have a nasty gash on your head and aren't quite yourself at the moment. It's best you keep still until they come.'

'So angry . . .'

'Why was he so angry?' Konrád asked, after speaking with Emergency Response and requesting an ambulance.

'He came here soon after you left,' Regína said. 'I looked out into the garden and saw him standing there looking lonely and forlorn, which gave me quite a surprise, of course, but I asked him in. He said he'd been standing there for a while, and was really quite calm, at first. He started talking about my daughter and said he thinks about her sometimes. Recalled how kind she'd been to him. He said he remembered it very clearly when she fell ill and went to the hospital and didn't come back. He knew that was why he couldn't have stayed with me any longer. He's been drifting here and there ever since then, in fact all his life, and never known exactly who he was or where he came from.'

Regína rubbed her forehead and grimaced with pain. She was starting to recover a bit from the blow.

'He wanted to ask me about his mother. That was why he came and I felt as if something had happened to him recently. He asked if I had any photos of her. He'd always known he was a foster child but hadn't thought much about it, but now he'd seen a familiar face somewhere and couldn't shake it . . .'

'What did you tell him?'

'The truth. The whole truth. I had no other choice. He has every right to know it, of course. He should have learned it long ago. I told him about the rape. I didn't know what else to say. I didn't want any lies. I tried to break it to him as gently as possible, and said it wasn't certain, but that you can't rule it out.'

'And?'

'He just smiled.'

'Smiled?'

'As if life had stopped surprising him long ago. Then he broke down. I tried to console him but it had the opposite effect – he started swearing, and before I knew it he was in a rage. He turned his anger on me. Screamed at me, asking why I hadn't told him anything. I should have contacted him years ago. I should have told him the truth at the church when Sunnefa died, and then this might not have happened. He wanted to know what had possessed us, and then he went on the rampage, smashing everything here and then . . . then he attacked me . . .'

'Do you know where he's gone?'

'He felt so awful,' Regína said. 'I told him about you, what you were doing. That you were trying to track him down because

Valborg had asked you to, and that you wanted to help him. He might want to talk to you.'

'Where did he go?'

'I don't know, maybe . . . maybe he's gone to see his father . . . I don't know.'

'Bernódus? Did you tell him who his father is?'

'Yes,' said Regína. 'He felt so bad, the poor boy, so terribly bad . . . I really don't understand how . . . how it could have happened that he, that it was him who . . .'

'What?'

'Dear God,' Regína groaned, grabbing Konrád's arm. 'It's no wonder he feels so awful, the poor boy.'

62

The young woman stood at the window looking out into the evening darkness. The curtains were still open and a faint light shone from inside the flat. The woman stood there, smoking, and blew the smoke out the window. She was wearing a tracksuit, as if she'd been out jogging and decided to have a cigarette to reward herself.

In the house next door, a woman sat hunched over a laptop in the kitchen. A man in the living room was looking at a tablet computer. They weren't talking to each other. The television was on and its bluish gleam illuminated the living room, but no one was watching it. They looked up simultaneously from their computers and the woman called something out. The man put down the tablet, stood up and walked into the master bedroom.

The young woman stubbed out her cigarette and left the window, started pulling off her tracksuit and disappeared into the bathroom. The door closed behind her.

The man in the basement flat came out of a bedroom, holding an infant who appeared to be crying. He held it closely and tried to comfort it by walking around the living room. His wife, in the kitchen, didn't move.

The bald man with the glasses and his wife were sitting on the sofa in front of the telly, with a bowl of popcorn. The man kissed her lightly on her mouth. Then they sat and watched telly together, munching their popcorn.

The bathroom door opened and the woman who'd been smoking came out with a towel wrapped around her, then went into the living room and took something from her bag. It was a shampoo bottle. She took it back to the bathroom and shut the door behind her.

The man in the next window buried his face in his hands. He appeared to be home alone and quite upset, and then he kicked some Lego blocks lying on the living-room floor. He picked up a mobile phone, and in no time at all appeared to be shouting into it. The call ended abruptly and he went to the window and stared into the darkness. He turned round, grabbed a decorative vase from the living-room table and flung it across the room. Then he shoved aside other ornamental objects before falling onto the sofa and burying his face in his hands again.

The bathroom door was still shut.

The woman on the first floor of the block of flats was sitting alone in her living room. She had a half-empty glass of beer in front of her and shook her head as she spoke on the phone. She seemed agitated and when the call ended, she threw the phone onto the sofa and it bounced from there onto the floor.

Above her was the flat of the woman whose murder had thrown

everything into turmoil. The flat was dark, as on the previous evenings, with not a soul about.

At the next stairwell, no one was home on the ground floor. On the first floor, people sat staring at the telly, but looked up every now and then and the woman nudged the man as if she wanted him to do something.

On the floor above them, young people were having a party. Some were dancing, others stood chatting, drinking straight from beer cans or downing shots. The door was opened, and the man from the floor below was standing there on the landing.

The young woman's bathroom door opened a crack, revealing her standing naked in front of the mirror . . .

Someone had switched on a light in the murdered woman's flat and was now standing in the living room. He appeared to stare straight into the lens of the spotting scope.

Then the light went out.

The bathroom door slowly closed.

63

Konrád thought about the irony of fate. About how few people there were in Iceland. About the coincidences that ruled people's lives. How they created life. How they destroyed it.

Marta wasn't happy when he finally got round to calling her and telling her what he'd learned about Bernódus and Ísleifur and Valborg and Daníel, and how it all seemed to be one giant tragedy far beyond his understanding. She chewed him out for not speaking to her sooner, for withholding information from her that was important to the investigation, for being a damned idiot. She said she would hold him accountable if everything took a turn for the worse, the investigation was botched, and even more tragedy ensued. Konrád let her rant and moan over the phone. It was just a distant buzz in the tragic story that had unfolded itself before his eyes.

He parked his car in front of the elegant villa by the sea and looked at his mobile phone. He'd managed to charge it briefly at

Regína's, and hoped it would last. All was quiet. This time, there was no clacking of golf balls being hit into the sea. To his surprise, the door was half open and he stepped carefully inside and called out to ask if anyone was home. He knew the police were on their way there and to Ísleifur's place, and that a search would begin for Daníel.

He entered a large, richly furnished living room with a white grand piano, huge paintings on the walls and a view out to sea, and there sat Bernódus's wife, whom Konrád had met earlier that evening. Her back was turned to him and she seemed to be entirely in her own world.

'Is that you, Klara?' she asked without turning round when she heard Konrád.

'No,' said Konrád, 'it's me again.'

'You?'

'Sorry for the inconvenience. Are you expecting your daughter?'

'What are you doing here?'

'I wanted to know if you'd had a visitor.'

'A visitor?'

'A man named Daníel.'

'Where's Klara?' the woman asked suspiciously. 'She isn't with you? I called my daughter. She's on her way. I need to talk to my daughter. Tell her what happened.'

'Yes, I understand,' Konrád replied, and he saw that the woman now had a black eye and had been bleeding from one ear. 'Can you tell me if someone's come to visit? Daníel?'

'Why are you asking that?'

'It may be that . . . Where's Bernódus? Are you all right?'

'No one has been here. Except you. Earlier. Why did you come here to see him? It was such a beautiful evening and he'd been so decent.'

'Decent?'

'Yes.'

'What do you mean?'

'I'm not blaming you,' said the woman. 'I should thank you, in fact. Thank you for telling me about the poor woman. Valborg. I didn't know about it. And neither does Klara. But I know my husband. He's forced me to have sex more times than I can count. Cheated on me. Whored around on his trips overseas.'

Just then, they heard quick footsteps coming from the hall. Both of them turned and saw Klara hurrying towards them. She looked at Konrád in surprise, but then took her mother in her arms and hugged her tightly.

'Are you all right?' she asked.

'Don't worry about me. I'm fine. I'm glad it's over. Glad this is over.'

'Where's Dad?'

'I don't know where I got the strength. Maybe it was the story of the woman at Glaumbær. Your dad told it to my face. Screamed it at me. That he'd done it. Raped her. Then he hit me. For the first time in three years. After being so decent.'

'Oh, Mum,' Klara whispered. 'Where is he? Has he gone? Where did he go? What are you doing here?' she asked, looking at Konrád.

'I think the police are on their way,' said Konrád, 'and will want to talk to both of you. And Bernódus in particular.'

'Because of that woman . . . that Valborg?'

Konrád said yes.

'Mum, where is he?!' Klara asked. 'Where's Dad?'

The woman looked at her and then pointed at a half-open door. Klara walked towards it.

Konrád watched her and saw her stop in the doorway. She

didn't go any further. His mobile started ringing and he answered it. It was Marta. He didn't speak to her straight away, but went over to Klara and looked into the room, where he saw Bernódus lying helpless on the floor. Blood welled from his head and his body twitched. His eyes were open and he stared up at the ceiling, but he couldn't move. On the carpet next to him lay a broken marble statuette. Konrád rushed into the study, but Klara didn't move; she just stood there in the doorway and watched him start giving first aid to her father.

'Send an ambulance to Bernódus's house,' Konrád said when he finally answered Marta. 'He's taken a hard blow to the head and is losing consciousness.'

'Damn it!' groaned Marta, and Konrád heard her order someone to call an ambulance, right now.

'I don't know where I got the strength to do that,' said Klara's mother, who'd made her way slowly to them and stood behind her daughter in the doorway. 'Suddenly, it was just so easy.'

Klara started to cry and buried her face in her mother's neck. Her mother held her and spoke soothingly to her.

'Some idiot has broken into Valborg's flat,' Marta said. 'He says he wants to talk to you. It's probably best to be cautious and do as he says. Do you know anything about it? Why does he want to meet you? How does he know you? What's going on? What the hell have you been up to?'

'I thought he might be on his way here,' Konrád said.

'Who? Who is it?!'

'It's Daníel. Valborg's child.'

64

Marta blew jets of vapour as she waited impatiently for Konrád in front of the block of flats. Another officer was with her whom Konrád didn't know. All was quiet on the street. There was no sign of any special response team to deal with the man in the flat. Light shone from most of the block's windows. Valborg's window was dark.

'That fool Emanúel called earlier and said he saw a man in Valborg's flat,' Marta said as Konrád hurried over to her. 'No one has bothered to take his spotting scope from him. The man refuses to come out. He's switched off all the lights and claims to be unarmed. It could be a lie. I'm mainly worried that he'll harm himself. Why do you think he's Valborg's son?'

'Did he know me by name?'

'Yes. He asked for Konrád. Have you met him before?'

'No,' Konrád said, looking up at the windows of Valborg's flat. 'What are you going to do?'

'You try talking to him,' said Marta. 'If it works, we won't break down the door. If he turns out to be a threat, we'll call in the SWAT team. Evacuate the building. Try to calm him down. I don't want any tragedies here.'

'Yes, too late for that, unfortunately,' Konrád said.

Marta showed him how to signal with his mobile phone if he needed help. Konrád set his phone, went to the front door, and opened it. He entered the stairwell and made his way slowly to the second floor, then went to the door of Valborg's flat. It had been forced open.

He knocked lightly on the door, not wanting to be too aggressive if this was Valborg's son. He called Daníel's name several times. Put his ear to the door. Heard nothing. He pushed the door. It opened further and he walked cautiously into the flat.

'Is that you, Daníel?' he called out. 'Are you all right? I've spoken to Regína. She'll be OK. She's very worried about you.'

'I didn't mean to hurt her,' Konrád heard from within the darkness.

'She knows that.'

'Nor did I mean to hurt Valborg or anyone else. I didn't know who she was . . . that she was . . . was . . .'

Konrád, peering into the darkness, inched his way forward.

'They said she kept her money here. The ones at the shelter. I don't know what I was doing with the plastic bag. Thought I could just make her sleep. Knock her out for a while. My head was all fucked up. Didn't know what I was doing. I've felt so bad about this. I never meant to do it. Not to her. Not to anyone.'

Konrád saw the man in silhouette, sitting on a chair. He saw no weapon in his hands. He appeared to be leaning forward with his elbows on his knees, staring at the floor.

'Strange that it happened to be her. I've never done any real searching for her or my father . . . Is what Regína said true? Was that why she gave me up? Because he raped her?'

'I'm afraid everything points to that,' Konrád replied. 'I take it you're Daníel?'

'I don't know who I am.'

There was another long silence, and Daníel didn't move in his chair. Konrád ventured a little closer until he was standing opposite the man. He noticed that the balcony door was open.

'That bloody bastard.'

'Yes. That bloody bastard.'

'Strange that it happened to be her,' Daníel said again.

'Of course, it isn't normal,' said Konrád. 'That you should find each other in this way. She thought of you all these years and finally asked me to track you down because I was once a cop. We didn't know each other at all, and I pushed her away. I feel like I failed her. And you. Maybe I could have brought you together. Before this disaster happened. She wanted to get in touch with you because, as the years passed, she came to regret what she did more and more, and maybe she also wanted you to have some of your father's money. He's a wealthy man. She had the idea that she might finally do you some good.'

'I would have liked to have known her.'

'Of course.'

'I would have liked . . . I wish I hadn't . . .'

'She bore her grief in silence,' said Konrád, inching closer to the man. 'The rape. That she'd had a child and given it up. It seems to have had a profound effect on her. She tried to live her life as if nothing had happened, but I don't think she ever succeeded.'

'Sometimes I asked the people around me, but no one knew

anything or else just kept what they knew secret, until Regína told me everything this evening. Why I was always so unsettled. She told me about the people in the congregation and Sunnefa, what she did.'

'Let me help you.'

'There's nothing you can do for me.'

Daníel looked up from the floor and at him, silent and serious.

'I never meant to do it. I'm no murderer.'

He'd started to drawl a bit and Konrád asked if he was OK, but got no answer. He said he wanted to switch on the light, and Daníel didn't object. Konrád reached for a switch by the kitchen door and a light above the dining table came on. The soft light fell on them and they looked each other in the eye. Daníel's face bore signs that life had been unkind to him. At some point, he'd broken his nose and a scar remained from a gash over one eye, maybe from a fight. His lips were chapped, his strong hands were dirty and scarred, and his nails were cracked and yellow-brown from constant smoking. Konrád regarded him and thought he saw his mother's mien in Daníel's facial features, his high forehead and arched eyebrows. And he saw that beneath his brows shone the same deep pain that was in Valborg's eyes the day they sat under the arched windows and she talked about motherly love.

'I wish I'd been there with her,' Daníel whispered.

'Yes, of course.'

'She didn't deserve this.'

'No,' Konrád said.

'And neither do I.'

'You sure don't,' Konrád said. 'Nobody deserves such a thing.'

'I'm thirsty,' said Daníel. 'Can you get me some water?'

He gave a joyless little smile and Konrád got up and went

into the kitchen, took a glass and filled it with water. When he returned, Daníel was sitting in the chair with his eyes closed. Konrád nudged him gently and said he'd brought water for him, but received no response. Seeing that something was wrong, he put down the glass, grabbed Daníel's head and asked if he was all right, said his name over and over, slapped him lightly on the cheek, lifted his eyelids and saw that his eyes were hard and lifeless. Konrád pressed the button on his phone and laid Daníel on the floor. He tried CPR and noticed boxes of Valborg's cancer drugs and a few other pills.

Saying Daníel's name over and over, he continued doing chest compressions until the police and paramedics arrived, accompanied by a doctor. The doctor pushed Konrád away and took over the resuscitation efforts himself, and before long, they'd carried Daníel out to an ambulance.

About three-quarters of an hour later, Konrád learned that Valborg's son had died on the way to the hospital.

65

The weather was mild and Konrád watched the tourists admiring the *Sun Voyager* sculpture standing down by the sea, on its eternal voyage out to the stars.

His mobile rang. It was Marta.

'He'll probably never fully recover,' she said. 'Bernódus. She managed to damage some nerves.'

'I got there too late,' Konrád said, as if it were a cliché.

'You should have kept in better touch with me,' said Marta, yet not in any sort of accusatory tone. 'The wife has been telling us about her difficult home life with him. Violence. Oppression. He threatened to kill her if she left him. The whole package. The daughter says she hadn't known all of it. Just some things. She thought he was getting much better. One big game of concealment and co-dependence. She herself has asked for a DNA test and wants to find out if she and Daníel were siblings.'

Konrád remained silent on the phone.

'You're not really bothered about them, are you?' said Marta.

'No.'

'You're thinking about Daníel?'

'Yes.'

'Could this have happened anywhere besides Iceland?'

'I don't know.'

They said their goodbyes shortly afterwards and Konrád looked in the direction of the eternal voyage, and then at the pavement. He hadn't had much of a chance recently to think about the window of a smokehouse. He'd figured out several years ago, after the Butchers' Association buildings were replaced by newer ones, that in the place where his feet now rested, the smoking kilns had once stood and his father had bled out. He tried to envision where the window had been and if it had played any part when his father was attacked. Whether the murderer had hidden in the smokehouse or entered the building through the window during his escape.

He was pondering these things when his mobile phone rang again. It was Eygló. They'd talked about Regína and her daughter and Daníel, and Eygló recalled how she'd once visited their home along with a psychic healer, and how that visit had been the impetus for her not to pursue medium work.

'Do you still have that music box of yours?' she asked after they'd talked for a while.

Konrád was holding it in his hand.

'Yes,' he said.

'What are you going to do with it?'

'I don't know,' he said.

Eygló wanted to talk about their fathers, but sensed that he was distracted and said she would talk to him another time.

Konrád stuck his phone in his pocket and walked back towards his car. He continued looking at the *Sun Voyager*, sailing into eternity. The artwork conveyed a feeling of freedom that he liked. He walked past a rubbish bin and for a moment stopped and considered the object in his hand, before tossing it in the bin and continuing on his way, slightly lighter of step.

66

A strange silence fell over the cluster of Butchers' Association buildings on Skúlagata Street, and Konrád's father stomped his feet to try to stay warm. The smell from the smokehouse hung over everything, but he didn't mind it. He tried to keep a low profile, but it was unnecessary. There was no one else in the neighbourhood. The petrol station down at Klöpp was closed. West of it loomed gloomy oil tanks marked BP. He looked out to sea. It was a short distance to the boulders on the other side of the street and he could hear the waves rising and falling under a cold veil of fog.

He'd waited for some time in the biting cold and had finally decided to leave when he heard someone approaching from out of the darkness.

About the Author

Arnaldur Indridason has won many international prizes, including the CWA Gold Dagger Award for *Silence of the Grave*. He is the only author to win the Glass Key Award for Best Nordic Crime Novel two years in a row, for *Jar City* and *Silence of the Grave*. He is an international bestselling author whose books have been translated into more than forty languages, and have sold over twelve million copies. He lives with his family in Reykjavik.